CHURCH
OF THE
GRAVEYARD
SAINTS

ALSO BY C. JOSEPH GREAVES

Hard Twisted

Tom & Lucky (and George & Cokey Flo)

AS CHUCK GREAVES

The Jack MacTaggart Mystery Series

Hush Money

Green-Eyed Lady

The Last Heir

CHURCH
OF THE
GRAVEYARD
SAINTS

a novel

C. JOSEPH GREAVES

TORREY HOUSE PRESS

Salt Lake City • Torrey

This is a work of fiction. Any resemblance to actual events or persons, living or dead, is entirely coincidental.

First Torrey House Press Edition, September 2019
Copyright © 2019 by Charles J. Greaves

Published by Torrey House Press
Salt Lake City, Utah
www.torreyhouse.org

International Standard Book Number: 978-1-948814-12-6
E-book ISBN: 978-1-948814-13-3
Library of Congress Control Number: 2019932479

Cover art "Mt. Sinai" by Julia Buckwalter
Cover design by Kathleen Metcalf
Interior design by Rachel Davis
Distributed to the trade by Consortium Book Sales and Distribution

For the warriors

What becomes of our earliest childhood—its sights and sounds, its textures and smells? Of diapers and talcum, nursing and teething, babbled words and first baby steps? All of life's novelties, miraculous and shining and, one would think, indelible. Yet their memory, so dear and enduring to the parent, is lost somehow to the child in the way that breath is snatched from the rising in a whoosh *of sudden acceleration.*

Intellectually at least, Addie Decker knew the answer. Something to do with the hippocampus and an infant's inability to bundle memories in the absence of a functional vocabulary. Not, as Freud would have it, because of some repressed infantile sexuality. That was the thing Addie had learned about Freud—that practically everything he'd written was about sex and yet what he'd actually known about sex you could fit on the back of an envelope.

Which was not to say forgotten wounds couldn't leave a permanent scar.

Attachment Theory, a post-Freudian model, holds that children's earliest interactions forge the die from which their later relationships are cast. So at one end of the spectrum, secure infants—those that in a clinical setting become upset when left by their mothers and embrace them when they return—grow into emotionally healthy adults who will trust and find comfort in their later life partners. At the other end of the spectrum, so-called insecure avoidants—infants that demonstrate indifference to maternal absence—grow up to have intimacy issues and are much more likely to distrust even good and supportive relationships.

So went the theory. But unlike Freud's speculative musings, Attachment Theory had been tested and validated and found to be highly accurate. And yet to Addie's way of thinking, its predictive value still suffered from two major shortcomings.

The first was that without childhood memories of our own, we're forced to rely on those very same parents—be they nurturing or neglectful, truthful or treacherous—to fill in our early-life blanks.

The second problem with Attachment Theory was that it failed to answer the basic question: What happens when your mother leaves you and never returns?

PART ONE

1

"Hey. Are you asleep?"

Addie blinked her eyes open. They were approaching Kayenta and the cutoff that would take them northbound through the iconic buttes of Monument Valley into the vast and rugged canyonlands of southeastern Utah. The part of the drive, she'd promised Bradley, where things would finally get interesting after nine bleary hours of scrolling blacktop and sere desert scrubland.

Except that the long fingers of dusk were closing around them like a fist.

"We'll want to take a left at the light."

"Which light?"

She yawned as she stretched in the passenger seat. "The only light."

"Are you sure? There's a map there in the door pocket."

Addie couldn't suppress a smile. Raised in Southern California, Bradley's concept of directions involved a series of freeway numbers followed by a street name. Like taking the 110 to the 10 to the 405 and getting off at Sepulveda. Those incantations still challenged Addie in a way she imagined the Navajo Code Talkers' rhythmic grunts and mumbles must have befuddled the Imperial Japanese Navy.

"Trust me. Besides, I thought real men didn't need maps."

"Naps." Bradley passed his cell phone over the dashboard like a Ouija plank. "Real men don't—" He sat upright, squinting over the wheel. "Now there's something you don't see every day."

What Addie saw through the bug-flecked windshield was a horse—a scrawny bay mare with an unkempt mane wearing neither halter nor tack as it ambled through the crossroads, pausing midway to rub its dirty muzzle on a foreleg. It brought them to a stop before clopping over the sidewalk onto the weedy macadam of a shuttered gas station.

This maddening indifference to animal welfare was one of the things that infuriated Addie about the Diné, the Navajo people. She'd had friends in high school that wouldn't even enter the reservation without first packing a leash and a bagful of dog treats. She herself had once rescued a starving rez bitch and driven it to Cortez where the veterinarian's x-rays had revealed over a hundred BB pellets embedded under the poor animal's skin.

In Los Angeles, that CinemaScope womb of Technicolor fantasy, her classmates thought Native Americans great stewards of the land and its resources—noble aboriginals living in simple harmony with earth's flora and fauna. Addie had long since given up on explaining the more nuanced reality.

Or take the Navajo Generating Station, the largest and dirtiest coal-fired power plant west of the Mississippi, and one of Bradley's personal bugaboos. While girls she knew from college were tying feathers in their hair and driving to North Dakota to join with the Standing Rock Sioux to protest a pipeline, the Navajo plant was quietly burning twenty-four thousand tons of coal from its nearby Kayenta strip mine each and every day.

Not that Addie blamed the Diné for that one, or the Hopi people for that matter, who shared in the mining royalties. With a majority of their households still lacking electricity or running water, the tribes were in desperate straits when the mine's promoters showed up in their shiny new pickups promising economic opportunity. It was only after the paperwork had been signed that the tribal elders discovered their lawyer had been on the promoters' payroll, which explained the paltry 3.3

percent royalty rate they'd contracted to accept. Still they'd come to depend on those royalties—and even more on the jobs that the plant and mine created—for their economic survival.

"Hey." Bradley brushed at her hair with his fingers. "Are you all right?"

"I'm fine. Remembering, that's all."

"You've been unusually quiet."

"I've been thoughtful. Pensive."

"Brooding."

"Not brooding. Contemplative."

"Wistful."

"Preoccupied."

"Melancholy."

"Let's settle on abstracted. But only by outward appearances. Inside I'm turning cartwheels."

They both knew that was a joke.

"We could still turn back." He glanced at the thermonuclear sunset filling his rearview mirror. "Plus there's an airport out by the tribal park."

"Do they have a time machine? You'll recall that my father's expecting us."

"Hence your anxiety."

"Hence we can't just turn around."

"My point is we don't *have* to do this. Or at least you don't."

"Hah. You think I'm a coward, is that it?"

"I think you're a force of nature."

"Right. Like gravity, pulling everything downward."

"I was thinking more of a tornado, standing everything on its head."

They'd turned into a Martian landscape; a volcanic wasteland sculpted by eons of pebbling wind whose dust cloud yet darkened the far horizon, shrouding the land of her forebears—land that six generations of Olsens and Deckers had claimed and defended, cleared and plowed, watered and seeded, transforming barren tracts of sage and saltbrush into settlements that had grown into towns and that might someday grow into cities.

Moths flared in the Prius's headlights. Plastic grocery bags raced ghostlike across the blacktop, swirling and snagging on the roadside wire to flutter there like pennants heralding Adelaide Decker's return.

For a school genealogy project Addie once had interviewed Jess and Vivian Olsen, her maternal grandparents, about their family's history. She'd learned how Dag Olsen, her great-great-great-grandfather, had answered the prophet John Taylor's call for Mormon pioneers to settle the Utah Territory's southeast quadrant, the contours of which, since beyond the diagonal gash of the Colorado River, were as unknowable in the parlors of Salt Lake as the dark side of the moon. In the company of eleven-score colonists that included his young bride Chastity and their infant son Ethan, Dag had set out from Escalante in the fall of 1879 in a covered wagon drawn by oxen and fueled by a zealot's certainty in the righteousness of his task.

Expected to last but six weeks, the journey from Fortymile Gulch to Montezuma Creek took over six months instead. Building roadway as it went, the Hole-in-the-Rock Expedition, as it came to be known, chopped and scraped and blasted its way to the west rim of the Colorado only to be confronted with a sheer drop of some two-thousand vertical feet to the muddy waters below.

By then, of course, there was no turning back. And so, in what counts as perhaps the single greatest feat in the history of a nation born of such superhuman efforts, the Hole-in-the-Rock pioneers set about carving a makeshift passage that none but the maddest among them would ever have dared to envision.

They began at a cleft in the rim rock where forty roped men with picks and crowbars chipped and hacked and spalled a slanting trough through an opening they'd blown with dynamite. The job once begun had lasted for fifty days and when it was finished the men had hewn on hands and knees through solid rock and bitter cold a chute through which they hoped their wagon wheels might find purchase against the fatal pull of gravity. Where they could not carve—where the rock bowed or fell away—men were lowered in wooden barrels to chisel holes into which pegs could be set and driftwood laid in cantilever.

The work at last completed, all that remained was to test it. First they sent their livestock down and were pleased when only nine horses plunged to their deaths on the jagged scree below. Next they fitted the first of their wagons into the rut they'd made, its axles roped and its wheels chained, and with teams of twenty men straining at the lines lowered it to safety. In this fashion each of the expedition's eighty-eight wagons made its way to the narrow mud beach, there to be rafted across the river.

Not a single pioneer was lost. Two, in fact, were born in that cold desert waste under the diamond banner of heaven. And after their struggles on its western rim, the east side of the Colorado seemed as nothing by comparison, taking the expedition only two backbreaking weeks to reach the top.

What lay beyond the river was a kind of fever dream—a dizzying maze of red-rock cliffs and gorges, buttes and mesas slick with snow and studded with twisted cedars. There the expedition traveled another hundred zigzag miles to cover ground a hawk might glide in a leisurely hour. But cover it they did, and in the spring of 1880 arrived at a broad floodplain of the San Juan River warmed by the morning sun and cooled by the evening shadow of a high sandstone mesa. It was there they built their fort, and their homes of log and mud, and christened their little settlement Bluff City.

Reaching their destination was one thing; taming it proved another matter entirely. Ute, Paiute, and Navajo people—some of whom had never laid eyes on a white man—greeted the 225 exhausted newcomers with attitudes ranging from indifference to curiosity to outright hostility. Misunderstandings festered into disputes, and disputes into gunfights. Then the river rose with the summer monsoons, wiping out months of trenching and plowing. Then winter returned with a frigid vengeance.

From those hardscrabble origins the Olsen family began its slow migration eastward to Colorado's remote and scenic McElmo Canyon where the Red Rocks Ranch, Addie's point of entry into her family saga, lay nestled in a broad side-canyon of slickrock and sage. It was on the Triple-R that Addie had pedaled her first tricycle, and raced her first pony, and branded her first calf. It was where Jess Olsen, her octogenarian grandfather, still lived in the creek-side cabin his own grandfather had built from hand-hewn logs in the summer of 1921.

Logan Decker, Addie's father, had never managed to convince her Grandpa Jess or Grandma Vivian to move into the ranch's main house, two stories of timber and stone that had been their gift to Addie's mother—Carole's dowry, in effect—upon her marriage to Logan in 1993. Even after Carole's death in '98—before Addie had acquired the language of memory—Grandma Vivian had insisted Logan would need both space and privacy for the new wife that would surely come along to help him raise her only granddaughter.

Except Logan never did remarry, and now Grandma Vivian was dead. Which is how Addie Decker found herself speeding through Mexican Hat as nighttime fell, bound not just for her grandmother's funeral but also for a reunion with a family whose indomitable will to settle the land around her was matched only by Addie's iron determination to escape it altogether.

"Besides," Bradley said, nudging her from her reverie, "it'll probably be fun. See some old friends. Visit your old haunts."

"Yup."

"You're making much ado about nothing," he said, reaching for her hand, finding it. Giving it a squeeze. "I mean, what's the worst that could possibly happen?"

2

The drive from the front gate to the main house measured half a mile, and in the sweep of the Prius's headlights Bradley could make out a hay barn, and a riding arena, and a sleepy cluster of farm equipment. The house itself, when they'd rounded the final curve, stood backlit by a faint incandescence that seemed to emanate from atop the towering mesa behind it.

It was after midnight, and all was eerily quiet.

"Maybe we caught a break." Addie leaned into the windshield. "Maybe we can sneak upstairs without waking him."

"Maybe we should get a hotel room."

"We will, don't worry. After the funeral. Just remember, whatever you do don't mention the Warriors. Daddy thinks climate change involves moving his cows to a higher pasture."

Light from the porch, yellow and sudden, set a dog to barking.

"Uh-oh," she said. "There goes the element of surprise."

Bradley studied the house as he unlatched his seatbelt. It appeared more Evergreen Lodge than Bates Motel, and its canine guardian proved a blocky shape awkwardly navigating the four wooden steps from its front porch down to its long flagstone walkway.

"Is it true what they say? That they can actually smell fear?"

"He growls, but he doesn't bite."

"I wasn't talking about the dog."

"Neither was I."

No sooner had they stepped from the car than Addie was set upon by the dog—a gray-muzzled Labrador that whimpered as it circled, its licorice tail lashing her shins.

"Waylon," she cooed, bending and offering her face. "Oh, Waylon. Did you miss me?"

Bradley examined the midnight sky, vast and clear and gaudy with stars. He lifted their bags from the hatchback. Reddish dust, finer than flour, had coated the back of his car. At the house, another figure appeared in silhouette, this one nearly as tall and lean as the porch posts that flanked it.

A shrill whistle. The dog wheeled and galloped toward the sound. Addie and Bradley followed, their footsteps crunching the driveway gravel.

"Hello, Daddy. I hope we didn't wake you. This is Bradley Sommers. You can thank him for delivering me safe and sound."

"I was expecting you hours ago." Logan Decker held his watch to the porch light, ignoring Bradley's hand. "Must've dozed off on the couch. Come in, come in. Are you hungry? We got more food than the Safeway store."

They settled in the great room where sprays and bouquets, incongruously festive, seemed to fill every nook and corner. Where the fire Logan had kindled sent shadows to dancing on the high raftered ceiling. Where the piñon smoke and the cloying fragrance of lily and rose blossom grappled with the yellow odor of cigarettes. The room's décor suggested some nightmare amalgam of Ralph Lauren and Charles Addams—all Indian blankets and riveted leather and, above the stone fireplace, an elk's head whose glass-marble eyes seemed to flutter in the firelight.

Addie sipped her tea. Logan Decker smoked and slouched with his stocking feet outstretched toward the fire. Tired but wary, self-conscious of his interloper status, Bradley watched them both from the far end of the sofa where, the pleasantries exhausted, father and daughter seemed to have reached a layer of conversational bedrock whose penetration would require new and different tools that neither had brought to the job.

Somewhere behind Bradley, a grandfather clock ticked.

"So," Addie said. "How's he doing?"

Her father grunted. "You know your grandpa. He ain't the type to sull. But still."

"What?"

Logan straightened and tilted forward, searching for words and seeming to find them, finally, somewhere in the fire.

"Remember when you were five or thereabouts and I took you up to McPhee? I was afraid you'd be too squeamish to bait a hook. Shows you what I knew. Then when we did catch ourselves a bass, I set it down there on the rocks and you talked to that fish and petted it like a housecat till the light went out of its eye. Do you remember what you said then?"

Addie shook her head.

"You said maybe that fish had a mommy in the lake and it had died of sadness from being taken away from her. Jesus Christ almighty. I haven't thought about that for, what? Almost twenty years? But when I seen the old man's face that morning he come in for his coffee, I knew right away. It was the light. It just seemed to of gone from out of his eyes."

Logan slid from his chair to squat at the hearth and poke at the fire with an iron. The flames coppered his face, animating it, highlighting its creases and crags. He was lean in the manner of other alcoholics Bradley had known; dissipated men for whom food was merely an afterthought. His profile, though, belonged on a Roman coin.

"As a widower yourself," Bradley ventured, "I'm sure you could empathize with what he was going through."

The iron paused. Logan nodded.

"In high school," Addie said, shifting the conversation to Bradley, "I was the class salutatorian. The only B I ever got was in Calculus my senior year. The Calculus teacher, Mr. Hoover, had a son named Grant who got the only A in the class. He was the valedictorian."

She set her mug on the table and rearranged her legs.

"I applied to four colleges: Harvard, UCLA, Colorado State, and a local school called Fort Lewis. I was accepted at CSU and Fort Lewis, and I was rejected by Harvard. But for some reason I never heard back from UCLA."

"Addie," her father said.

"The registration deadline for CSU was coming up fast and the frustrating thing was, there was no one I could talk to. I mean, nobody here had ever applied to a college, and if I'd asked my guidance counselor Mrs. Melton she'd have recommended I take cosmetology classes at the community college. I think Grant and I were the only two from our class who'd even applied out of state."

At the sound of Addie's voice the old Labrador emerged from out of the shadows. It padded over and rested its head on her knee.

"So anyway I moped around for a few weeks pretending everything was fine. But Grandma Vivian, she could see I was troubled about something."

"Abstracted," Bradley said, and was rewarded with a smile.

"She asked me what was wrong, and when I told her she said when she was a girl, all the men in the county were off fighting the war in Europe, or in the Pacific, and that she and most of her friends had to quit school to work on the ranches and farms. That's why she never got past the ninth grade. She and her mother would work until sundown doing chores outside and then they'd work until bedtime doing the baking and canning and whatnot, and then they'd wake up and start all over again. Just the two of them tending a ranch with fifty-some head of cattle, day in and day out, for something like four years straight."

Addie rescued her mug from the dog's swinging tail and took another sip.

"And when the men finally came home, those that did, she was already eighteen and wasn't about to go back to high school.

So what she did, she taught herself to type. She practiced for months, and then she drove into town and applied for jobs at maybe a dozen different places, but she was turned down every time. Either because she had no experience or else no diploma. So at this point in the story I'm thinking, okay Addie, your stupid college problem is a big fat nothing so quit whining and get on with it. Which is probably what I needed to hear, but that wasn't the point she was trying to make."

She scratched at the old dog's ear, and its tail accelerated.

"What she finally said was, 'Addie, don't you be that worn-out girl with the callused hands who lets some man in a bolo tie decide her future.' And that was better advice than any parent or teacher or guidance counselor ever gave me."

Logan, still squatting and smoking, lowered his head. He replaced the poker in its caddy.

"So where did Grant Hoover end up?" Bradley asked, and Addie smiled.

"The Colorado School of Mines. And when he told me I thought, 'Oh, I didn't know he wanted to be a mime. Why would anyone want to be a mime?'"

Logan took a final drag off his cigarette and dropped it into the fire. He stood, stiff in his movements, and wiped his palms on his jeans.

"Well," he said. "Big day tomorrow. The viewing's at one o'clock, then the procession back here to the graveyard. Then we get ourselves pawed and clucked over by half the women in Montezuma County." He regarded Addie where she sat. "I believe those horses could use some work in the morning, in case you was of a mind."

She hesitated before nodding. "I'd like that."

"All right then. You'll find your room is right where you left it."

Logan circled behind the sofa. "As for you," he said to Bradley's back, "you'll find clean sheets on the guest bed. I'll trust Addie to show you the way."

* * *

Bradley lay on his back with his fingers laced over his ribs. He heard a toilet flush downstairs, then the faint and skeletal clatter of dog claws on hardwood, then quiet. In the room next door he heard drawers open and close, then the telltale squeaking of bedsprings. Other movements whose import he could only imagine. *Did* imagine, picturing Addie in her bra and panties, in only her panties, in nothing at all. Bending and straightening, her dark hair brushing the milky white of her shoulders. Her eyes glowing electric blue in the moonlight when she turned her face toward the window.

He waited ten minutes more, then eased to the edge of the bed.

Downstairs he heard nothing. Next door there was only silence.

The door creaked on its hinges. The hallway lay dark and empty before him. Holding his breath to listen, he heard only the quickening pulse of his own guilty heart.

He opened her door slowly. What moonlight there was cast a crooked oblong on the bed, on the wooden floor, on the otherwise dim and empty room.

"Addie?" A whisper. "Hello? Anyone home?"

He stepped inside, leaving the door behind him ajar.

The room was small and tidy and appeared to have been stripped of its personal effects. A bookshelf held a fish tank, cracked and empty. The bed was a queen, still neatly made, and thumbtacked above its iron headboard was a poster advertising some sort of equine dietary supplement. The poster depicted a cowgirl on horseback, her body leaning and her blond curls flying as they twisted, horse and rider together, around a teetering barrel.

Opposite the footboard, two pairs of cowboy boots stood by a scarred wooden dresser. Above the dresser hung a mirror and wedged in the mirror's oval frame were three curling photographs Bradley bent to study in the meager light from the window.

The first showed Cowgirl Addie sitting horseback in fringed leather chaps and a straw cowboy hat. She appeared to be thirteen or so, with braces on her teeth and hair tumbling halfway to her waist. She beamed into the camera as a sunflower-sized ribbon was affixed to the horse's bridle by a woman in a bright floral dress.

The next photo was of Graduation Addie, older and more familiar, standing between an elderly couple with her say-cheese smile as pure and bright as her white satin gown.

The last photo featured Prom Queen Addie: a stunning woman-child in a gown of pale organza with her hair upswept, her dark radiance eclipsing the lanky farm boy fumbling to pin an orchid corsage to her shoulder strap.

This last photo Bradley removed to examine in the light from the window. The boy was pool-hall handsome, his long hair bleached by the sun. His lips, viewed in quarter profile, offered just the faintest hint of a smile.

Bradley wondered at that smile—at what, exactly, it foretold. Cockiness? A shared joke? A kind of easy familiarity? He wondered if this had been Addie's first lover. Or, worse somehow, was about to be. He wondered also if Addie's father had been the photographer and if that were the case how the boy had managed even half a smile under Logan Decker's wilting gaze.

He replaced the photo and re-crossed the room to the window. A gravel walkway bisected the lawn as it ran in back of the house, the lawn's flat expanse ending at the bank of a narrow streambed. There, some forty yards distant, stood a modest log cabin, vaguely lopsided, the glow from its lone facing window framing in sharp cameo the two seated figures within.

One of whom, he realized, was Addie.

"Just like I figured."

Bradley jumped, nearly banging his head on the window frame. He turned to see Logan Decker in a robe of plaid flannel filling the doorway behind him.

"I was only—"

"Saying goodnight. I know."

The taller man advanced, hands in pockets, to join Bradley at the window. Together they watched as the two backlit silhouettes conversed across a small kitchen table.

"Well, professor. Looks like you ain't the only one couldn't wait until morning."

3

Lying in darkness, listening to Waylon's ragged breathing, Logan Decker had things on his mind.

He was not a bad person; of this he was fairly certain. On the other hand, what man actually knows his own true nature? If such a thing were possible then who among men would choose cruelty, or vanity, or ignorance? And yet the cruel, the vain, and the ignorant seemed to him in no short supply. No, it was a simple fact of the human condition that life was a rearview mirror and that a man could only see himself, his pure and honest self, in that which had already happened. And that, Logan decided, was the source of his disquiet.

That was better advice than any parent had ever given me.

Should it surprise Logan that his Adelaide was stubborn? Wasn't that a word, stubborn, that others applied to him? That he himself had applied to Jess and Vivian both? That they, in turn, had applied to Carole? The fact was that Addie was third-generation stubborn. Stubborn on both sides of the ledger. And if that was one of the things Logan saw in his own life's reflection, well, it certainly wasn't the worst.

Still there were times he wanted to shake her. To tell her, Wake up, dammit! To show her that life isn't some empty book in which you take up your pen and start scribbling on page one. That life is just a chapter in a volume that's part of a whole shelf of books that goes back generations. That he'd all but finished his own chapter, and even if the words he'd written weren't those she chose to live by, it was a by-God chapter just the same, and in it were notions and stories and lessons that could help her and guide her and that she could accept or reject however she saw fit just as long as she had sense enough to quit her own scribbling long enough to sit down and give it a read.

Take that man. That professor, or whatever he was. Old enough to be her damn uncle. Gold wristwatch and new penny loafers and pressed khaki slacks. A man Logan pictured sniffing the garden every fall and plucking the freshest bud, the prettiest blossom, and pinning it to his lapel. Then come the next year and a new crop to choose from and he does it all over again. Eeny, meeny, miny, moe. Addie by then just another wilted bloom on a path of faded flowers he'd trampled underfoot, and not a one of them ever sticking to those shoes.

This he could have told her. This and other things. Things you don't find in textbooks. Tales of grit and courage. Lessons about character. Whole passages on duty and honor and family. A life full of lessons he'd learned the hard way and for no useful purpose but to share with his own flesh and blood. His and Carole's. Lessons that, okay, maybe he hadn't always got around to sharing, busy like he was putting food on her plate and clothes on her back. Busy playing father and mother, cook and nursemaid, all while running a goddamn ranch.

I'm sure you could empathize with what he was going through.

This too was in Logan's mirror. The fact that sometimes even now he could feel his Carole right there beside him. And not just her memory—not some fading echo of her voice or her laugh, although there certainly was that—but her actual physical body. The actual thing. In bed it was, mostly, where some nights he'd roll in his sleep and drape an arm on her hip or bury his face in her neck. Feel the tickle of her hair. The smell of it. Hear her breathing, soft and steady, right there beside him. He'd smile to himself on nights like those, the feeling no longer a wish or a dream but something more than dream, more even than memory. Lying in darkness and daring not move for fear of losing her all over again.

Lord knows, he'd wanted to tell somebody. How many hours had he and Jess ridden together on horseback or on ATVs or in old pickup trucks talking beef or water, hay or horses? Mostly not talking at all. Mostly just looking sideways, as if Carole's death was some kind of sleeping bear they both knew to tiptoe around. Some hornets' nest that once kicked would only unleash a thousand painful stings.

I seen her last night, he could've told the old man a hundred different times. I honest-to-God touched her!

But he never did tell, not even once. Because somehow he never could. Just as Jess never could, the two of them jawing about this or that, about one thing or another, but never about the one thing—the one true and honest thing—they actually shared in common.

Choriocarcinoma. Logan had written the word on a strip he'd torn from a waiting room magazine and gone straight to the public library. A rare form of cancer, the textbook said, caused by pregnancy and childbirth. Caused, in other words, by Logan. The doctor had called it a blessing Addie'd been born at all; a miracle Carole'd survived for as long as she did. Except that miracles—another one of those lessons—don't always come clouded in stardust.

And now Vivian. So what do you say to a man like Jess who's outlived his wife and his daughter both? I'm sorry for your loss? You're in my thoughts and prayers? Because that was bullshit, plain and simple. What you do, Logan decided, is you shut your mouth and you give him the time he needs to brush himself off and get his ass back in the saddle. Give to him, in other words, the very gift he gave you.

Logan knew a man once, a rancher who'd been a guard down at Huntsville back in the gas chamber days where he'd witnessed over a dozen executions. And the damnedest thing, the man told him, was that when the gas started to rise those condemned men all did the exact same thing. What was that? Logan asked, and

21

the man's answer was that they all held their breath, every last one of 'em. After years of caged misery and strapped like they were to a hard wooden chair, they'd all held their breath in the hope of hanging on for a few extra seconds. Which just goes to show, the man said, how precious life is.

How precious life is. So maybe Jess at that very moment was feeling Vivian beside him; the weight of her in his bed. And then tomorrow, or the day after, or whenever things got back to normal around here, maybe Jess and Logan would sit down and talk about that. Talk themselves blue, and have a good cry, and maybe a laugh or two.

But probably not. Most likely they'd just cinch it up tight and get back to it, keeping to themselves whatever it was that troubled them on nights like these, alone in their beds in the dark.

This too, Logan knew, was written on Addie's ledger.

4

They saddled the horses at daybreak. Feather, her old sorrel mare, pressed her blaze into Addie's shirtfront as Addie patted her and stroked her and whispered to the horse a guilty confession of greetings and apologies, excuses and promises.

"She look fat to you?" Her father led Lightning, his big Appaloosa gelding, from inside the darkened barn. The two horses bobbed and snuffled, their mingled breath clouding the cold morning air as Waylon, his tail wagging crazily, snaked between and among their dozen legs.

"Has she been getting any work?"

"Your grandma Vivian used to chase her in the arena till Jess made her quit. Jess still rides her now and again, but mostly she just eats."

Logan stepped into his stirrup and hopped once and swung himself into the saddle.

You never used to hop, Addie thought.

"She looks good. Better than good. Thank you for even keeping her."

"Hell," her father said, snugging his hat and pointing his horse toward the sunrise. "Waylon, you stay."

The road had been graded, the footing firm and sandy. Running eastward from the horse barn it followed a line of ancient cottonwoods flanking an irrigation ditch whose lyric splash and gurgle joined with the twitter of birdsong to form a bright morning melody. At Red Rock Creek, a mile or so upstream, both roadway and river would fork with one branch climbing steeply through a rocky forest of piñon and juniper while the other curved gently onto the mesa behind the house.

"Now there's a woman can sit a horse," Logan said as Addie's sorrel eased alongside the Appaloosa, the two animals falling into a familiar rhythm. "I don't see how you could go five years without riding."

"How do you know I haven't been riding?"

"In Los Angeles? Riding in cars is more like it. Sitting in traffic all day."

"Have you ever been to Los Angeles?"

"I been to big cities. I don't care to go back is all I'm saying."

The cottonwoods under which they passed formed a colonnade and the air beneath it bore the fallen-leaf fragrance of autumn. Sunlight dappled the road and flared at the gaps in the trees. The trees themselves were already changing—more yellow now than green—and there was something vaguely ecclesial in their procession, horses and riders together, through the golden light and the massive trees and the vertical red-rock cliffs.

How many times, Addie asked herself, had she ridden this way before? Five hundred? A thousand? It seemed to her that little had changed and yet somehow that everything had. The horse, so familiar beneath her, was no longer her horse; the road no longer her road. She was a visitor now, a *guest*, and she felt in that single blunt syllable a sadness whose weight seemed to burden the mare, slowing her step and forcing Addie to close her legs and cluck her forward again.

Mindful humans evolve, she reminded herself, and grow, even if the world around them—and especially the people around them—do not. It was Bradley who'd warned her against what he'd called the false comfort of nostalgia. Change, he said, was life's only constant—just as inertia was death and entropy—the invisible force that drives molecules careening and joining into new and different combinations: the very essence of life.

By that measure, Addie Decker was finally living. As a freshman at UCLA she'd visited Disneyland and Universal Studios and she'd splashed in the teeth-chattering surf at Zuma Beach. By the end of her sophomore year she'd learned to speak passable French and to wait tables, offering advice on the optimal pairing of food and wine. By her junior year she'd seen the LA Philharmonic, and been to an actual Hollywood party, and visited world-class museums like the Getty and the Broad. She'd spent her summers working at Le Petit and her spring breaks with her girlfriends in places like Palm Springs and Ensenada.

In an elective called Cultural Anthropology she'd taken her senior year, Addie had studied traditional rites of passage, from the walkabout rituals of the indigenous Australians to the Jewish *bat mitzvah* and the Mexican *quinceañera*. Intended to mark the transition from adolescence to adulthood, all shared the common elements of separation, liminality, and incorporation. College being such a rite, she'd recognized the inherent paradox of studying a phenomenon whose very study was itself the phenomenon, like the mirror's reflection of itself in a mirror, the images cascading into dizzying infinity.

Where she'd stood in her own life's transition had been no less disorienting. Separated, obviously, but when would she know for certain that a threshold had been crossed?

Then, in her first semester of graduate studies, she'd met Bradley Sommers. Addie had expected some silver-haired eminence, stern and jowly, to head the university's Center for Climate Change and so was surprised when a boyish man in jeans and running shoes bounded to the head of her classroom. He was, she would later learn, only twelve years her senior and yet he brought to the course curriculum a worldly perspective and the kind of fiery passion Addie had been disappointed to find lacking in most of her other professors.

There'd been an elemental attraction between teacher and pupil—a planetary pull, as Bradley described it—from the day of that very first meeting. Before long their after-class discussions had spilled into afternoon coffees, and then dinner dates, and then, more dizzying still, into clandestine sleepovers.

It happened so quickly. Addie's love life to that point had been largely anticipatory, the campus hookup culture so alien to her sense of propriety. In truth, the boys she'd met at college all seemed either loud and drunk or else so painfully tongue-tied as to make even casual conversation a chore. Bradley in contrast was confident and wise, urbane and witty. His interests were varied and his viewpoints mature. Most of all he respected Addie and never spoke down to her opinions or presumed on her affections.

Not that it had been easy. Inside her body, desire and caution had circled like wrestlers, ducking and feinting, each probing the other's defenses. That their relationship would violate a central tenet of the university's *Faculty Handbook on Conduct and Ethics* was, she supposed, the very thing that made their relationship possible since it was precisely its transgressive nature—the career-ending power Bradley had ceded to her on their first night together—that had enabled Addie to cross what was for her that most daunting of thresholds.

When, a month into that first graduate semester, Bradley was approached by Naomi Lopez, executive director of the fabled Western Warriors, with a request that he travel to Colorado and lead opposition to Archer-Mason Industries' planned expansion of carbon dioxide extraction in and around the Canyons of the Ancients National Monument—literally Addie's backyard—it was she who'd urged him to accept. Bradley had agreed, but only on condition that Addie accompany him as his graduate assistant.

At first she'd demurred, citing the promise she'd made to herself five years earlier. But there was no use denying that her vow seemed petty once vocalized, and in the discussion that followed Addie confided for the first time to anyone the depth of her schoolgirl yearning for a life beyond honky-tonk weekends and early motherhood and church bake sales—beyond the stultifying orthodoxy she'd feared was her lot in a town like Cortez, Colorado.

They'd talked until daybreak, she and Bradley, and when they'd finished talking the catharsis Addie experienced had been almost, well, Freudian in its effect. Then came news of her grandmother's passing, and evasion was no longer an option.

But still there was the matter of the letter.

It had been a Saturday evening in June, some two weeks after her high school graduation, and Addie had just returned from the fairgrounds rodeo. Suspecting her father might have been drinking, she'd gone to check on the horses before turning in for the night. A light still burned in his empty barn office where, opening the door to investigate, she saw his tooled leather checkbook open on the desk. She sat in his oak swivel chair, and when she slid the drawer open to replace the checkbook, something inside caught her eye.

Something gold, and baby blue.

The heavy envelope lay buried beneath slabs of other paperwork—seed catalogs and invoices and old bills of lading—with only one corner showing. She unearthed it carefully and held it to the light, noting the date on its postmark.

March 21.

Her hands now trembling, she tore at the flap and slid the brochure from inside. After it, like the *snick* of a switchblade, came the letter printed on thick paper stock.

"Dear Bruin," it began.

At first her father pled innocence. The envelope must've gotten overlooked, or been buried somehow among all his other papers. It wasn't until Monday, some forty hours after its discovery, that Logan finally confessed.

"There is such a notion," he told her, "as doing the wrong thing for the right reasons."

Addie, heaving her last duffel into the bed of her pickup, pretended to ignore him.

"When I was your age," he continued, stepping into the driveway, "the thing I wanted more than anything was to go to CSU. Your uncle Luther went. Only there wasn't money enough for the both of us, so one of us had to stay home."

She stood on the wheel, leaning and stretching bungie cords to secure her cargo in place.

"Fort Collins is only eight hours away. Heck, you could drive home on weekends. Bring your laundry, eat some home cooking. That's what Luther used to do. To this day he'll tell you those were the best years of his life."

"*His* life, Daddy." Addie wheeled, red-faced, to where he stood in the driveway. "This is *my* life we're talking about."

"It's your life I was thinking about. Your life here, with Waylon and Feather. With your friends and your schoolmates. With your grandparents, for goodness sake. Have you thought about them for even a minute?"

"Don't try to make me the guilty party."

"They want you here as much as I do. You know they do. Here where you were born. Here where your mother is buried."

Addie circled the truck, inspecting. "I'll call Grandma when I get to California," she said, yanking the driver's door open.

"And what about Colt? Ain't you even gonna say goodbye to him?"

The driver's door slammed and the engine caught and roared. Addie lowered the passenger-side window as she leaned over the console.

"You can call him! Tell him goodbye for me! You can invite him over and the two of you can watch baseball and drink beer and make plans for my future!"

She'd jammed her truck into gear then, and stomped on the gas, and she never looked back at the tall man receding in the driveway behind her, bending double as she sped from view.

"Colt ought to be there today."

"What?"

Her father drew rein, halting the big Appaloosa. To Addie's surprise they'd arrived at the fork where the first stony riffles echoed in the pine trees. Where somewhere beyond them a hissing sound, faint and serpentine, seemed to hang in the wind.

"Colt called to say he'd like to pay his respects to your grandma. You'll recall she was right fond of that boy."

"Daddy. I don't know what you're thinking, but Colt Dixon is a married man."

"Was a married man. Him and your friend Brenda, they divorced around four months ago."

"Divorced? How come?"

Logan shrugged. "I reckon their baby had something to do with it. Born dead is the story I heard."

Addie turned the sorrel on its haunches and urged it up the trail toward the mesa.

"Hold on!" her father called. "I thought we might ride to the waterfall!"

She spurred the mare into a canter. After a long minute of uphill pounding she heard Lightning's anvil hooves thundering behind her.

Addie was first to the cattle guard where the dry fork of the irrigation ditch passed under the track through a culvert. From this higher vantage the hissing she'd heard at the fork sounded more like an idling jet engine. She dismounted and held the reins in one hand and unlatched the gate with the other.

She walked the horse forward, then froze.

"Oh my God," she said.

5

Bradley had overslept, and by the time he descended to the kitchen he could sense from the deafening stillness the house was already empty. He checked his phone for the umpteenth time, turning a circle where he stood.

A coffeepot warmed on the counter. In a cupboard he found a single porcelain mug, chipped and stained, amid a jumble of mismatched glasses.

On the porch out front he got his first sunlit view of the Red Rocks Ranch in all its autumnal splendor: Emerald fields framed by massive cottonwoods ablaze in greens and golds. Girdling walls of terra cotta rising to a sky of glacial blue. Elongated shadows, black and canted, running in chiaroscuro. He was reminded of Klimt somehow, or maybe van Gogh. *The Mulberry Tree.* He'd seen it once at the Norton Simon and now stood witness to that same arsenic palate of madness and wonder.

"You must be that professor."

The old man sat in a rocker with his back to the risen sun. He was swaddled in a faded quilt while across his lap rested a twin-barreled shotgun that, by Bradley's estimation, may well have outweighed him.

Bradley recognized him immediately, from the photo of Addie's high school graduation.

"Bradley Sommers. You must be Mr. Olsen. I'm terribly sorry for your loss."

The old man tossed a hand.

"Addie's told me stories about her grandmother. I only wish

I'd had the chance to meet her in person. I know Addie held her in high esteem."

"You could say the feelin was mutual. My Vivian, she clucked over that girl like a mother hen. I reckon we both did." The shotgun barrels lifted. "Reckon I still do."

"Not for warding off suitors, I hope."

"This? Hell no. This here is for wolves. We get packs of 'em around these parts, daytime and night."

Bradley's gaze shot to the Prius; to where they'd parked it in darkness some thirty long yards from the house.

"I'm funnin you, sonny. There ain't wolf one in the whole state of Colorado. Used to be, many years back. They come clear up from Mexico. I hear where they're bringin 'em back on the Gila. On purpose, I mean. As if gettin quit of 'em in the first place wasn't chore enough. Ranchers down there are fit to be tied, and I can't say as I blame 'em." He fished a handkerchief from his pocket and half sneezed, half coughed into it and examined it closely before returning it to his pocket. "Whatever you teach at that college of yours, I hope it ain't nothin about animals."

"I co-chair the university's Institute of the Environment and Sustainability, but my academic background is in geology."

"Geology. You mean like rocks and such."

"That's right."

"What about oil and gas?"

"That's also part of it. And alternatives like wind and solar and geothermal."

"And that's what Addie's been studyin? Environment and sustainability?"

"I believe she was a psychology major at one point, but her degree is in environmental science."

"Huh. There any money in that?"

Bradley rested his weight on the railing and took a sip of his coffee. He nearly choked.

"Well, there's always teaching. And research, of course. Environmental consulting and TES surveys, that sort of thing. And quite a few governmental positions. Not to shortchange the value of knowledge for its own sake."

"Sounds like farming. If you can't grow rich, at least you can grow food."

Bradley smiled. "I'm guessing that's alfalfa." He pointed his chin toward the nearest hayfield, a darker shade of green than those beyond. "What else do you grow around here?"

"Hay mostly, all kinds. Well, mostly we grow beef, but there's folks in these parts that grow grapes and stone fruits—peaches, plums, apricots. Some apples and pears. Did you know that the fruit from this bitty canyon took the gold medal at the St. Louis World's Fair?"

"I did not know that."

"There you go, professor. You learnt somethin today. They say folks is growin marijuana now, but no place I ever seen it. Course I'm not sure I'd recognize it if I did."

"There goes my second guess."

"How's that?"

Bradley nodded to the gun.

"Oh. Had me a spot of trouble yesterday. Got into it with this fella and told him if I seen his truck again, I'd fill it with buckshot." His blue eyes twinkled as he smiled. "Call me old fashioned, but I abhor idle threats."

"What sort of trouble are we talking about?"

"Listen for a second." He cupped a hand to his ear. "Can you hear that?"

Bradley listened. Only then did he realize that the breeze he'd heard whispering in the cottonwoods had in fact been nothing of the kind.

"What is it?"

"I don't hear so good, but if it's a low kind of humming, then it's the compressor station. If it sounds like steam from a busted hose, then they're venting that new gas well."

Bradley set his mug on the railing and walked off the porch and around to the side of the house. The sound seemed to come from atop the high mesa in back.

"Carbon dioxide?"

"That's right." The old man craned his neck. "They pump it from here and pipe it clear down to Texas. 'Advanced recovery' is what they call it. Say it gooses the oil right out of the ground. Claim we're settin on the mother lode."

"You mean Archer-Mason Industries?"

"That's right."

Bradley shielded his eyes with a hand, scanning the edge of the mesa. "What they say is true enough. The McElmo Dome is one of the largest and purest known CO_2 repositories on earth."

"So that fella said. Right before I run him off."

Bradley circled back to the porch, pausing again to survey the canyon—its lithic walls and its dizzying colors.

"Who was this fellow, exactly?"

"Oh, some Denver boy. Silverbelly hat and crocodile boots. We own this section of land outright, y'see. That's six hundred and forty acres. That thousand acres on top we lease from the government. But the BLM, they went and auctioned off the mineral rights. Double-dipped is what they done. Leased the grazing to Logan and the minerals to Archer-Mason. Never mind that cows and compressors don't mix."

"Isn't that part of the national monument?"

"That's the damnedest part. You try and hike up from here and the BLM will cite you for trespass. You gotta stay on the trails, they say, on account of the monument. Don't want you steppin on no pottery sherds or climbin into them cliff dwellings. As if folks ain't been doin that for two hundred years. But if Archer-Mason wants to doze a new road or lay a new pipeline, why hell, the feds say go right ahead."

"Or overrun it with cattle?"

The old man's eyes lost some of their twinkle.

"That's a different ball of wax. My family's been runnin cows on this land since before there was a monument. Since before there was a BLM for that matter."

Bradley wasn't about to argue, though he was sorely tempted. The fact was that over three hundred million acres of Western public lands, including 90 percent of all Bureau of Land Management holdings—an area three times the size of California—were leased for private livestock grazing at rates well below market. The resulting litany of environmental impacts included denuded rangeland, polluted streams, evaporated wetlands, eroded soils, invasive flora, endangered native species, mile upon mile of barbed-wire fencing, and an annual bill to the American taxpayer of five hundred million dollars. In short, America was subsidizing a handful of livestock permit holders—welfare ranchers—to turn the public landscape into a private feedlot, all to provide less than 3 percent of the national beef supply.

"So this fellow we're talking about, he's a land man for Archer-Mason?"

"That's right."

"Then why run him off? I had the impression from Addie that you and her father were in favor of resource development."

"Hell, son. I know you can't make a omelet without breakin some eggs. That's why we didn't say boo when they first started drillin. We didn't like it, but we didn't complain. But there's only so much you can ask a man to endure. Here, come see for yourself."

He leaned the gun against the railing and struggled to his feet, shedding the quilt as he stood. He bade Bradley follow him down the steps and across the lawn to the western side of the house. There a tractor—a green John Deere model—rested under a buzzing nimbus of flies. A trio of magpies, screeching in protest, flapped off at their approach.

Bradley covered his nose with a hand. In the tractor's front-end loader lay an oleaginous mass of raw and putrid flesh.

"Jesus. What is it?"

"Two yearling calves," the old man said, rising on tiptoes. "Logan found 'em in a wash Monday morning. Not a mark on 'em, and nary a coyote nor bear nor cat track to be seen. It's like they just laid down and died. And that's not all. We had half a dozen stillborn before these. We normally don't have but one or two stillbirths a year, and that's with near three hundred head."

Bradley stepped back to snap a photo with his phone. "So you think—"

"I don't *think*, sonny, I know. Once Archer-Mason started drillin up there, this here is what's happened. Now they say they're fixin to double the number of wells."

He turned on his heel and stalked toward the house. Bradley hurried to catch up.

"Methane and hydrogen sulfide are common by-products of well venting," Bradley explained. "And carbon dioxide, although generally non-poisonous, tends to settle in low spots, displacing atmospheric oxygen. That's probably what happened here."

The old man didn't answer. Back on the porch, he folded his quilt into a cushion and settled into his rocker, replacing the shotgun across his thighs.

"So what are you planning to do about it?"

The old man grunted. "This part of the ranch you see here, this hundred and sixty acres, it come with the mineral rights. On the other quarter-sections the owners sold off their minerals during the Depression. When my daddy bought 'em out he wound up with what you call your split estate."

"Meaning you own the surface land but not the underlying minerals."

"Denver, he's paid me four visits so far, each time with a different deal. First it was wantin to lease the minerals under the homestead. I was neighborly about it, but I told him I wasn't interested. Then he come back a few days later and offered more money. All puffed up, like he done me a favor. Time after that he wasn't so friendly. Said they could force-pool my minerals with the BLM's minerals and I wouldn't have a say in the matter. Then the last time he said if we didn't want a road or a well pad right here in our yard then by God we'd have to pay money to Archer-Mason. And that's when I run him off."

Bradley heard the dog barking. To the east he saw two riders in silhouette approaching from under the trees.

"You said Archer-Mason is planning more wells. They call that down-spacing. It means they've applied for permission to increase the drilling density in this particular unit. As a mineral rights owner you should've received written notice of that application."

"Maybe I did. That Denver, he brung me a whole stack of papers. It's all up there at the cabin."

"And when was that, exactly?"

"Let's see. That would've been day before yesterday."

When the riders had reached the barn, the shape that was Addie swung down from her saddle and bent to quiet the dog.

"You're right about one thing." Bradley extracted the phone from his pocket and studied the photo he'd taken. "That man from Denver is not your friend. But if we play our cards right, he may have done us both a very big favor."

6

A rusting Ford Bronco, Creamsicle orange with a white driver's door, pulled to the graveled shoulder along a wooded stretch two miles from the state highway. The strapping young man who alighted slung a rifle case over his shoulder. He locked his door and pocketed the keys and looked both ways before wading into the roadside brush.

His hike through the tangled bulwark of oak brush and elm was but twenty or so yards, and once to the clearing he set down the case and paced off his distance and removed four thumbtacks from his pocket. From another pocket he removed a folded page he'd torn from a magazine. He slapped the page onto the bark of a cottonwood and tacked it in place and stepped back to study the effect.

What breeze there was came from the west. Gently, like a breath. He figured it for two miles per hour. Facing it with eyelids closed he could smell the coming winter as he listened for cars on the highway.

Before returning to his rifle he climbed the bank of a low earthen dike behind the tree. The stock pond, ankle-deep when last he'd seen it, today was a dried flower arrangement of cattails and cockleburs bleached by mud and sun to the color of cold chicken gravy.

Again he listened in silence. From a treetop behind him a blackbird whistled a single mournful note. To his right, insects buzzed and jumbled. Of life there was no other sign.

He shed his coat, a faded brown Carhartt, as he strode back to the rifle. Draping it on the ground, he knelt and slid the gun from its case along with two foam earplugs and one new box of .30-30 cartridges.

He stoppered his ears and cradled the weapon in his elbow and thumbed six of the cartridges into the receiver while humming an Aerosmith tune, "Dream On," his head nodding in time to the beat.

He stood. The distance he'd paced was a hundred yards. The breeze held steady at two, maybe two and a half. His rifle was a lever-action Marlin 336C, his scope a Weaver K4. His target was a color photograph in the upper-right quadrant of the torn magazine page, the photo depicting a smiling man in a button-down shirt with his sleeves rolled to reveal tanned forearms and a fancy gold wristwatch.

*Boomchacka**Boom**chacka**Boom**chacka**Boom**chacka**Boom**chacka**Boom*. He squeezed off the rounds with a rapidity that bespoke either skill or anger, and when the echo of the last report had died in the trees he lowered his weapon and ejected the final casing.

After returning the rifle to its case, he unplugged his ears and stood and shrugged back into his coat. He bent once more to collect the ejected shells, counting them as he did. Shouldering the rifle this time, he re-paced the distance to the tree.

The tacks he removed with a blackened thumbnail to examine what was left of his target. The man in the photo—his dimpled smile, his fancy-ass watch—had been obliterated by a tight cluster of five bullet holes that had overlapped into one. The sixth shot—high and right by an inch—had altered the headline above the photo to read "One Man's Quest to Save t   merican West."

"Dream on," the young man sang aloud, folding the page into his pocket and turning again toward the road.

7

Addie knew that, try though she might to simply accept his bolstering presence, she was fated to see the day, and her old hometown, and the people who lived there, through Bradley Sommers' eyes.

The Bradley Sommers, she reminded herself, whose father was a Caltech professor and whose mother had once served on the Pasadena city council. The Bradley whose boyhood home had been a meticulously restored Craftsman bungalow in a leafy enclave of other historic houses whose owners needed something like three city approvals and a special variance before they could replace so much as a front doorknob.

Montezuma County in contrast had virtually no zoning, since it interfered with a man's God-given right to live as he damn well pleased. It had no building department because it neither licensed contractors nor inspected their work. Instead it had as part of its Comprehensive Land Use Plan a "Code of the West"—commonsense tips for country living—inspired by the writings of pulp novelist Zane Grey. Things like, "Children are exposed to different hazards in a rural setting than they are in an urban area," or "Be aware that adjacent mining uses can expand and cause negative impacts."

The result, not surprisingly, was an architectural hodgepodge in which the custom log-and-glass aeries of urban retirees might overlook a warren of singlewide trailers. In which automobile graveyards or mini storage units might sprout, weed-like, in the middle of residential neighborhoods. In which even the pristine beauty of McElmo Canyon had been marred by the odd junkyard or gravel pit or, in the case of one enterprising neighbor, an off-road racing track.

So what was Bradley thinking, riding in front with her grandfather as their procession snaked the twelve wending miles from the Red Rocks Ranch to the faux-stone solemnity of the funeral home in Cortez? The route took them past four pawn shops, and three liquor stores, and two defunct service stations. It traversed rubber-tomahawk tourist emporia and weekly-rate motels. And once onto the state highway that ran like a scar through downtown Cortez, they passed a succession of faded billboards for the likes of Denny's and Wendy's, Arby's and JESUS SAVES.

For her part, seeing it all again, Addie thought how much better off Cortez and the surrounding communities might have been had they been settled a century later, when the area's centrality to forested peaks and high-desert mesas might have attracted the sorts of seekers and dreamers who'd settled in places like Santa Fe or Taos, Sedona or Moab. She imagined, and not for the first time, a cosmic pulse erasing man's first muddy footprints and giving the town, the county, the newly pristine landscape the second chance they deserved.

Amid the wood-paneled quiescence of the viewing room, where her grandmother's rouged propinquity reduced all conversation to murmur, Addie watched as Bradley, standing apart from her family, fielded the tremulous handshakes of curious mourners whom Addie recognized from the Historical Society, or the Cowbelles, or the Episcopal Church. Several with canes, still others bent over walkers, their shuffling parade past the casket left a slipstream of Old Spice and Mineral Ice and the faintish redolence of mothballs.

Addie herself proved an object of no small curiosity. The hands squeezing hers were blue-veined and spotted, their skin like waxed paper. Carole's girl, she heard herself called. Vivian's pride and joy. Do you remember? they asked her, but mostly she did not. Mostly she felt numbed by grief and guilt at the realization that she among all those present had probably been longest in seeing her own grandmother alive.

Once the torrent of new arrivals had slowed to a trickle she joined Bradley where he stood by a sideboard display of framed family photographs.

"She was very beautiful," he said, restoring one to its place. Addie recognized it as her grandmother's favorite—she and Grandpa Jess on their honeymoon at the Broadmoor on the morning after the night on which, she'd once confided to Addie, they both had lost their virginity.

"You're a saint for doing this."

"I feel more like the bearded lady." He turned to survey the room. "Everyone seems to want a closer look."

"The rubes lining up to watch, corndogs in hand, while the fat man and the bearded lady watch them right back."

"That sounds overly judgmental. They seem like decent people."

"I never meant to suggest otherwise."

"Your grandmother's friends, after all."

She took up the photo in its ornate silver frame. "You would've liked her. She was plainspoken, and God knows she could be prickly, but at least you always knew where you stood."

"I like him."

She followed his nod to where Grandpa Jess stood in the same place Addie had left him, in the same vested suit and polished brogans he'd worn to her graduation. Like a rock he was, in a stream running cold and warm, swift and slow, season upon season, but that somehow never budges.

"He's putting on a brave face, but I know he's devastated. Did he tell you they'd been married sixty-two years?"

"Wow."

"In all that time I don't think they spent a single night apart. I'd also bet he never once mopped a floor or made a bed or washed a load of laundry. On the other hand I've seen him buck hay and shoe horses and split a cord of hardwood. And that was well into his seventies."

They watched together as Jess nodded and chatted and even smiled at the occasional anecdote or rib-digging reminiscence shared with his old friends and neighbors. Never, Addie noted, moving more than an arm's length from the casket.

And that's when she saw him, standing with her father. He wore a faded brown jacket and blue jeans and brown cowboy boots. His hair was short now, but there was no mistaking the slouching posture or the easy laugh she could read in quarter-profile even as the sound of it was lost in the burble of other voices.

Her father's glance over Colt Dixon's shoulder, the judgment in it, pierced her like an arrow.

"Are you all right?"

"I'm fine. Come on, let's look at pictures."

She steered Bradley to another table on which more photos were arrayed along with some yellowed newspaper clippings.

"I know this isn't the time," she said, "but I learned something this morning. Archer-Mason is drilling wells on our grazing allotment. There's a new pad up on the mesa, plus a road and some sort of pumping station."

"I know."

"What do you mean you know?"

"Jess told me all about it. That well you probably saw is part of the drilling unit Archer-Mason wants to down-space. I don't know about your father, but your grandfather's against it." He slipped his phone from his pocket and showed Addie the image. "He thinks the vented gasses are harming his cattle."

"They're Daddy's cattle," she said, frowning at the photo, "but it's still Grandpa's ranch."

"And Grandpa's minerals. Did you know he owns the entire estate on a quarter-section of land that sits atop the McElmo Dome?"

"He does?"

"That's not all. As a mineral rights owner he's entitled by statute to written notice of any down-spacing application. Under Colorado law, that opens a seven-day window in which to request what's called a local public forum. They're almost never held, because nobody bothers to read the regulations. Also because the regs are set up in a way that makes citizen recourse all but impossible. But a hearing like that, right here in Cortez, could be our key to the mint. It's the perfect vehicle to rally opposition not just to the down-spacing application, but to Archer-Mason's entire play."

"Okay . . ."

"But there's a catch. Jess can't request the forum on his own. It has to come from the county commission acting on his behalf. What's more, they have to do it immediately. Or at least no later than Wednesday."

"Why?"

"Because like I said, the regs are stacked in favor of industry."

Addie turned to study the room, her eyes sweeping past her father and Colt Dixon in the way a phonograph needle skips a scratch in the vinyl.

"Montezuma County has three commissioners. You see those two by the door?"

She nodded toward a fleshy man in a Western-style suit and a shorter, jug-eared man beside him. Both were addressing a circle of attentive listeners.

"The big man is Mr. Hawkins. He owns a ranch up near Cahone. He was president of the Cattlemen's Association when I won their senior class scholarship. The man with the ears is Bud Wallace. He runs an oilfield services company."

She watched as Bradley took their measure. Hawkins did most of the talking while Wallace, as though heeding some silent alarm, slid his eyes in Bradley's direction.

"What are you thinking?" she asked him.

"That the oilman's a tough sale, but the rancher could be an ally. Like your grandfather says, cattle and compressors don't mix. Who's the third commissioner?"

"Mr. Holcomb. He owns the movie theater in town." She scanned the room, which had grown even more crowded. "I don't see him here, but I went to school with his daughter. Brenda is her name. She actually married my old boyfriend."

Her glance toward the casket was reflexive. Her father was leaning forward now, listening to an older woman who'd taken hold of his coat sleeve.

Had Colt already left? Was she wrong about why he'd come here in the first place?

"Maybe you could introduce me."

"What?"

"To Hawkins. I'd like to know where he stands."

"Okay, but wait a minute." She moved in front of Bradley. "You said Jess owns some mineral rights. What might those be worth?"

"Hard to know for certain, but at today's prices I'd say in the range of several million dollars."

Addie was flabbergasted. Nobody—not her father, not her grandparents—had ever so much as hinted at such a thing.

He asked, "What is it?"

"Nothing. It's just . . . you said Jess is opposed to the down-spacing. Are you sure he understands what he'd be giving up?"

"I am, but go ahead and ask him yourself. Meanwhile, what about our Mr. Hawkins?"

"Okay, but look. Even if Jess is on our side, do we really need to be bothering him or his friends on the day he's burying my grandmother?"

"Of course not." Bradley placed both his hands on her shoulders. "That was thoughtless of me. But let's not forget that seven-day window. Today is day three, and tomorrow is Sunday. That leaves Monday and Tuesday to bring at least two of the commissioners on board."

"I know, but—"

"And the forum doesn't have to involve Jess. We'd be raising issues on behalf of the entire community. Water quality, air quality, public health and safety. All the cattlemen will be affected, as will the farmers."

"I understand that, but—"

"Good." He gave her shoulders a squeeze. "Just think of all the good we can do."

"Hello, Addie."

She blenched as from a spark. Colt Dixon's proximity—his adult face in close-up—sent a bloom of warmth to her face.

"Hey. Hey, you! What a nice surprise."

They embraced awkwardly, then she stepped back to regard him. There were crows' feet at his eyes and furrows spanning his brow. His once-long hair, sun-bleached and curly, had darkened to the color of sand. Features that had seemed sculpted of clay by a slippery hand—his cheekbones, his chin—now appeared chiseled and of a piece with his broader shoulders. He looked windburned and rugged in that infuriating way young men managed to age, and she wondered reflexively if the years had been as kind to her.

"Colt Dixon," she said, drawing a breath, "this is my friend Bradley Sommers."

The men shook hands for what seemed longer than was traditional.

"Bradley is a professor at UCLA," she heard herself saying. "We'll be in the area for a month or so doing environmental consulting."

"That's what your dad was telling me."

Bradley said, "We're hoping to raise awareness of some of the long-term consequences of carbon dioxide mining and other extractive industries on things like air quality and groundwater. Issues that impact not just the ranchers and farmers in the area, but also the sportsmen. The hunters and anglers."

Colt glanced down at his camouflage shirtfront.

"I don't know if you appreciate this," Bradley continued, "but as pressure mounts to open up wild places to the fossil fuel industry, the conservation and outdoor recreation communities are finding common cause. If you have friends or coworkers in the area who hunt or fish, they might want to know what Addie and I are up to."

"Oh, I guarantee I got coworkers who'd like to know what you're up to."

"Great. Where do you work?"

"Pleasant View. For Archer-Mason Industries."

Bradley's smile remained in its place. "I see. As a roughneck?"

"Motorman. Going on three years now. A year in Aneth before that."

"Drilling for oil on the Navajo reservation?"

"That's right."

"Well then. Common cause may prove uncommonly difficult."

"Oh, we got a thing or two in common." Colt redirected his smile at Addie. "It's just that bankrupting my hometown ain't one of 'em."

"That's not what Bradley—"

"Don't think I'm unaware of the short-term stimulus oil and gas provides to rural communities like this," Bradley said. "I get it. But the resource is finite don't forget, and fickle, and even a modest drop in oil prices will stop a play like Archer-Mason's dead in its tracks."

"Exactly. Carpe diem, that's my motto."

"And what are you left with then? Formerly pristine wilderness scarred by roads and well pads. Methane and fracking fluid leaching into your groundwater. Not to mention the public health bill that local taxpayers will be footing long after the Archer-Masons of the world have pulled up stakes."

"Look at the bright side. If it wasn't for the likes of me, smart guys like you'd have nothing to consult about. And then Addie here would have no reason to helicopter in and honor us with her presence."

"There's no need to be rude," she told him.

Colt scuffed at the floor with his boot. "You're right, there was no call for that. I genuinely am sorry. But hey! Maybe Bradley'll let me make it up to him. I don't suppose you're a deer hunter? The reason I ask is we're already two weeks into rifle season and I ain't been out but the one time."

"I'm sure Bradley doesn't want—"

"I'm sure Bradley can decide for himself what he wants. Ain't that right, Bradley? You talk about your pristine wilderness, but have you actually seen it? Around here I mean? Heck, I'll show you some places that'll make your head explode. So what do you say? Get the lay of the land? Observe the locals in their native habitat?"

"Something to think about, certainly."

"There you go. Something to think about."

He clapped the older man's arm.

"And as for you," he told Addie as he backed toward the door, "I hope I'll see you around somewhere. Decker and Dixon! We could get together and *consult*."

8

The graveyard sat on a flat-topped rise overlooking the horse pasture from which Feather and Lightning looked on as, a hundred feet above them, a score of black-clad mourners had gathered in a semi-circle. At the center of their hushed assembly lay the oblong grave that Jess, ignoring Logan's entreaties, had spent the better part of the past three days stubbornly digging.

The closed walnut casket rested on a canvas tarp. Standing over it, his eyes downcast and his Bible open to Romans, was the ramrod figure of Edmund John O'Connell, rector of the Episcopal Church of St. Barnabas. Several of the mourners had their own Bibles open, paging with mottled hands clutching handkerchiefs or tissues or delicate glass-bead rosaries.

"Who shall separate us from the love of Christ?" the priest began. "Shall trouble or hardship or persecution or famine or nakedness or danger or sword?"

To Bradley, it was a timely question indeed. Stated differently, what more would it take for modern man—for humans alive in a twenty-first century of space probes and nanobots, gene sequencing and artificial intelligence—to cast aside the Bronze Age tethers of ignorance and superstition?

In the year 1800, the world's human population was fewer than one billion. By 1960 it was still only three billion. Today it was approaching eight billion, and growing exponentially. Billions upon billions more people—nearly a quarter-million per day—needing potable water and arable soil even as the fact of their very existence served to deplete both. It was, in short, a relentlessly vicious cycle that even the greatest fool or fanatic had to know was no longer remotely sustainable.

So where did the world's major religious denominations stand on what, in any rational universe, would be the moral issue of our time? An issue that presaged war and famine, mass migration and genocide—calamities, in other words, of truly biblical proportion? All preached the importance of procreation, that's where, and the largest and most influential of all—Roman Catholicism—forbade contraception entirely.

So go ahead, be fruitful and multiply. And while you're at it, don't forget to exercise dominion over the earth and all its creatures. Like cattle, for instance. Never mind that it took three thousand liters of water to produce a single hamburger, or that the United States alone ate over fourteen billion hamburgers a year.

That would be forty-two trillion liters of water per year. Just for hamburgers. Just in the US of A.

And never mind the four liters of water it took to make a one-liter plastic bottle, part of the 320 million metric tons of plastics produced in the world each year. Or the fact that, since the invention of polypropylene in the mid-1950s, every single molecule of the stuff ever created is still in existence, floating around somewhere, mostly in our garbage-strewn oceans.

These were the thoughts that haunted Bradley Sommers on a daily basis; the dark ruminations that kept him awake each night. His university tenure, his academic writings, his speaking and consulting engagements—these weren't just jobs to Bradley, they were his *mission.* He'd often imagined himself a herald; an envoy from a dystopian future sent back in time to awaken a bovine populace lulled into drooling obeisance by Fox News and Facebook, Xbox and Netflix—by the bread and circuses of a capitalist-consumer culture intent on devouring the very planet over which it sought hegemony.

"Amen," the priest intoned, closing his Bible.

Amen, Bradley agreed.

By some rehearsed prearrangement six men, Logan among them, surrounded the casket and lifted it by the tarp on which it lay and carried it to the foot of the grave. There, after some awkward jockeying, they managed to slide their heavy burden into the pit. Jess moved from where he'd been standing beside the priest and took hold of the shovel jutting from the mounded earth nearby. He stepped into a heaping scoop and pivoted and dumped the reddish clay soil onto the casket where it landed with a hollow thud.

One scoop, purely ceremonial. He replaced the shovel and dusted his hands and started back to the house.

Elderly wives leaned on the arms of their rickety husbands as all the mourners followed, murmuring quietly and stepping reverently around the other headstones so as not to disturb the eternal rest of those beneath. Bradley watched as Hawkins, the county commissioner, placed a bracing hand on the priest's slender shoulder. Addie waited until the crowd had dispersed before moving to stand before an upright slab of polished granite on which was incised:

CAROLE OLSEN DECKER
MAY 12, 1964 – AUGUST 4, 1998
BELOVED WIFE AND MOTHER

"Do you even remember her?" Bradley asked after doing the math.

"I'm not sure. I was only three when she died. I have these memories, these sort of phantom images, but I don't really know if it's my mother I remember or Grandma Vivian or someone else entirely."

"What images?"

She shook her head. "Nothing I can describe. Just . . . like holding a hand, or running ahead of somebody. Having my shoes tied. That sort of thing. The problem is, I've tried so hard to remember for so many years now that I can't even say what's real anymore."

"Does it matter? I mean, as long as it's real to you?"

She took a moment to reflect on that.

"You find yourself wondering how your life might've been different," she said. "I mean, I know it'd be different, but . . . would I be the same person? And if not, then who would I be? Would this version of me even like that version of me? Would we even recognize each other?"

"I imagine you'd be the same person but with a few different memories."

"No, I don't think so. I mean, is a person with different memories really the same person? It's like having this other life moving in parallel with your own but no matter how fast you run you'll never quite catch it. It'll always be out there, just beyond your grasp."

"The life you would have had if your mother had lived?"

"Psychology tells us that maternal interactions are the foundation on which the rest of our lives are built."

"And yours is built on a dream?"

"A dream, a figment. Thin air." She turned to face him. "If you've only—oh! Here." She dug into a pocket. "Your nose is bleeding."

More flowers had arrived with the casket; great clouds of lilies, carnations, and colorful hyacinth spilled from the living room through the dining room and into the kitchen where ovens hummed and crockpots bubbled and bustling women in sensible shoes fussed over plastic tubs of potato salad and coleslaw and cling-wrapped platters of deviled eggs, the warm aromas of the cooking and of the coffee in rented urns reminding Bradley it had been nearly six hours since he'd eaten.

Dabbing his nose with the tissue, he eased his way through the crowded dining room and into the high-beamed living room where he positioned himself by the grandfather clock at the foot of the staircase to watch and wait for the men who smoked and laughed and ate from paper plates to achieve the desired alignment.

Addie was still in the kitchen. Her grandfather Jess stood by the fireplace with one hand on the mantle and one foot propped on the hearth. Logan with Waylon beside him had been cornered by a gaggle of women near the open hallway to the rear of the house. Hawkins, meanwhile, was orbiting clockwise, slapping backs as he went. As the big man approached the nodal vector of the mounted elk's head, Bradley pushed off from the wall and headed in his direction.

"Hello, son! You must be Addie's new beau I been hearing about."

Bradley had to switch hands with the tissue to shake Hawkins' meaty paw.

"Mile-high elevation and 5 percent humidity will do that to your nose. I warn out-of-towners all the time. On the plus side, you do get your money's worth from the liquor."

Bradley slipped the phone from his pocket and swiped to the image. He handed it to Hawkins without speaking.

"What the hell is this?"

"Yearling calves," Jess said, butting into the conversation. "Dropped dead on their feet by that new gas well up top. The professor here says it was carbon dioxide from the venting what done it."

"Bullshit. Carbon dioxide never hurt a fly. It's what comes out of our mouths when we breathe, ain't it?"

Bradley examined the tissue to confirm his bleeding had stopped.

"In cases like this," he explained, "carbon dioxide isn't the proximate cause of death. It's suffocation from lack of oxygen when the CO_2 settles in creekbeds and arroyos. Have you ever heard of Lake Nyos? It sits in a volcanic crater in Cameroon, in

52

central Africa. In 1986, a huge bubble of carbon dioxide burst out of the lake and settled in the surrounding valleys, killing over three thousand head of cattle. It also killed seventeen hundred people."

"Well, hell," the big man said, returning the phone. "Sounds to me like some kind of a freak accident."

"Oxygen displacement is the least of your problems. I understand you're involved with the Cattlemen's Association. Out of curiosity, have you had any members who graze near a drill site complain of an uptick in stillbirths?"

"Well. Now that you mention it."

"We had half a dozen this year," Jess told him. "All since they started their drillin'."

Hawkins' eyes narrowed on Bradley. "And you think it's the carbon dioxide?"

"No. It's either the hydrogen sulfide or the methane, depending on the well. Or maybe it's sulfur dioxide, or benzene, or any of a dozen other VOCs. The point is that it's happening, and until there are independent testing protocols in place you'll never know for sure what you're dealing with. Do you happen to know any midwives?"

"Any what?"

"Midwives. Or neonatal nurses. Anyone dealing with newborns."

"What's that got to do with the price of cheese in China?"

"If you're seeing stillbirths at this rate in cattle, you might also see them in humans. Not as frequent, of course, but doubly important to monitor."

"There was that nurse in Durango," Jess said. Bradley shook his head, and Hawkins took up the story.

"That was around ten years ago. Some drill monkey came into the ER at Mercy covered in fracking fluid. He turned out to be fine, but the nurse who treated him damn near died from organ failure. Spent something like thirty hours in the ICU. Her doctors wanted to know what she'd been exposed to, but the operator wouldn't say. Claimed it was proprietary, like the formula for Coca-Cola. Never mind that the woman had one foot out the door."

Bradley remembered the incident. He also recalled that when Colorado's Oil and Gas Conservation Commission proposed a rule requiring such disclosure, Halliburton responded by threatening to pull all of its fracking products from the state. Faced with the loss of some twenty-nine billion dollars in taxes and royalties, the commissioners backed down.

"Look," Bradley said. "If you own only the surface estate, and if an operator decides to run a pipeline through your hayfield or an access road past your front door, what legal recourse do you have?"

"None to speak of," Hawkins admitted. "It's a problem, I'll grant you that. But most operators in these parts have been willing to work with the ranchers. We've had a few ruffled feathers, but nothing we couldn't smooth over."

Bradley looked to confirm that Addie was still in the kitchen.

"And what happens when they double the well density, making those compromises harder to come by? Or when they double it again? What happens when the resource plays out and the responsible operators are replaced by the fly-by-night outfits?"

"I see your point. But oil and gas pays the bills around here. Archer-Mason alone makes up half the county tax base. We'd be tarred and feathered if we did anything that might chase 'em away."

"Away to where? The McElmo Dome isn't moving. They can't take the resource with them."

"He's right," Jess said. "The boy is right."

"Even so, you're forgetting one thing. I'm just a county commissioner. We got sixty-four counties in this state, and not a one of us sets the goddamn rules. The COGCC and the state legislature, they're the ones calling the shots."

"With one important exception."

"What exception?"

Bradley returned to Jess. "Right now Archer-Mason is allowed one well site every forty acres. Down-spacing to twenty acres means they've had to submit a formal application to the COGCC. I haven't seen it but I can guarantee it fails to address the public health and safety implications, let alone the environmental impacts. And that includes how the cattlemen in the area will be affected." He pivoted back to Hawkins. "Families like yours and Jess's, who've been ranching out here for generations."

"So what can I do about it?"

"The rules allow for a government designee to request what's called a local public forum. It's like a public hearing that's held right here in the county. That way the ranchers can testify, and so can expert witnesses. You can raise issues like the ones we've been talking about. Things like setbacks and monitoring and other protections for ranching and farming operations."

"And you're saying the county commission is this government whatchamacallit?"

Bradley nodded. "Talk to your county counsel. But understand that the clock is already ticking. You'll need to request the public forum no later than Tuesday."

"Then there's another problem. We don't meet but twice a month, and it takes two votes just to fill a pothole. Plus I'll tell you right now that if the industry is against what you're talking about, Bud Wallace is damn sure against it."

Bradley again looked to the dining room. This time he saw Addie sidling toward them, getting waylaid by every third guest she passed.

"You don't need a formal meeting. All you need are two signatures on a fax to Denver before Wednesday. Which means we'll need the theater owner. What was his name again?"

"Holcomb. Marty Holcomb."

"Where do you think he'd stand on the issue?"

The older men shared a look. Jess said, "You know his daughter lost that baby."

Bradley asked, "Is her name Brenda?"

"If you could prove Archer-Mason had a hand in that," Hawkins said, "Marty'd not only fall in line, he'd lead the damn parade."

"And what parade is that?" Addie appeared among them, slipping her hand under Bradley's arm.

"The parade of horribles stemming from oil and gas development. I'm afraid I've been boring these men on a day when our thoughts should properly be elsewhere."

"You'll have to forgive Bradley, Mr. Hawkins. He's very passionate on certain subjects, and once he takes the bit in his mouth, there's no use trying to turn him."

"I can see that. And in my experience a horse that can't be turned eventually winds up in a ditch. Well, it was nice chatting, son." He patted Bradley's shoulder. "I got a feeling it won't be our last."

Across the room, Logan had extricated himself from the women and was zigging in their direction.

"I'm about dead on my feet," Jess said. "Think you and your pa can manage from here?"

"Of course. But what about . . . ?"

"Your grandma? Don't worry, I'll tend to her later."

Logan joined their circle, and Jess took hold of his elbow.

"We got us an appointment tomorrow morning with Tom Boudreau. You and me and Addie, ten o'clock at his office, so don't go wanderin off on horseback. Now if you'll excuse me, I'm sneakin off for a nap. Anyone asks, you tell 'em I'm plumb wore out but I thank 'em for everything they done." He started toward the back door but stopped. "You tell 'em Vivian would've been tickled."

* * *

Several hours later, Bradley stepped onto the porch. The sun had slipped behind the peak of Ute Mountain making it glow in silhouette at the western mouth of the canyon. He was drying his hands on a dishtowel that he slapped over his shoulder before dragging the empty rocker alongside Addie's.

"Thank you for helping," she said absently, her eyes remaining eastward where the horses grazed in twilight.

"You're still angry with me."

"I'm not angry."

"Upset."

"Really, I'm not."

"Vexed."

"Stop doing that."

They sat in silence, watching the canyon darken and the golden tips of the treetops fade to bluish-gray.

"Tom Boudreau is a lawyer," she finally said. "What did you say to Jess to make him think he needs a lawyer?"

"It sounded to me like he already had an appointment."

"You think? On a Sunday morning? You promised you'd keep him out of all this."

"Look, I'm sorry he happened to be standing there when I talked to Hawkins. Who initiated the conversation, just for the record. All I did was answer the man's questions."

She shifted but didn't reply.

"And I already told you, this has nothing to do with your grandfather. Hawkins, on the other hand, could be the key to what we came here to accomplish."

Addie drew her knees to her chin. "Was he receptive?"

"Hard to say. The art of politics is appearing to be on both sides of any given issue. In any event, I was glad to hear you have an appointment tomorrow. I was thinking about taking your friend up on his offer."

"What friend?"

"Colt's offer to take me hunting."

"What?"

"Is that so shocking? He works for Archer-Mason. There's a lot we might learn from him, and maybe vice versa."

"Wait a minute. You're going *hunting*? With my old *boyfriend*? How am I supposed to feel about that?"

"I'd hoped you wouldn't feel anything, to be perfectly honest."

"Please. That's not what I meant and you know it."

He sighed. "Colt could be useful, Addie. He could be our eyes and ears on the ground."

She unfolded her legs and stood. "I'm tired, and I'm going to bed. Have you even talked to Colt about this?"

"Your father had his number. We're meeting tomorrow at seven."

She snatched the dishtowel from his shoulder and left him alone where he sat. After the door had closed behind her—not a slam, at least—Bradley stood and paced a circle, listening to the night songs of crickets and bullfrogs. Listening and pacing and although he hadn't smoked in years, finding he wanted a cigarette.

He was a herald, he reminded himself. There were over fifty thousand oil and gas wells in Colorado alone. According to NASA's satellite imagery, a methane hot spot hung like a pall over the entire Four Corners region, an invisible plume of some two thousand square miles caused by the six hundred thousand metric tons of methane released from the area's leaky wells, pipelines, and related facilities each year. Methane, which is eighty times more effective than carbon dioxide in trapping the sun's heat. Bradley was standing, quite literally, at ground zero in America's battle against global warming—in humankind's fight for survival—and though the last thing he wanted was to stoke Addie's ire, he wasn't about to let anyone's fragile feelings deter him from his mission.

A new sound interrupted his thoughts. East of the house, the cold white light of a lantern moved horizontally in the darkness, like the floating blip of a heart monitor.

When the lantern finally stopped and its bearer stepped away, Bradley saw it was Jess, and that he'd arrived at the gravesite.

And that he'd already taken up the shovel.

9

Decker and Dixon.

Dixter. Deckson. Colt's invocation of their high school portmanteau had rattled inside Addie's skull for most of the night like a pebble in an empty can. Or like a hit song from summers past that drags you back in time—a riptide sucking you further and further from the shores of present tense. And though the tug is backward and the waters deep and dangerous, what sweet release to float for just awhile and give your arms a rest.

Vignettes as in a slideshow clicked behind her eyelids.

Freshman year, first day of school. Addie at her locker breathing the heady perfume of fresh paint and new textbooks and sharpened No. 2 pencils. Colt in his jayvee jersey, number nineteen, loose mesh over a tight black T-shirt, doing a double-take in the hallway and stopping to ask her name. Just like that, with none of the usual fumbling or hemming or my-friend-thinks-you're-hot preliminaries. Just Colt Dixon with his acne and his mullet, his slouch and his smile, oblivious to his own limitations.

Junior year, the rivalry game. Cortez versus Bayfield, fourth quarter, Panthers down five. Fourth and goal from the Bayfield nine with eight seconds left on the clock. Colt in motion, driving and planting and zigging to the near sideline. Calvin Longhouse's fadeaway pass wobbling in the stadium lights, floating out of bounds until Colt leaps and twists, tightroping into the end zone as time expires. His teammates swarming. Colt shedding his helmet and shaking his hair loose as he races down the sideline past the officials and the benchwarmers and the coaching staff to find Addie still jumping and waving her pom-poms. Lifting her and crushing her against the chain-link as the team on one side and the town on the other bounces and chants with Addie and Colt—Decker and Dixon—together at the center of the universe.

Senior year, Brenda Holcomb's bedroom. Downstairs, the thump of music and the peals of drunken laughter mask the pounding of her heart as Addie watches Colt unsnap his shirt and unbutton his jeans and step from his boxer shorts. Watches him crawl, catlike, to where she sits hugging herself against the cold wooden headboard. Feels his mouth on her mouth, on her neck, on her navel. Arches her back as he slides the underwear over her hips.

These were the memories on which she floated in the raft of her childhood bed. These, and not the others that followed.

Not Addie on the toilet, silently praying. Not Grandma Vivian, solemn and wordless, counting out twenties from the pewter box she kept on her bedroom dresser. And not Brenda Holcomb, her mascara streaking, insisting to Addie that Colt had a God-given right to know.

And what did Addie expect? That Colt would be tender, that's what. Tender and solicitous, but secretly relieved.

Certainly not that he'd propose. And definitely not that he'd grow angry, condemning her selfishness and her stubbornness and her fucked-up priorities.

We could rent us a trailer, he told her, his eyes shining. Maybe share with Calvin and Deb. I could work at the garage by day and the Sinclair at night and I could hunt on the weekends. Get us a big ol' freezer. Sell deer and elk to the restaurants and save up for a few years and maybe buy us our own patch of dirt.

Decker and Dixon, he said, imploring. Dixon and Decker.

Brenda had been the closest thing to a sister Addie would ever have—a BFF in whom she could confide and conspire, deliberate and dream. Ever since the sixth grade theirs had been a confederacy of kindred spirits whose zany energy had pro-pelled them through the cratered minefield of cooties, braces, acne, tampons, bras, makeup, gym class, tryouts, drinking, dating, and the dozens of wonders and blunders that in the sum of their accretion constitute adolescence.

It was only natural, therefore, that Colt's attentions toward Addie would nettle, relegating Brenda as they did to the role of faithful sidekick. And while it was a role she'd played with stoic cheer, enduring Addie's breathless confidences and Colt's incessant probing, the personal toll for Brenda Holcomb had been solitary weekends and unanswered phone calls and unreturned texts—slights that had they been visited upon Brenda by another girl would have provoked Addie to violence but that Addie had come finally to recognize, and to regret, only in hindsight.

The end of Addie's pregnancy marked the last of Decker and Dixon. Its *termination.* Yes, they saw each other at the graduation parties—terse nods across crowded rooms before looking away—and yes, Brenda still labored to bridge their stubborn divide, but the combustive combination of Colt's wounded pride and Addie's whirling blender of emotions had created a kind of vortex—a black hole from which the light of their future together could never quite seem to escape.

Had Addie been shocked when, three years later, she'd received the invitation to Colt and Brenda's wedding? She'd decided she was not. What had surprised her, however, was the relief she'd felt, as though the union of her two best friends had been a kind of karmic penance from which she might at last receive absolution. Because as she'd been warned that day in Grandma Vivian's bedroom, you're not punished for your sins in this life, you're punished by them. That the invitation had been mailed to an old dorm address and had only reached Addie after the wedding added what she supposed was a further glaze of healing balm.

When at last the slideshow ended Addie slept and dreamt a dream both fantastic and familiar: Of wobbly footsteps in baby-sized shoes. Of the glimpsed hem of a woolen overcoat. Of a little girl stopping and starting, hurrying forward but not too fast, not too far from a vaguely parental presence looming somewhere behind her.

Then she was alone, this little girl, with a corridor stretching before her, its floor tiles the black-and-white squares of a chessboard. Strange to her, and doubly so because she'd just been outside. A door at the end of the hallway separated her, she somehow knew, from her mother.

Adults were observing her: earnest men and ponytailed women in lab coats with clipboards and serious eyeglasses jotting notes on the behavior of the little girl behind the glass divide whose image was overlaid by the reflected lights of the machinery behind them, the metered blinking of a mainframe computer whose hum and whirr contrasted with the total silence of the corridor beyond the glass.

The girl, awash in that silence, advanced. Cautiously now, it seemed to those observing. But would she cry this time? Would she collapse into a fitful ball of tears? Alas, she would not. Of course she wouldn't. She never did, this girl. Instead she tottered to the door and raised, almost in defiance, her tiny little fist . . .

"Adelaide?" Three sharp raps. "It's nine o'clock! Better shake a leg!"

When she emerged from her room a half-hour later, Addie was towel-drying her hair and reliving the final moments of her dream. The odd synchronicity of that knock. Had she somehow anticipated it, bending the narrative to that precise point in time or, more unnerving still, had the entire dream been lived in that fleeting nanosecond when flesh contacted wood?

Barefoot, she paused in the hallway and noticed that the door to the guest bedroom had been left ajar.

The door creaked on its hinges. Bradley's suitcase lay splayed on the floor like a nylon clamshell; his travel clock ticked quietly by the bed. The bed itself was hastily made, and centered on its pillow lay a bulging envelope marked ADDIE in bold capitals.

She sat on the edge of the mattress and tore at the envelope and poured its contents onto the quilt.

They were Hearts. Dozens of blood-red hearts snipped from a deck of playing cards Bradley must have found downstairs. Fifty-odd little squares that Addie scooped and hefted and watched as they ran through her fingers.

Sharp they were, and cold to the touch.

Law Office of Thomas R. Boudreau. Gold-leafed on pebbled glass, the words appeared backward to Addie where she sat in a hard wooden chair flanked by her father and grandfather, the muffled thrum of Main Street wafting through the open windows behind her.

Mr. Boudreau was a rumpled man in a rumpled suit whose office smelled of yesterday's cigars and tomorrow's laundry. He began by apologizing for having neither coffee on offer nor a secretary available to make it. After settling into his swivel chair he squared some papers on his desk and relocated a pen from one side of his blotter to the other before addressing himself to Jess.

"First off, I want to offer my condolences. Vivian was a fine woman and a pillar of this community. Why just the other day Ruthie was saying that without Vivian to ride herd at the Historical Society, they wouldn't know whether to spit or wind the clock." For Addie's benefit he added, "You'll pardon my French."

She smiled tightly, and Jess only nodded. The lawyer cleared his throat, moving the pen back to where it had been.

"All right then. To the business at hand."

He lifted one of the documents from his desk and seemed to consider it for a moment before half-turning to Logan.

"As you may or may not know, I prepared an estate plan for Jess and Vivian some years back, creating what we call a revocable inter-vivos trust with a pour-over will. Now it gets a little complicated, but the upshot is that this particular trust terminated upon Vivian's death and a new trust sprang into being, what we call a survivor's trust. And that trust is irrevocable."

Logan blinked at the man without speaking.

"Like I say, no need to get too deep in the weeds. What's important for now is that Jess here is the sole trustee of this survivor's trust and is what's called the income beneficiary, meaning he's entitled to receive all net proceeds therefrom during his lifetime. But because the trust is irrevocable, he has no power of appointment over the trust corpus and in effect enjoys what we call a life estate."

"For shit sake, Tom—"

"Hold your horses, Jess. I'm getting there."

The lawyer opened the folder on his blotter and handed Logan and Addie separate copies of a multi-page document titled *Olsen Family Trust.*

"Now if you'll look at Article Four at the bottom of page five, you'll see what I'm talking about. Under the terms of the survivor's trust, certain tangible personal property of a household nature that was the separate property of the deceased settlor— that's Vivian—is to be distributed in accordance with any written instructions the deceased settlor may have delivered to the surviving settlor and co-trustee—that's Jess—during her lifetime. I understand that Jess has such a list in his possession."

Jess leaned in his chair and drew a folded sheet from his seat pocket. He passed it across the desk to the lawyer who opened it and smoothed it flat and donned his reading glasses. After a moment, he handed the sheet to Addie.

"Everything seems to be in order," he said. "These are the personal items Vivian wished you to have."

The list was in her grandmother's handwriting. It described various pieces of jewelry, most of which Addie recognized. The last item on the list was the pewter box Vivian had kept on her dresser.

"As for the rest and residue of the estate," the lawyer continued, "or what was formerly held in the revocable trust, I'm afraid there isn't any cash or negotiable securities to speak of. Those items, if any, having expressly been excluded from the trust corpus. What does constitute the trust residue, however, remains in the survivor's trust until the death of the surviving settlor—that's Jess—at which point it passes into a residuary trust—"

"Christ almighty."

"—a *residuary* trust which will then distribute the residuary estate as therein provided. You'll find those provisions at page ten."

Logan flipped the papers in his lap. "So what's the bottom line here?"

"The bottom line," the lawyer said, "is that as of Vivian's death, the terms of the trust cannot be amended. Jess remains the trustee and the income beneficiary of the survivor's trust until he dies, at which point the trust corpus passes outright to the beneficiary of the residuary trust free and clear. Provided, of course, that she survives Jess."

Addie looked up from her copy. "She?"

The lawyer smiled. "Congratulations, young lady. For all intents and purposes you are now the beneficial owner of the Red Rocks Ranch."

PART TWO

10

"I hope you ain't fixin to die on me."

Colt Dixon stood near the top of the hill with his rifle slung over his shoulder. He waited as Bradley struggled to join him, and again as the older man collapsed forward with his hands pressed to his knees.

"This elevation," he gasped. "Takes some. Getting used to."

"So they say. I reckon we're close to ten thousand feet. But things'll flatten out up ahead."

Bradley, still wheezing, made no move to straighten. They'd been hiking for twenty minutes since leaving their ATV by the side of a single-track trail shaded by tall ponderosas. Their vertical death march had taken them through a forest of blue spruce and fir that bled into oak brush and aspens whose blazing fall foliage of reds and golds had given way to skeletal woodland of bare aspen trunks with their skin-like bark and darker knots that evoked in Bradley's imagination a thousand unblinking eyes.

"Better sightlines this far up," Colt said. He adjusted his rifle and his camouflage backpack and studied the ridgeline above them. "Plus fewer fat-ass hunters."

Colt's gun was a lethal slash of blued steel and checkered walnut whose virtues he'd extolled to Bradley with a reverence one normally reserves for newborns or religious icons. Bradley, meanwhile, lugged Colt's older and heavier bolt-action .30-06 which, Colt assured him, had killed more deer than the night-time traffic on Highway 160.

That conversation had taken place amid the shambolic clutter of Colt's singlewide trailer, part of a grid of similar structures surrounded by swing sets and Big Wheels, rusting appliances and vehicles under repair—a scene of communal decrepitude that had only confirmed Bradley's long-held socioeconomic hypothesis that the less prosperous a neighborhood, the more cars its residents owned.

Bradley had arrived there at the appointed hour bearing a dozen donuts from City Market, half of which Colt, tousled and shirtless, had eaten while cleaning the guns and then chased with a sixteen-ounce Red Bull. There followed for Bradley's benefit a camouflage fitting and a rudimentary lesson in firearm safety whose pedagogic essence seemed to be (a) Don't aim at anything you don't plan to shoot, and (b) Try not to shoot anything at which you didn't aim.

When they'd left the trailer park, Colt's ATV had been hitched to his orange Ford Bronco, a boxy mid-seventies model with mismatched doors. Amped by the sugar and the energy drink and an ear-splitting Aerosmith CD, Colt drummed on the steering wheel as they roared like teen truants past the overflow lots of a dozen different churches—Catholic and Baptist, Presbyterian and Mormon—en route to the forested headwaters of the Dolores River.

"Don't I need some sort of hunting license?" Bradley shouted over the music as they followed the river northward, its narrow valley snaking through rocky outcrops and steeply furred foothills. This was the Colorado of Bradley's imagination, with its crashing clear water and pine-scented air—a stark contrast from the high-desert dreamscape that was McElmo Canyon.

"You got a hunting license!" Colt reached for the glovebox and groped for a folded paper laminated in plastic. "Anyone asks, what you forgot is your wallet!"

So Bradley today, should anyone ask, would be Calvin Longhouse of Towaoc, Colorado, who, having recovered his wind, finally stood upright.

"Okay," Colt said. "Let's rock and roll."

The mountain as promised topped out onto a flattish bench through which a narrow streambed wended. They followed the stream's meander with Colt in front and Bradley behind stumbling to keep up while aping the younger man's increasingly stealthy gait. They moved through sunlight and shadow, the thin air cold and crystalline and the mossy ground spongy underfoot.

Some ten minutes later, Colt halted and raised an open hand.

"Hear that?" he whispered.

Bradley listened. From a point maybe fifty yards distant came a faint rustling sound that might have been footfalls in leaf litter. Then the rustling ceased.

Colt touched a finger to his lips.

Practically on tiptoes, Colt eased the rifle from his shoulder. Bradley, following behind him, did likewise although he'd promised himself before leaving the Triple-R that he'd not fire on anything short of a charging bear, and even then that his first shot would be over the poor animal's head.

Colt's crouch deepened as they crept toward the spot from which the sounds had come. The trees seemed thicker here, as though the bench had once been burned or logged, its old-growth aspens replaced by a dog-hair forest of thinner and younger trees.

A sudden eruption of sound and movement brought Colt's rifle to his shoulder. The splashing gave way to a wet and furious flapping as several green-winged teals flashed over the treetops. Colt's muzzle tracked the birds as they swung a quacking arc toward higher ground.

"Bang!" he said, lowering his rifle.

A half-hour later, they entered a clearing. There the stream had widened into a small lake or wetland thanks to a beaver dam complex whose mounded lodge rose from the water's center like a giant overturned nest. Colt unshouldered his rifle and leaned it against a tree. He rolled the kinks from his neck as he unzipped his fly to urinate.

"You gettin hungry yet?"

"I'm afraid I didn't—"

"I did. That is if you don't mind store-bought jerky."

Colt curtsied as he re-zipped his camouflage pants. He unslung his pack and sat on a downed aspen log. Bradley watched as he opened the pack and fumbled around inside. He came out with a canteen, and a sealed plastic package, and a folding knife that appeared of military origin.

"Considering the fact that you work outside all week," Bradley said as Colt sliced open the package, "I appreciate you making the time to bring me up here."

"It's like my old man used to say." Colt proffered the jerky, which Bradley declined. "Better to be outdoors thinking about God than to be holed up in some church on Sunday thinking about hunting."

"Is that what you think about when you're up here? God?"

"Nature, God, creation. Whatever you want to call it, I'd say it's all of a piece."

Bradley didn't respond.

"How about you? What do you think of this high country?"

"Spectacular." Bradley turned to regard the beaver pond and the mounded lodge and the cordon of skeletal trees. It was a composition straight from a painting, perhaps of the Hudson River School, lacking only some woodland Indians huddled around a campfire. "It's hard to say which is prettier, this or the red-rock country in McElmo."

"Here. You just said a mouthful, brother."

Bradley accepted the canteen and took a swig and returned it to Colt, who sat chewing with focused intensity.

"Not to broach a difficult subject, but I understand you suffered a loss recently. I was terribly sorry to hear it."

"How's that?"

"I overheard at the memorial service that your wife had recently miscarried."

Colt took a long drink and wiped his mouth on his sleeve. He screwed the canteen's cap back into place. "My ex you mean. But yeah, you heard right."

"That must've been difficult for both of you."

Colt didn't reply. He returned the items to his pack, then stood and dusted the seat of his pants.

"Brenda's her name? Brenda Holcomb?"

Colt shrugged into the pack. "You got somethin on your mind, professor, just come right out and say it."

"It's just that I was speaking with Addie's grandfather the other day. We were talking about cows. He told me that since the drilling began on the mesa above their ranch he'd noticed an uptick in stillbirths. Way more than anything he'd seen in all his years of ranching."

"So?"

"So I assume you've heard about the methane cloud that hangs over the Four Corners? What you might not realize is that there's a power plant on the reservation called the Navajo Generating Station. It burns over fifteen tons of coal every minute, twenty-four hours a day, seven days a week. It pumps over sixteen million tons of carbon dioxide into the atmosphere every year, not to mention dangerous levels of nitrogen oxide and sulfur dioxide."

"No shit."

"It's a big shit, actually. Especially since Cortez is downwind. I've seen studies suggesting that Navajo cancer rates have more than doubled since the plant went on line."

"Yeah, but you ever seen the crap those people eat?"

"This isn't a dietary issue. The Four Corners region has been a national energy sacrifice zone ever since the Nixon administration. Uranium mining, coal mining, shale oil. Industry was given free rein to do as they pleased, and the consequences be damned."

"And I suppose you aim to change all that?"

"I aim to try. In addition to the air you're breathing, I assume you know that the chemicals you work with on a daily basis are known carcinogens?"

"Meaning they cause cancer. Supposedly. And that's if you're dumb enough to get splashed."

"Or breathe the fumes."

"Look, Bradley. Cancer had nothin to do with it. Shit happens, in case you ain't heard. And I seen pictures of Los Angeles. Who are you to criticize the air in these parts?"

Colt retrieved his rifle. Bradley followed as he set out in the direction from which they'd come.

"Do you even know what caused the miscarriage? Did the doctors ever say?"

"I'd file that under None of Your Business."

"The reason I ask, there was a study done recently in Pennsylvania. They tracked over a million births over a ten-year period and found that babies born to parents living within one kilometer of a fracking site were 25 percent more likely to suffer from low infant birth weight."

Colt didn't answer. They continued as before, in silence, with Colt in front and Bradley behind. With the thousand knothole eyes silently watching.

"Okay then, here's a new subject. Brenda's father is on the county commission. I'd like to talk to him about a problem I have. Actually, it's a problem Addie's grandfather has."

"So call him up. Or better yet, drop by the theater. He's there every night."

"Actually, I was hoping to speak with Brenda first."

Colt halted and turned. "And why is that?"

"Because her father doesn't know me from Adam. Because he'll listen to his daughter before he'd listen to me."

"And because you think Brenda'd be easier to convince than her old man."

"I was hoping so, yes."

"And you figure our baby's the way to convince her?"

"Wait a minute. I never said that."

"You don't have to say it, Bradley. I can read you like a book. Too bad them books Addie's been reading don't seem to have taught her a whole lot of anything."

He marched on, and Bradley followed.

"Look. If it will assuage your concerns, I'm more than happy to make you part of the conversation. Maybe we could all get together for dinner some night. Maybe tonight as a matter of fact."

"By all, you mean Addie too?"

"Certainly. I understand that she and Brenda were good friends."

They'd reached the edge of the bench from where Bradley again could see the blazing calico of greens, reds, and golds in the river valley below. Colt lifted his chin and raised a hand for quiet.

They stood in silence. Bradley heard nothing.

"I'm gonna flank around thisaway," Colt whispered. "You count to sixty and head straight down, nice and quiet. If you get a clean shot, take it. If you don't, then maybe you'll drive 'em my way."

Colt unshouldered his rifle and vanished among the aspens. Silently, like a woodland Indian, leaving Bradley alone with his thoughts.

Bradley waited, counting to himself and feeling foolish for doing it.

Colt had been right, of course, about his intentions, which were to convince Brenda that Archer-Mason was damaging not just the public's health in general but neonatal health in particular. To convince her to intervene with her father and persuade him to join with the rancher, Hawkins, in demanding a public forum. And these were still his intentions, only now with Colt as part of the matrix, he would need to refine his strategy.

Of one thing he was certain—that the offer of a reunion with Addie, even with he and Brenda present, had been exactly the right lure. If Bradley had learned anything from his years observing students it was that female youth and beauty were comic-book superpowers to which even those who wielded them seemed strangely oblivious. He could name a dozen different coeds who, if he'd dressed them right and walked them into any law firm or talent agency in LA, would have every man in the building, from the mail-room clerk to the corner-office partner, trading elbows for their attention. Yet here were these same women—these girls, really—dating pimple-faced frat boys in backward ball caps, blithely ignorant of their true potential.

Colt Dixon, on the other hand, was trailer-park trash—a loser and a redneck and the personification of everything Addie had spent her college years escaping. So yes, Colt would bring Brenda Holcomb to the table; of that Bradley was certain. And once there, Bradley would close the deal with Brenda while Colt sat mesmerized by a chimera that had already eluded him.

At the count of sixty he started down. Except that the wooded mountainside, which during his ascent had appeared so uniform, now seemed to undulate in a way Bradley found oddly disorienting. Just follow the fall-line, he told himself, but doing so sent him zigging and zagging until he reentered the tree canopy and found his sightlines reduced to mere meters.

He paused a moment to gather himself. It was a silly notion, getting lost on a mountain. Impossible, really, since one need merely descend.

Bradley fished the phone from his pocket to confirm what he already knew. How did these people live without Wi-Fi or cell service? He pocketed the phone and resumed his trek even as the terrain flattened again, and then tilted, until once more he stopped for his bearings.

He felt a pinprick of panic. Which was doubly silly because, in a worst-case scenario, he could always just fire his rifle. That would bring Colt running, and to avoid embarrassment he could claim to have sighted a deer.

Then paranoia, like a hazy beach sunrise, burned through his other anxieties. He'd heard no sound earlier—no deer rustling in the trees. So what if Colt hadn't either? What if Colt had planned all along to bring Bradley up here and then to abandon him without food or water? That would explain the absurdly remote location, and the single ATV, and even the salty beef jerky that Bradley, thank goodness, had had sense enough to refuse.

The ATV. If that were Colt's plan, then Bradley would surely have heard its engine by now. So maybe that wasn't the plan. Maybe he was just spooked by the isolation, and the thin air, and the numberless trees that seemed to crowd him, jostling from all sides.

Then again, what if he'd underestimated Colt's malevolence? What if the plan wasn't to abandon Bradley, but to actually *murder* him? Abandonment meant a search party, perhaps a single cold night on the mountain. But a hunting accident? Bradley could hear Colt's explanation to the authorities. He was a city boy, Colt would say. I told him to wear orange.

I'll show you some places that'll make your head explode.

Bradley unshouldered his rifle and weighed it in his hands. Was it even loaded? Had he actually *seen* Colt inserting the bullets? More importantly, how could one tell? You could fire off a round, that's how, and bring Colt running.

But is *that* what Bradley wanted?

He turned a circle, noting the sun's location high overhead, then resumed his downward progress. Walking stealthily now, avoiding twigs where possible, his gun poised at the ready. Looking less like a woodland Indian than a soldier in a movie. Like the hard-luck kid from Brooklyn who gets it between the eyes.

Something warm tickled his lips, his chin. He swiped at his face, and his hand came away bloody. Wonderful. He imagined Colt as a shark—a circling, dead-eyed predator scenting Bradley's blood in the water.

He soon entered a different clearing. But with his nose pinched and his head tilted skyward, he tripped on a root and stumbled and did a full forward roll, losing his rifle in the process. Rising to his knees, he brushed at his jacket then froze at a sight in the distance.

A camouflaged figure—Colt Dixon—stood at the far end of the clearing, his gun leveled. The lens of the scope, the muzzle, aimed directly at Bradley. Their eyes locked, and Colt smiled, and in that fraught nanosecond Bradley heard his bowels go slack.

"Bang!" Colt shouted, lowering his rifle.

11

Logan's irrigation boots sucked and sloshed as he walked the high side of the hayfield kicking pipe gates open or shut as the water's flow required. As he paused for a moment to survey the results, afternoon sunlight on a distant windshield flashed at the edge of his vision.

The car was practically flying. It rounded the curve and skidded to a stop on the gravel driveway and before the dust had even settled the professor was out and trotting up the porch steps and pushing through the front door of the house.

Without even knocking. Just making himself at home.

Congratulations, young lady.

The lawyer's words were like a scab that Logan, try though he might, just couldn't stop picking. Was that because they'd surprised him, bursting some bubble of expectation he'd unconsciously been inflating? Or had he felt rebuffed somehow—disrespected even—given the years he'd spent breaking his back to keep this ranch afloat? Or had it simply never occurred to him to ponder the Triple-R's future once Vivian and Jess were gone?

Except that he had pondered it. He'd presumed, in fact, to wind up in Jess's shoes someday—living in the cabin while Addie and her husband and a passel of grandkids filled the big house and raced through the hayfields and tackled the daily chores. In that hopeful vision the cabin served as a playroom, and a bunkhouse, and a toy-repair shop, with Logan the stable nucleus around which the chaos of ranch life might orbit.

And the thing of it was, neither his dustup with Addie nor her departure for California had ever changed those assumptions.

That she would one day return and resume her place in the natural order of things was something Logan had accepted as an article of faith, like the sunrise and sunset or the changing of seasons. Like life and death, inevitable and unyielding, preordained in their infinite cycle.

And now she had. But the cold slap of the lawyer's words had awakened Logan to a new reality, forcing him to confront the fact that nothing was happening the way he'd figured it, and hadn't been for years.

First off was the drought. Though he'd never acknowledge as much to Addie and invite some high-minded lecture, this was the first year in five the ranch had had water this late in the season. Meaning that absent some new setback he'd eke out a fourth cutting and avoid buying hay for the winter. But the Farm Bureau boys had made clear that this year was the exception—something to do with the ocean currents off Mexico—and warned they were still in a jackpot. A *trend* or some such, part of a larger weather cycle that might last decades, or even a century.

It seemed to Logan that whatever snow fell on the La Platas these days got coated over by dust blowing up off the dry hardpan of the Navajo reservation, peppering the peaks and accelerating the snowmelt on which their irrigation ditch depended. Snowcaps that a decade ago might last into July now were gone by June, and sometimes as early as May. Less and faster snowmelt meant that the big upstream irrigators would husband the water they held with their dams and their reservoirs and dole it out to their shareholders, reducing the flows on which McElmo Creek depended. The result was a cycle within a cycle whose centripetal pull threatened to leave the smaller farmers and ranchers of McElmo Canyon circling the drain.

So maybe they'd break even this year, if prices held steady and if nothing went haywire that Logan couldn't fix. But that was this year. The issue long-term was competing with Canadian beef and Argentine beef and beef from wherever the hell else it still rained and snowed like it used to. The point being that even if Addie wanted to stay and raise a family, the Triple-R was a different ranch from the one she'd grown up on. For most of her lifetime, beef and hay and the henhouse and garden had provided bounty enough to meet their modest needs. Those days, Logan feared, were already behind them.

He'd tried to explain all of this to Jess, to show him the numbers, but found it like talking to stone. It was only now, only today, that what Logan had mistaken for the old man's natural obstinacy finally made sense. Jess hadn't doubted him and wasn't ignoring him. It was just that the old man had known all along these wouldn't be Logan's problems to solve.

And as for the carbon dioxide, well, Logan had been around long enough to know that oil and gas was a boom-and-bust proposition. That you'd better make hay while the sun shined because if oil prices in London or Riyadh dropped below a certain benchmark, then the pump jacks went quiet in Texas. Once that happened, then everything else shut down up the line, often for years at a time. And these days, that line ran straight through McElmo Canyon.

Which was maybe the damnedest thing about what that lawyer had said. According to the Olsen Family Trust, Jess, while he was still alive, was entitled to receive whatever net income the Triple-R generated. That meant the sooner he started drilling, the bigger his share would be. But rather than throw the gates open and wave the rigs in, the contrary old goat had pulled a shotgun on Archer-Mason's land man.

All of which made perfectly clear that what Jess and Vivian wanted all along was for Addie to have everything—the ranch, the minerals, the whole shooting match. To drill or not to drill, that would be her call to make. It was probably something they'd discussed there toward the end. What are you gonna do with a million dollars? he could hear the old girl say. Buy a gold-plated walker?

So now it was all up to Addie. Her future, the ranch's future, and Logan's future as well. And that would be fine, except for the one goddamn thing.

In Logan's hazy notion of his golden years it was always Colt Dixon he'd pictured for a son-in-law. Colt had been the only boy ever to turn Addie's head, and in their years of high school courtship Logan had grown to like the boy and to trust him and to respect the man he'd become. Colt had had it rough, what with his mother's health and his father's wild ways. A boy raised like that, dirt poor and without supervision, already had two strikes against him. Yet Logan had seen no quit in the boy; no signs of anger or malice or self-pity.

Colt Dixon was a sure cowhand and a helluva mechanic. He was a stellar athlete and a crack shot with a rifle. He said *yes sir* or *no ma'am* and he looked you in the eye when he said it. He was exactly the sort of polite, hardworking, capable young man Logan would have been proud to call his own son.

Logan remembered the story Addie told him, about the night she and her girlfriend Brenda had left the movies by the back door to the theater and found Colt in the dumpster behind the sandwich shop. This would've been tenth grade or thereabouts. Addie had been mortified, but Colt had just grinned and waved to the girls and asked how they'd liked the picture. It wasn't until later that Addie, reflecting on the incident, told her father that Colt had had nothing to be ashamed of. That it was she who should be ashamed. Colt, she said, should be proud for doing whatever it took to take care of his ailing mother. But it was Logan who'd been proud—proud of his daughter for seeing the nobility that comes from meeting hard times with hard choices and hard choices with hard work.

Which was not to say Addie was perfect. If Logan had learned anything about his daughter it was that if he really wanted her to do something all he had to do was tell her she couldn't. Tell her she was too small or too young or, God forbid, that she was just a girl. The only problem was that as she grew older, the converse became true as well.

So maybe it was Logan's fault Addie had left Colt to twist in the wind. Maybe his affection for the boy had rubbed off on Colt in the way the smell of a human hand can cause a mother bird to abandon her chick. And if that were the case, then Logan had no one but himself to blame for Bradley Sommers.

So far he'd been careful not to bad-mouth the professor in front of Addie for fear of driving them closer together. But it was clear to Logan that the man had gotten into his daughter's head and filled it with lofty notions, the kind that come from living in a place like Los Angeles where your water comes out of a tap and your food comes out of a store and your cash comes out of a machine. A man who'd never broken so much as a sweat or grown so much as a callus was exactly the type who'd try to talk Adelaide into leaving the carbon dioxide—her birthright, and now her inheritance—to waste in the ground while the ranch dried up and blew away from under her feet.

From under all their feet.

Logan wanted to believe that if Vivian and Jess had foreseen a man like Bradley Sommers they'd have revised their estate plan. And though it was too late for that, it wasn't the end of the story, not by a long shot. He was still Addie's father. It was still his duty to watch over her and protect her from the dangers she was either too naïve or too stubborn to see. Hell, it was what he'd been doing for all of her life. It was what he aimed to keep on doing, whether she liked it or not, for the rest of his.

Whatever that might involve.

12

They'd parked the Prius two blocks to the west and were strolling arm in arm in the deepening twilight past the slumbering cars and the familiar downtown storefronts and the flashing carnival neon of the Fiesta Twin Cinema where, inside its glowing lobby, a lone man, slight and balding, stood behind the counter with his back turned to the street.

"That's Mr. Holcomb," Addie said. "He doesn't look busy. Why don't we just go in and talk to him?"

"We've already been through this." Bradley checked his watch. "Plus I told Colt we'd meet him at eight thirty."

"So you'd rather dangle me as bait than have to face Brenda's father? This from the man who only yesterday was accosting the guests at a funeral?"

"It's not a question of reticence. I told you, he won't be persuaded by some stranger off the street to vote against what he thinks are the county's best interests."

"Ah, but I'm not a stranger."

"You're not his daughter either. Besides, you'll have to see Brenda eventually. You said so yourself. So who's the one being reticent?"

It was true Addie was reluctant to confront her former best friend who, as soon as her back was turned, had run off and married her boyfriend. Worse, who'd been the one that persuaded Addie she'd had some moral obligation to tell Colt she was pregnant. Secretly hoping, no doubt, that their differing views on the subject—views known only to Brenda—would be the narrow end of a wedge that might separate them forever.

Which, lo and behold, it did.

But it was equally true that Addie was in no mood for an argument with Bradley. Not now at least, with their larger objective—the systematic defanging of Archer-Mason Industries—requiring a united front.

"Okay," she said. "I'll take another one for the team."

"Addie." He took both her hands in his. "Don't think for a moment I don't appreciate the sacrifice you're making. And I'm not talking about Brenda. The fact is that very few people in your position would act the way you're acting. And if I haven't said as much, then let me say it now. I'm enormously proud of you."

"Thank you. That's pretty much what Jess said."

"There you go. With great age comes great wisdom."

They continued along the empty sidewalk. Across the street, on the second floor of the sandstone bank building, the lawyer's darkened windows watched them, offering no counsel on the subject.

"I finally spent some time with those regs," she said. "The idea of a local public forum is actually pretty inspired. I suspect the community's only heard Archer-Mason's side of the story. In any event, I promised Jess we'd do whatever we can to stop them. Or at least to slow them down."

Addie had spent time with the state's oil and gas industry regulations, followed by an hour with her grandfather to go over the papers he'd received from Archer-Mason's land man.

The essence of their offer was that Archer-Mason would pay Jess a signing bonus of fifty thousand dollars in exchange for a three-year lease of the mineral rights beneath the original 160-acre Olsen homestead where most of the Triple-R's structural improvements—the home and cabin, the garage and workshop, the barns and hay sheds—presently stood. Once drilling was completed, Archer-Mason would pay a royalty equal to 12.5 percent of the wellhead value of any extracted minerals. A subsequent, revised offer had upped that royalty rate to 15 percent.

And, the land man had assured Jess, since carbon dioxide flowed from the McElmo Dome like tequila in Tijuana, that 15 percent represented several million dollars in surefire royalties.

But those were just the highlights of the offer, spelled out in bullet points. The details, set forth in a proposed Oil, Gas, and Mineral Lease, told a more nuanced story. The lease term, for example, wasn't just three years, but would continue for as long as operations continued, and operations were broadly defined to include not just drilling the wells but also laying pipelines, constructing roads, digging canals, installing tanks, building power stations, constructing employee housing, and using either surface ponds or injection wells to dispose of the drilling waste.

As for the royalties, they would be net of all operating expenses incurred by Archer-Mason, including the cost of drilling the wells and treating the extracted minerals to render them ready for market. And should energy prices fall or should other circumstances arise to make further extraction unprofitable, Archer-Mason had no obligation to continue pumping and no duty to restore the surface estate.

Last but not least, the fine print gave Archer-Mason the right to use as much flowing water on the Triple-R as was needed for its operations, the right to assign its obligations under the lease to another operator, and a long-term easement for access to each well site even after they'd been abandoned.

Jess had told the man he wasn't interested. The man, however, was insistent, and soon became hostile. The Triple-R, he explained, was part of a larger drilling unit. That meant Archer-Mason could force Jess to pool his minerals with the BLM's neighboring minerals whether he liked it or not. In that event, the man said, Jess would get no signing bonus and only the lower royalty rate, and then only after all of Archer-Mason's costs had been recouped. His share, moreover, would be charged a holdout penalty equal to double the cost of drilling the wells.

However you sliced it, the resource would be developed. And while it was true that in a forced-pool scenario Archer-Mason couldn't drill wells directly on the homestead, it was also true that they alone would decide where to site their new well pads and other infrastructure on the split-estate portion of the ranch from which they would use those wells, essentially drilled at Jess's expense, like giant straws to suck the carbon dioxide from under his feet.

Jess could take the goose in the pot, the man said, or else he could chase a chicken around the yard. Either way, he'd be eating bird for supper.

So, Jess had finally asked her, his bony hand clamped to her knee. What did Addie think?

She didn't have to think. She'd replied that the idea of wells and tanks and pipelines on her childhood home made her literally, physically ill. That she didn't care how much money there was to be made, the Red Rocks Ranch wasn't for sale to Archer-Mason at any price.

Only then had Jess relaxed. Your grandma'd be proud, he'd told her, patting her knee. Only how do you figure on stopping them?

"You can begin by making peace with Colt Dixon," Bradley said as they approached the corner bar on Main Street. "He's pigheaded, but I still think he can be useful. When I mentioned the stillbirths at the ranch, he made the connection right away."

"Wait a minute." Addie stopped on the sidewalk. "Are you saying Colt's *job* had something to do with Brenda losing their baby?"

"Does that surprise you? You know what's in fracking fluid, right?"

"Not exactly."

"That's the problem. Nobody does, thanks to the Halliburton loophole. If Colt worked in Aneth, then he was into the stuff up to his elbows. God only knows what Brenda's been exposed to.

Did you know that she and Colt were living in Pleasant View, right on the edge of the play?"

Addie didn't know that. She knew, in fact, virtually nothing of Colt and Brenda's marriage, and the fact that Bradley did seemed bizarre to her, and somehow like an invasion of her privacy. As for Colt being pigheaded, well, Bradley had no idea.

"Let me tell you a story about Colt Dixon. He played on the football team in high school, and toward the end of every summer, he and his friend Calvin would train to get in shape for the coming season. What they'd do is they'd meet at the junior high stadium at lunchtime and run up and down the bleachers in the midday heat. We're talking ninety degrees and like zero percent humidity. They'd do that for as long as it took for one of them to throw up. Then they'd go back to work and meet again the next day and do it all over again. They kept doing that every day until neither of them could throw up. That's when they knew they were ready."

It was darker inside the bar than on the street. The band—a guitar and a mandolin, an upright bass and a fiddle—was just tuning up as Addie and Bradley entered and stood and waited for their eyes to adjust.

The place had changed since Addie last had seen it. Once a neighborhood bar catering to the area's biker crowd—tattooed and leather-clad, their chromed Harleys lining the curb on weekend nights—the thematic emphasis had shifted to hunting, as the dozen or more mounted trophies mutely attested.

All the barstools were occupied, as were the tables. From somewhere in back, an arm waved for Addie's attention.

"There's Colt," she said.

He rose to greet them. Pink-scrubbed and shaved, Colt had dressed in faded jeans and cowboy boots with a white cotton shirt stretching tightly across his chest. His sleeves were rolled, exposing muscular forearms and the tooled Zuni bracelet Addie had bought him for his eighteenth birthday—the gift Colt later described as his conciliation prize.

They all sat.

"Sorry to hear you got skunked." Addie addressed herself to Colt but rested her hand on Bradley's knee. "But thank you for bringing him back in one piece."

"If maybe a few pounds lighter."

"What do you mean?"

"He's joking," Bradley said, taking up a menu. "Is anyone else thirsty?"

The crowded barroom bustled and hummed but Colt's eyes, blue and unblinking, never left Addie's even as the waitress arrived and took their order then returned to set coasters and mugs on the table alongside a frothing pitcher of beer. Even as the band launched into a rollicking two-step that had half the women out of their seats and dragging their men onto the dance floor.

"Grant Hoover was in before," Colt announced over the music as Bradley poured their glasses full. "He said to send his regards."

"The Colorado School of Mimes," Bradley deadpanned, setting down the half-empty pitcher.

Addie smiled. "What's Grant doing back in Cortez?"

"He's district foreman for Archer-Mason. My boss, as a matter of fact."

"Grant was the school's alpha dork," Addie explained to Bradley, shifting in her chair. "Clark Kent eyeglasses, chess club president—the works. One time I ran into him outside Walmart. It was summertime, and he'd stopped to pet a dog through the open window of a car. It was like an Irish setter or something, with long red hair, and it was sitting in the passenger seat."

She lifted her glass and tasted the ice-cold beer.

"After we'd finished our shopping, we happened to leave at the same time. We were pushing our carts through the parking lot when Grant stopped to pet the dog again. Only it was the wrong car this time, and while he was talking to me he started stroking this woman, this redhead, who was sitting there waiting for her husband. So the woman screamed, of course, and when she did, Grant jumped back and said, 'I'm sorry, lady! I thought you were a dog!'"

Colt howled with laughter. "Hoover the groover," he said, shaking his head.

Addie looked to Bradley for approval, and he nodded.

Colt set down his glass and wiped his mouth with his hand. "Okay, so you never heard this one. When Calvin turned twenty-one his old man figured to buy him his first official drink, right? So they sat right over there, and old Mr. Longhouse told the bartender somethin like, 'I'd like to buy this young man a cocktail.' And Carly the bartender, she said, 'Sure thing, Calvin. The usual?'"

Colt roared again. Only this time, Addie noticed, his gaze had shifted over her shoulder. She turned to see a familiar figure standing on tiptoes, scanning the darkened barroom.

"Look who's here." Colt waved his arm as before. "Show must've just let out."

Brenda Holcomb approached their table as a penitent approaches confession. Her hair was streaked with henna, and her sweatshirt failed to conceal the dozen or more pounds she'd gained, but Addie still recognized, even with Brenda's eyes downcast, the boisterous spirit that had made them all but inseparable for so many years.

Until they weren't.

"Hello, Addie," Brenda said, her hands clenched and wringing.

Emotions flooded Addie where she sat. The first of these was jealousy, cold and irrational, and whether directed at Colt or at Brenda she wasn't quite sure. But the stronger feeling, the warmer current, flowed toward her best and oldest friend who'd braved Colt's enmity and Addie's harsh judgment to stand before them and accept whatever was coming.

Addie stood, and they embraced.

"I've missed you," she whispered into Brenda's hair, to which Brenda, hugging her tighter, only nodded. Her cheeks when they parted were blotched and streaked and Addie reached to smudge one with a thumb. "Brenda Holcomb," she said, "I want you to meet my friend Bradley Sommers. Bradley's a professor at UCLA, and he's been very eager to meet you."

Smiling, already standing, Bradley pulled a chair away from the table. The band had launched into a country waltz, and Colt was up on his feet.

"Two's company," he said, taking Addie's hand and leading her onto the floor. Over his shoulder, Addie watched on tiptoes as Brenda, her head turned toward the dance floor, took the seat Bradley had offered.

"We shouldn't be doing this."

Colt pivoted, turning her away from the table. "Course we should. This way Bradley can talk to Brenda and you can dance with me and we can all make each other jealous."

"I didn't realize jealousy was on the agenda."

He lifted her arm and spun her once and reeled her neatly into his body. He was still, Addie thought, the best dancer in town.

"The agenda is complicated," he said, rocking her gently, his breath warm in her ear. "A man would need a scorecard to keep track of the agenda."

"I'm not sure I know what you're talking about."

"Then let me spell it out for you. There's a play on for your grandfather's ranch, and the professor there wants Brenda's dad to help shut it down. But what he really wants is to put Archer-Mason out of business. Never mind what that'd do to the town."

"Cortez survived for over a hundred years before Archer-Mason came along."

"Survived is right. Scraped by is more like it."

"Farming and ranching are what built this valley, not oil and gas."

"Here's what I know. Twelve bucks an hour for ranch work or thirty for work on a rig. More if you got yourself a specialty."

"So now you're all about money? Mister live-off-the-land, eat what you kill?"

"I'll tell you what. Money comes in handy when you got a family to support."

He shoved her away, then spun her on an inside turn. They were hip-to-hip now, holding hands and stepping in time with the music. Brenda, Addie noticed through the scrum of other dancers, had ceased watching them and instead was focused on Bradley.

"I reckon you heard about the baby. Bradley did, so I guess everyone knows."

"I heard, and I'm terribly sorry."

He pivoted and turned her again, and again they were face-to-face. They'd probably danced a hundred times over the years, but never could Addie recall being so conscious of Colt's hand on the small of her back.

"So what about you?" he asked. "You ready for a lifetime of baby food and diapers?"

"I wasn't planning on motherhood any time soon."

"Motherhood? I was talkin about Bradley. That guy's like your grandfather's age."

"And here I thought we might be having an adult conversation."

His smile wilted. He hesitated for half a beat and then guided her backward again.

"Our marriage was on the rocks anyway, in case you were wondering. The baby was Brenda's idea. Not that I didn't want it once she got pregnant but . . . I guess it's complicated. Hell, you know that. Then when she lost it, all's I felt was guilty. Guilty about the baby. Guiltier still about feeling relieved. Feeling like I'd dodged a bullet. Does that make me a horrible person?"

"No, that doesn't make you a horrible person."

"Thanks. I think I needed to hear that."

She leaned away to study him. "Are you all right?"

He shrugged. "The Lord works in mysterious ways, that's what my mom used to say. I figured maybe it was all for the best. Like maybe the Lord knew I'd be a fuck-up for a father just like my old man."

"Don't say that, Colt. That's not true and you know it."

"I remember him telling me one time that marriage was like a deck of cards. My old man that is. He said you start off with two hearts and a diamond, and pretty soon you're out looking for a club and a spade."

"That's not even funny."

"I know, right? Okay, maybe a little funny."

He spun her again and then snugged her closer, denim pressed against denim, their hips moving as one. Addie felt a trickle of sweat on her ribs.

Colt said, "It's not like I'm against marriage or anything. It's just that my whole life growing up I'd seen what a bad one looked like and it scared me to see it again in my own mirror."

In the crush of moving bodies, amid the spinning and the swaying, Addie began to feel lightheaded.

"Colt, why are you telling me this?"

"You're still my friend, right? Who else am I gonna talk to around here?"

"Brenda. You should talk to Brenda."

"We talked it to tatters, believe me. And that was before she even got pregnant."

The song ended, and the dancers parted and clapped.

"Anyway, here's the main thing I wanted to tell you. Bradley's over there right now using our baby to get to Brenda. I warned him not to, but it ain't like he'd listen to me. And then it occurred to me that a man who'd use Brenda like that, vulnerable like she is, would sure as hell use your father or your grandfather to get what he wanted."

"Would use me, you mean."

Colt didn't answer.

"Well, thanks for the dance."

She led him back to the table where Bradley and Brenda were deep in conversation. Glancing up at their approach, Bradley flashed a thumbs-up from behind Brenda's back.

Colt rested a hand on Addie's shoulder. "Just watch your back-trail, cowgirl. That's all I came here to say."

13

From his childhood home in Pasadena, Bradley Sommers could pedal his bicycle up Lake Avenue to the old Cobb Estate, the vacant site of a former Altadena mansion that legend said had once belonged to Groucho Marx. There, beginning next to its orphaned gates of filigreed iron, a hiking trail skirted the eastern edge of the property before climbing sharply into seven hundred thousand acres of dense and rugged wilderness known as the Angeles National Forest.

For Bradley, then in middle school, the Angeles was itself a gateway of sorts. A quiet boy by nature, young Bradley eschewed the rough-and-tumble of peewee football and AYSO soccer for the hushed decorum of the Pasadena Central Library, his portal to the vicarious adventures of Nancy Drew and Frank Hardy, Sherlock Holmes and Nero Wolfe. It was there that his interests evolved beyond the escapist pleasures of mystery fiction and science fiction to biography and chemistry, to world and American history. And it was there that, on a still-memorable Saturday in the spring of 1997, Bradley first heard tales of a magical White City that once had overlooked Pasadena from a forested perch high atop nearby Echo Mountain.

The brainchild of a wealthy but eccentric Civil War balloon aeronaut named Thaddeus S. C. Lowe, the White City formed the northern terminus of what became known as the Mount Lowe Railway, a combination electric-traction railroad and cable-driven funicular Lowe completed in 1893 to ferry intrepid guests from the floor of the San Gabriel Valley to the sumptuous seventy-room Victorian hotel he called the Echo Mountain House and whose surrounding amenities included an astronomical observatory, tennis courts, riding stables, and a zoo. Within a few short years, however, Lowe's ambitious venture had collapsed under the treble burdens of flood, fire, and bankruptcy, leaving what had briefly been America's most popular honeymoon destination a ghost resort that, upon the railway's abandonment in 1938, gradually disappeared both from the mountain proper and from local memory altogether.

Did Bradley know that the ruins of the White City still existed? a roguish librarian asked the boy. And would he like to see a map that would lead him there?

Bradley's first expedition held all the fevered promise of a Hardy Boys adventure. He'd begged off Sunday service, citing a pressing homework assignment. He'd packed his usual lunch along with his map and his Boy Scout canteen. He'd arrived at the Cobb Estate at nine, locked his bike to the gate, then set off on what proved to be six-hour marathon of vertical climbs and dizzying descents on narrow trails through chaparral and yucca, Douglas fir and ponderosa pine. And while he found the remains of the old hotel site—a few slab foundations and the gigantic funicular wheel—he also discovered something infinitely more important.

He discovered his life's true calling.

The Angeles was a maze—a wooded ziggurat of interconnected trails that would over the ensuing months and years lead Bradley Sommers from high mountain meadows to crashing waterfalls, from primordial forests to panoramic vistas that on rare smogless days might encompass not only Pasadena and the skyscrapers of downtown Los Angeles, but also the Palos Verdes Peninsula and the Pacific Ocean beyond.

The forest became Bradley's personal looking glass, his enchanted wardrobe, the magical wormhole through which he could escape the crowds and clamor of urban living for the cool green solitude of a secret world in which hawks and lizards, deer and coyotes outnumbered the occasional hiker or biker he might encounter by at least a hundred to one.

Then, in a development that would shake Bradley's faith in the adult institutions of law and government, he read a newspaper account of a proposal to turn some three hundred pristine acres in Millard Canyon—home to some of his favorite riparian hiking—into an exclusive gated community of a thousand luxury homes.

The so-called Alpine Gateway Project was opposed by a grassroots alliance of neighbors and conservationists outraged by yet another commercial incursion into the public wilderness. It was opposed by the Altadena Town Council for its impacts on traffic and fire safety. And it was opposed by good-government watchdogs who detected a strong but familiar odor surrounding the land-swap arrangement on which the project's viability depended. But the developers had deep pockets and powerful allies who, after years of lobbying and litigation, delivered the approvals necessary to make their dream a reality.

Bradley followed the proposed development and the litigation to derail it with an interest bordering on the obsessive. He wrote letters to the local newspapers, and dragged his parents to community forums, and even titled his junior class essay "Block the Alpine Gateway!" More importantly, and unlike his more jaundiced fellow travelers, Bradley refused to accept the defeat all but assured by the final Ninth Circuit opinion.

On a Saturday morning in October, roughly three years to the day since he'd first read news of the project, Bradley Sommers drove his sister's SUV to the quiet intersection of Loma Alta Drive and Cheney Trail in Altadena. From the rented U-Haul trailing behind it he removed a large wheeled cage, a folding chair, an empty gasoline can, a cooler, and a hand-painted sign, all of which he carefully arranged in the roadside shade. Curled on a blanket inside the cage, compliments of a sometimes girl-friend who volunteered at the Eaton Canyon Nature Center, lay a weeks-old spotted fawn. The sign read: ON SUNDAY AT 3:00 P.M. I WILL BURN THIS FAWN ALIVE.

All day Saturday Bradley sat, and answered questions, and posed for pictures. He bottle-fed the fawn and answered more, increasingly hostile questions, including several from a harried reporter who'd arrived from the *Pasadena Star-News*. At dusk he repacked his singular cargo and drove it all home for the evening.

On Sunday morning, when he returned as before to his vigil, there were two television news vans filming his arrival. By two o'clock there were four, plus a handful of print reporters. Finally, at around 2:50, Bradley set down his book and rose from his chair to face a crowd of some fifty spectators, two sheriff's patrol units, and nearly a dozen video cameras.

"Good afternoon," he said into the microphones arrayed in the gutter. "My name is Bradley Sommers, and I'm a high school senior at Pasadena Poly. First of all I want to say that I'm not crazy or some kind of a sicko. I'm here today to make a point about a housing development that's planned for the hillsides you see directly behind me. It's called the Alpine Gateway, and if it goes forward as planned, then hundreds of forest creatures—not just this little guy, but also rabbits and skunks, owls and raccoons, snakes and bobcats—will be displaced or killed. These hills you see will be leveled, and millions of cubic yards of earth will be moved, burying several blue-line streams on which these animals depend. Over a thousand trees will be clear-cut or bulldozed, including hundreds of native oaks, all of which provide critical habitat for animals like my little friend here.

"I've sat here for two days now, and I've been called everything from a whack job to a psycho, all because I threatened the life of one little deer. So I ask you, what does that make the Alpine Gateway developers, men who'll knowingly kill dozens of deer, not to mention hundreds of other wild animals, all for their personal profit? And what does it make the people who'd buy the houses they know to be built on the crushed and buried bones of these little critters?

"I guess the point I wanted to make is that until animal cruelty becomes personal, we're all willing to turn a blind eye to it and go about our business. But it *is* happening, and it's wrong! It's wrong to build houses in places like this, and it would be wrong for anyone to ever buy one and thereby become complicit in the slaughter of these innocent creatures. And I guess that's all I came here to say."

That evening Bradley sat with his parents and watched his speech on the local news channels. On Monday morning the story of his protest, along with a photograph, appeared in the *Los Angeles Times.* Later that week it appeared in the *Pasadena Weekly* and the *Los Angeles Business Journal.* The week after that the developers of the Alpine Gateway, citing an unfavorable environment for mortgage lending, announced plans to postpone the project indefinitely.

"You really taught them a lesson," his father told Bradley when the postponement was announced. But it was Bradley who'd learned the lesson, and the lesson he'd learned was this: even an army of wealthy and powerful Goliaths can be slayed, or at least stayed, by a lone but determined David.

Following his graduation from Stanford, Bradley faced many such Goliaths at the behest of an alphabet soup of conservation organizations ranging from the Arizona Audubon Society to the World Wildlife Fund. These freelance assignments, coincident with his rise within the insular world of environmental academia, plotted a career trajectory that even his fiercest rivals could only describe as meteoric.

Also nontraditional. While his peers and colleagues wrote ponderous papers for academic journals no one actually read, Bradley's punchy prose was more likely to turn up in the *Utne Reader* or *Outside* or *High Country News.* His TED Talk on Spaceship Earth was still a minor YouTube sensation. He'd been profiled in *Time* magazine, and he'd debated a Republican congressman, a prominent climate-change skeptic, on the *PBS NewsHour*.

Bradley forged many alliances along the way, and he made many enemies. But what all of them, friends and foes alike, said about Bradley Sommers was that *he's a man who gets things done.*

All of that had transpired, however, in a different political climate. Since the last presidential election, since the new administration's gleeful assaults on the environment and public lands and endangered species, Bradley's successes had been sharply curtailed.

Curtailed? That was a laugh. The truth was they were virtually nonexistent, making new opportunities for environmental consulting—for effecting the kind of change the world so desperately needed—fewer and farther between.

Bradley extracted his phone from his jacket.

>   They're in closed session
>   right now.

> How would you rate our
> chances?

>   Better than even. I've been
>   on a charm offensive.

> So they don't stand a
> chance. ☺

>   You overestimate my
>   charm.

> Oh, but I've seen it in
> action.

Bradley checked the time. Thirty-five minutes, and not a voice raised in anger. Did that bode well or ill? He could envision two scenarios, mutually exclusive but equally plausible, like the opposite sides of a coin. In the first, Hawkins and Holcomb were holding firm against Wallace's sputtering tirade. In the second, the Montezuma County Commission had already agreed to close ranks against Bradley and moved on to discussing traffic congestion or parking at the county fair.

Bradley retraced the path in his mind—the step-by-step journey that had led him to this moment. Some of it had been calculated, certainly, but much had been improvised, and all had been flawlessly executed. He also thought of Vivian Olsen's admonition to her granddaughter: *Don't let some man in a bolo tie decide your future.* Because for all practical purposes that's exactly what Bradley was doing, and if the vote went against him—if the coin were to land just so on its thin and reeded edge—he'd be back to square one with nothing to show for his efforts.

The door finally opened, and the three men filed into the otherwise empty council chamber. Bradley pocketed his cell phone and stood to study their faces, searching for clues to the outcome.

He saw two tight smiles and one ominous scowl.

"All right, Mr. Sommers. Here's what you wanted."

Marty Holcomb, Brenda's father, handed Bradley the envelope. Inside was the letter Bradley had drafted for the county commissioners' approval. He opened the flap and peeked inside to confirm it bore two blue-ink signatures.

"So where do we go from here?"

"You fax this to Denver." Bradley returned the envelope. "Now, today. The COGCC will then have to hold a public forum at least two weeks before their hearing on Archer-Mason's downspacing application. Since that hearing is set for December, we can expect the local forum to be scheduled within the next several weeks."

Bradley pumped Holcomb's hand. "Time is short, gentlemen. We'll use it to organize our presentation and line up our experts."

"Experts?" Hawkins, the beefy rancher, stepped forward. "What sort of experts?"

"I work closely with an organization called the Western Warriors. They'll help us arrange testimony in areas like petroleum engineering, hazardous waste management, and water and air quality monitoring."

"And obstetrics?"

"Absolutely, Marty. And I'll count on you, Jimbo, to help organize the ranching and farming interests."

Hawkins glanced at Wallace, the lone holdout, before nodding.

"All right then. You've done the right thing, gentlemen. You may get some pushback at first, but your constituents will thank you in the long run."

Wallace shouldered past the others. "Our constituents," he snapped, "will hang these two in effigy. And you can bet I'll supply the rope."

14

The climb from the canyon floor to the shelf below the flat mesa top was nearly vertical. Addie paused midway to catch her breath and admire the downstream view of McElmo Creek, a thin copper thread snaking between and among the ochre cliffs and the pocket hayfields that suggested, from her bird's-eye perspective, outsized gems in a necklace of green turquoise.

There was no point in denying that McElmo Canyon was beautiful, and from that vantage, achingly so. Was this why the ancestral Puebloans—the so-called Anasazi—had chosen its rugged grandeur over the sheltering ponderosa forests that must surely have beckoned, even a thousand years ago, but a few days' trek to the east? Might there have been some aesthetic component to their grim daily calculus of water and forage, game and cover, fight and flight?

Were they, in other words, simply enchanted by the views?

The sculpted red walls and rockfall eyebrows directly above her were honeycombed with the remnants of dwellings and kivas and granaries painstakingly cobbled by ancient hands from stone and mud, branch and twig. Flint arrowheads and sherds of painted pottery still littered the ground up there despite the heedless cupidity of eight generations of explorers and settlers, pot hunters and tourists. The received wisdom of her childhood was that fewer people today inhabited the Four Corners region of the American Southwest than did in the first millennium AD; facing south, overlooking the unbroken forest of piñon and juniper unfurling in verdant waves beyond the red-rock canyon, Addie saw no reason to doubt it.

She shifted her gaze eastward, past the volcanic peak of Ute Mountain to the jutting and still-familiar contours of Mesa Verde some twenty miles distant. Had modern humans, she wondered, inured to the comforts and diversions of urban living, lost their love of wild country like this?

Even more pointedly, had she?

"If they catch us up here they could write us a ticket." Brenda Holcomb had stopped directly below where Addie waited on the narrow switchback trail.

"If who catches us? This is the only way up."

"I heard the BLM's been using, like, drones and hidden cameras."

"Great. If you'd told me that earlier, I'd have worn different shorts."

"What's wrong with your shorts?"

"For one thing, they make my butt look bigger than Battle Rock."

"Oh, please."

Addie waited as Brenda resumed her ascent. She passed completely out of view, then reappeared at Addie's level and raised a finger and leaned, breathless, on a tilting slab of sandstone.

"I'm not exactly in the best shape of my life."

"You're doing fine. I'm the one who's been living at sea level."

They stood together, a light breeze in their faces, gazing into the abyss. Halfway across the canyon, two ravens swooped and soared in an aerial ballet.

"Don't you miss this, even a little?"

Addie expected the question. Her first impulse was denial—a reflexive rote to the effect that she loved her new life and school and Los Angeles in general with its palm trees and its ocean air, its lush green lawns and its frenetic pace. That she loved the people, young and idealistic, a crazy-quilt patchwork of races and cultures. That she loved the opportunities it presented for education, self-improvement, entertainment.

But standing there as on the cusp of creation, such an answer could only ring false. Instead she asked Brenda, "Do you trust Colt?"

"You mean do I think he cheated on me?"

"No, not that. I mean like his judgment. Of people, for instance."

"Why are you asking me? You know him as well as I do."

"Don't be silly. The Colt I knew was an eighteen-year-old boy."

"And you think people change that much from when they're eighteen?"

"God, I hope so."

"You think *you've* changed? Because I don't." Brenda was stripping her outer shirt and tying it onto her hips. "I see the same badass chick who told Sheriff Janes where to shove it. The girl who kidnapped those dogs from the junkyard. The girl who wore cowboy boots with her prom dress."

"So did you."

"So did everybody, once they heard you were doing it."

Addie shielded her eyes. The ravens had vanished, vacating the foreground and leaving eternity in their wake.

"Was it hard, moving to a place like LA?"

"Are you thinking about it?"

"I wish. My dad would have a thrombosis."

"It was hard at first, I suppose. But the thing about college is that almost everyone comes from someplace else. Not just other cities or other states, but from all over the world. It takes a while, but you eventually find your tribe."

Her answer, while essentially true, was also incomplete. In reality, Addie had found campus life intimidating, and oddly hierarchical, with the richest and coolest girls—the celebrity daughters and the Olympic athletes and the Barbie doll cheerleaders—atop its golden apex. Hawaiian girls with their flip-flops and secret code of pidgin English occupied a stratum just above the California natives, who themselves sorted in a longitudinal progression that began at the beachfront and worked its way steadily inland.

To her surprise, Addie's cowboy boots and Cruel Girl jeans had somehow evoked snow-capped Rockies and ski weekenders—an outdoorsy exoticism that had made her an object of no small interest in her freshman dorm. Then came sorority rush, a kind of sorting-hat ritual that separated the girls with moneyed parents from those like Addie who owed their leisure hours to work-study jobs in places like the library or the rec center or the dorm cafeteria.

She'd actually looked into the campus equestrian team but found the girls there—sorority girls in tall English boots whose parents could afford to board sleek hunter-jumpers at private riding academies—even more cliquish than the rest. In the end, Addie's tribe proved to be girls like herself who'd come to school on scholarship and took their grades seriously and migrated from the dorms to the cheaper off-campus apartments where they lived on peanut butter and ramen and hopes for brighter tomorrows.

"I think he's totally hot, by the way."

"Who?"

"Bradley! And he's obviously nice and super-smart. He reminds me of one of those guys you see on television. Like a news anchor or a game show host."

"You don't think he's too old for me?"

"Hah. Remember Ashley Richmond? She smelled like a dead body in gym class? Guess who she married?"

"Who?"

"Mr. Epstein."

"The English teacher?"

Brenda nodded.

"My God. You don't suppose they were . . ."

Brenda shrugged.

"Come on. I think I just threw up in my mouth."

They topped out on the boulder-strewn shelf and picked their way through yucca and prickly pear and a crusted field of cryptobiotic soil. At the base of the first alcove they stood amid jumbled scree to gaze upward at the half-dozen rooms still standing in mute defiance of eight centuries of wind and sun, rain and snow, the naked walls of the cliff dwelling a crude mosaic in hues of buff and rust save for the end section on which a sun-bleached scrim of tan adobe had somehow managed to endure. Window openings, square and black, accentuated the ruin's haunted aspect, inviting visitors to imagine the terror and desperation that had forced an entire civilization to abandon its pit houses and cornfields and choose instead to live like human packrats.

"Can you imagine what it must've been like to live up here in winter?" Brenda said. "Or while you were pregnant? With no heat and no bathroom and no running water?"

"And all the while your enemies are down there waiting to attack during the night and eat your brains for breakfast."

"Kinda puts the problems of people like us in perspective, doesn't it?"

Addie assessed Brenda's upturned profile. "I haven't had a chance to say how sorry I am about the baby. That must've been awful for you."

Brenda shrugged. "It was what it was. Tell you the truth, I mostly felt sorry for Colt. He wanted to be a father so bad and then . . ." She turned to Addie. "I felt sort of like you wouldn't give him a baby, and then I couldn't."

"Wow. Did I really deserve that?"

"You asked me how I felt. And I'm not saying everything was all rainbows and roses before that, because it wasn't. You want to know the real truth? I don't think he ever loved me. At least not in the way I hoped he would. At least not in the way he loved you."

"Don't be ridiculous. He married you, not me."

"Because you turned him down. He told me. So you were like this . . . I don't know, this *presence* the whole time we were together. It felt like he was there with me, but not always. And never all of him."

Addie backed blindly, groping for a place to sit.

"So we were picking out baby names, right? And if it was a boy, do you know what he wanted to name it? Logan. He claimed it was after some comic-book character. Like I didn't know your father better than he did."

Addie didn't answer. In her darker moments she'd played a game, a kind of mental torture, in which she'd imagined her own child born. Its sex, and its chubby little body, and the weight of it in her arms. Its features an amalgam of hers and Colt's. And yes, even the names they might have chosen together.

"Look," Brenda said. "I don't mean to lay some kind of trip on you or anything. It wasn't your fault. You were, like, a thousand miles away."

"I'm so sorry."

"Don't be sorry. Now come to find out that the miscarriage might've been Colt's fault after all. Colt's or Archer-Mason's."

"We don't know that, and I wish Bradley had never mentioned it."

"Not me. Even if he's wrong, it was nice to hear somebody say that all this . . . this shit I've been eating this past year . . ."

She turned away. Addie stood to comfort her, but Brenda shrugged her off.

"So much for perspective." Brenda dabbed at her eye with a wrist. "At least nobody's trying to eat my brains for breakfast."

They climbed to the ruin and stepped through its broken walls. Peering out the windows, they imagined the canyon floor at nighttime aglow with the council fires of their enemies. Squatting to sift the powdery sand of the alcove floor, cold between their fingers, they found pottery fragments and charcoal fragments and a smattering of corncobs no larger than baby carrots.

"I forgot," Addie said, dusting her hands as she stood. "Is your mom still doing real estate?"

"Sort of. Only it's more like a hobby these days. Her full-time job is torturing me."

"Do you think she could help me and Bradley find an office to rent somewhere on Main Street? Nothing big, and strictly short-term. Maybe two months at most?"

"Call her. Just prepare yourself for the Spanish Inquisition."

On their descent back to the shelf they spotted an image—an ancient glyph etched in the burnished black lacquer of a tilting rock slab. Two triangular figures with ducks for heads stood hand-in-hand beneath a sun-like spiral a thousand years gone from the sky.

"That's really freaky," Brenda said, leaning in closer.

"Because it could be us?"

"Because I had that exact same hairdo, like, three years ago."

A hawk called in the distance, its lingering cry echoing among the cliffs. Silvery clouds floated down canyon—a balloon parade whose drifting shadows darkened the valley floor below.

"What would it mean for Archer-Mason," Brenda asked as they followed the cliff-face eastward, "if this hearing or whatever it's called goes down the way you hope?"

"I suppose it depends. In a worst case it'll be a waste of everyone's time."

"And the best case?"

It was an excellent question, and one she and Bradley had never really discussed except in broad abstraction. Things like increasing the setbacks from homes and farms, while worthwhile goals, were not the sorts of high-impact outcomes to which a group like the Western Warriors typically aspired. Nor, come to think of it, did they justify commissioning someone like Bradley Sommers to achieve them.

What might they realistically hope to accomplish? A complete fracking ban like the one in New York would certainly be a plum, but that was a matter for the state legislature. And as far as Addie could tell, Archer-Mason wasn't even fracking their carbon dioxide wells. Plus Archer-Mason was a huge multinational with billions in market capitalization and outsized influence in Washington thanks to all the former oil company executives and lobbyists holding key positions at the EPA and Agriculture and Interior. Denial of a down-spacing application in one tiny county in southwestern Colorado wouldn't cause so much as a blip in the company's stock price, and it would leave all their other operations intact and unaffected.

"I'm not really sure," Addie admitted. "But anything that hampers oil and gas extraction will help us as a nation move toward cleaner renewable energy. It's inevitable, of course, but as long as dead-enders like Archer-Mason can squeeze a final nickel out of the old paradigm they're perfectly willing to scar the landscape and foul the air and water for generations to come. They're only accountable to their shareholders, don't forget, and not to the people who live in the communities in which they operate."

"Okay, but what difference does it make if they drill a few extra wells around here? Aren't countries like China and India still burning coal and doing a lot more damage to the environment?"

"I suppose that's true, and it's one of the challenges we face as a planet. That's what climate treaties are for. I mean, did you know that half the world's coral reefs are already dead? But it's hard to ask a poor country like India to abandon fossil fuels when the US is providing over fifteen billion a year in government subsidies for drilling and fracking and strip-mining. Fighting a company like Archer-Mason will at least help demonstrate our commitment to the world's environment."

"I don't know," Brenda said. "That sounds pretty iffy. And what about the people who work around here? People like Colt, for instance."

"There'd be some displacement, obviously, in the short-term. But green industry jobs will more than make up for those lost in coal and oil and gas. It's just a matter of getting our priorities straight. And once that happens, the Southwest is uniquely positioned to lead the nation in wind and solar power."

They'd arrived at the next alcove, where a few crumbled walls were all that remained of a small dwelling complex. They both stared upward, weighing the risks and rewards.

"You sound just like a politician," Brenda told her. "Or one of those preachers on television. Send in your money and buy a ticket to heaven! Never mind if sending money today means eating cat food tomorrow."

"I didn't say—"

"If Colt gets laid off by Archer-Mason, he's pretty much fucked. You know that, right? He has no college, and he's spent four years learning a trade that you say is obsolete. And as far as this community goes, what do you care? I mean really. It's not like you've got any skin in the game."

Addie stifled the urge to defend herself. She hadn't told Colt about the ranch, and she wasn't about to tell Brenda.

And tell her what, exactly? That she was forgoing millions by rejecting Archer-Mason's offer? Because that wasn't entirely true. If she was going to own the ranch then she was going to own the minerals that came with it, simple as that. Selling the Triple-R would still mean profiting from oil and gas, and keeping it probably meant having her mineral rights force-pooled with the BLM's. She'd given thought to the matter and concluded that the only way to keep the CO_2 in the ground would be to persuade the community to join with her and Bradley in rejecting Archer-Mason entirely.

But really, what were the chances of that?

"If that's how you feel," Addie said, "then why'd you offer to help us?"

"I don't know. The way Bradley described it, it seemed like the right thing to do. And maybe it is. I mean, I'm sure it is. It's just that there's consequences, you know? Folks around here have a lot to lose."

"We all have something to lose. Look up there. It was drought that forced those people into the cliffs. Drought that led to starvation and warfare. But they had no alternatives. We have plenty of alternatives, and yet we're heading toward the exact same outcome because we're allowing the greed of a few to prevail over the welfare of the many."

"Wow. You really are a politician. You should run for county commissioner."

"So should you. We'll gang up on your father."

"Hah. We'll make him show nothing but Zac Efron movies."

"And a few Ryan Goslings."

"Now you're talking." Brenda squinted into the sun. "Who needs Colt Dixon anyway?"

15

He pulled to a stop on the flattened grass and let the engine idle for a ten-count before turning and extracting the key. He waved to Mrs. Nantz, whom he knew would be watching him as she watched everyone, guest and resident alike, through the screen door of her trailer. Hearing the telltale squeak of that door, he paused as she stepped into the evening sunlight drying her hands on her apron.

"I sprung another leak," she told him, as though reporting some personal ailment.

"Under the sink?"

She shook her head. "Toilet. Where that hose thingy runs into the tank."

"How bad is it?"

"Just a drip. Not like any emergency or nothing."

"Okay," he said. "Just give me a minute."

He tossed his keys onto the coffee table and ducked into his bedroom where he sat on the bed and untied his heavy boots. Standing again, he removed his wallet and set it on the nightstand and shed his coveralls like a dirty blue skin. He found some semi-clean jeans in the laundry pile and stepped into those and was sitting again to retie his boots when he remembered or else felt the crinkle of the folded page in his pocket.

One Man's Quest to Save t   merican West.

"You couldn't save a seat in church," Colt said to nobody, crumpling the page and banking it into the trashcan as he passed through the kitchen. He grabbed his toolbox off the floor and headed back outside.

"Like I said, it wasn't no emergency or nothing."

Mrs. Nantz was leaning in the doorway of her bathroom where Colt lay sprawled on his back with his head beside a toilet that wasn't presently leaking and probably never had, Mrs. Nantz being widowed and lonely and generally ignored by the other residents of the trailer park who thought her a busybody, or overly needy, or just bat-shit crazy.

She had a son in New Mexico who sold spas, Mrs. Nantz did, spas being another name for hot tubs. Or so she claimed. Colt had neither met the man nor seen him around. But then she also claimed to have known Colt's mother from bingo at the Ute Mountain Casino, except that Colt knew for a fact his mother didn't play bingo and had never set foot in the Ute Mountain Casino.

"I see the problem," he told her. "I'll have her fixed in a jiffy."

"Can I offer you some coffee? Or a glass of water?"

"No, ma'am." He held pliers aloft. "But could you hand me the ones that look like these, only with the blue handles?"

He closed his eyes and waited as she rummaged his toolbox.

"I heard that Decker girl is back in town. Didn't you two used to see each other?"

"Yes we did." Colt's eyes were open now. "How did you know that?"

"I saw Paulette Hawkins at the Cowbelles. She'd been to Vivian Olsen's funeral. Said she looked like a young Elizabeth Taylor. The Decker girl that is. Not Vivian. Vivian looked like a wax dummy. Are these the ones you wanted?"

Back in his own trailer, Colt reclined on the sofa with his feet on the coffee table and a beer bottle warming between his thighs. *Monday Night Football*, Lions and Dolphins tied at three in the third quarter in possibly the worst game of the season, neither team with a quarterback but both with a stout defense. Bunch of commercials for beer and pickups and pills to give you a hard-on, Colt doubly depressed both from watching them and in recognizing himself as their target demographic.

When his mother died senior year it had fallen to Colt to deal with all she'd left behind. Clothes and shoes, pans and dishes, photo albums and cheap bric-a-brac. A lifetime of accumulated crap that in any normal family he imagined the kids might've argued over but that Colt had either hauled to Goodwill or else tossed in the dumpster behind Walmart. Now as he looked around his own trailer, bathed in the bluish glow of the television, he wondered at what he might leave behind. More to the point, he wondered who would give a shit.

That was the thing about bachelorhood. It wasn't the here and now of it—the happy hour beers or the frozen pizzas or the nightly *SportsCenter* highlights—so much as the way it colored a man's long-term thinking.

Take those photo albums, for instance. Dozens of pictures of Colt in swim trunks, on horseback, in pads. Not a single shot of his father, the yellowed pages brighter white where photos once had been. He'd imagined its counterpart, an identical album in Reno or Vegas or in the trunk of a car somewhere from which all evidence of his mother had been removed. As though memories were so easily erased. As though the scars left by those missing photos would ever fully heal.

And yet Addie had a father, a flesh-and-blood parent on whom she'd willfully turned her back. Granted, a lot of folks around town thought Logan Decker a real hard case, but Colt wasn't one of them. They hadn't seen what he'd seen, which was a man who'd lost his wife young and had maybe overcompensated some by focusing so much attention on his daughter that he'd damn near burned her up. Fried her to a crisp, like when you were a kid if you weren't careful you might burn out a beehive or an anthill or whatever it was you were studying through a glass you held in the sun. And if that was a crime on Logan's part, well, there were worse crimes to be sure. But to Colt's way of thinking, there were few worse punishments.

Colt, of course, had his own set of photos—dozens of images on his cell phone, some dating back to high school. A bunch were of him and Addie, his favorite being the one Calvin took at Purgatory, both of them laughing like maniacs after Colt had done a header getting off the chairlift and had tackled Addie who'd somehow ended up in his lap. Photos that meant the world to him today but someday after he'd died would be tossed or deleted by someone, probably some stranger, who with a click or a swipe of the finger would make his entire life disappear.

Such were his views on bachelorhood.

"Cry me a river," he said aloud, flipping through channels in search of a movie. *National Velvet* maybe, or *A Place in the Sun.* But all he found were ads. Ads for pizza, and for insurance, and for rental cars. Ads for Xarelto and Humira, Lyrica and Zoloft.

Side effects might include headaches, dizziness, rashes, nausea, constipation, diarrhea, vomiting, bleeding, infection, depression, heart failure, death.

Call your doctor if you experience an erection lasting more than four years.

16

Logan pulled his truck to the shoulder and fished the sheet from his pocket and read it again in the ghostly glow of the dash. The printed instructions directed him to proceed exactly 3.2 miles past the third cattle guard where an unmarked driveway would lead to a gate with a twelve-button keypad. Tonight's entry code, the instructions said, would be 91101.

The sheet had arrived in an envelope delivered by a ponytailed man with a pitted face and a holstered sidearm who'd appeared in the hayfield like a walking scarecrow and had handed it to Logan and then disappeared without saying a word. Also inside the envelope had been an official-looking document headed "SUMMONS: Posse Comitatus" replete with Wherefores and Whereases commanding Logan's attendance and warning that not only the time and place of the meeting but also its very fact were to be held in strictest confidence.

Logan checked his odometer. He could still turn back, he knew, but then he'd never know for certain why it was he'd been summoned. He had a pretty good hunch though, and that alone made pressing onward all the more urgent.

The cattle guard, school-bus yellow with tubular pipes scuffed black by the tires of a thousand passing trucks, glowed in the headlights before him. He folded away the instruction sheet and took a final drag off his cigarette and flicked it onto the blacktop. He put his truck back into gear.

The gate once he'd found it opened onto a rutted track that curved through a rolling expanse of snakeweed and rabbitbrush. On a rise some half-mile distant he could make out a dark cluster of buildings and a single, beckoning light. Behind him, in the ruby glow of his taillights, he saw that the fence through which he'd passed was at least ten feet of chain-link and was topped with a coil of razor wire.

He counted eight vehicles in the graveled parking lot, all of them pickups, all with their beds angled toward the building. As he swung his own truck into the row his headlights swept two human figures standing at attention. Both men appeared to be young—no more than thirty—and both were dressed in makeshift fatigues that included black berets, Kevlar vests, and camouflage pants tucked into lace-up tactical boots.

Across his chest each of the men cradled what looked like an AR-15 assault rifle.

"Mr. Decker?" one of them called as Logan stepped down from his truck.

"That's right."

"You'll forgive me, sir, but I'll need to pat you down."

The young man handed off his weapon and pantomimed for Logan to spread his arms before frisking him neck to ankles including, Logan noted, his sternum area where, in the movies at least, a recording device might've been hidden.

"If you'll follow me, please."

The man recovered his weapon and led Logan around the main structure to a large and windowless outbuilding clad in corrugated steel. A caged light shone over the plain wooden door on which the man rapped twice before shouldering it open and gesturing that Logan proceed.

The first thing Logan noticed, aglow in the overhead lights, was a bright yellow flag that hung like a bedsheet from a central rafter. In arching block letters above the familiar corkscrew rattlesnake were the words MILITIA OF MONTEZUMA. Beneath the flag, in the lighted center of a concrete floor, a dozen or more men were gathered around a beer keg cocked and floating in a tub of melting ice.

The men wore Carhartt jackets or hunting camo or, in several cases, variations on the uniforms he'd seen outside. Many were stout and bearded and some had tattoos on their necks. Most wore ball caps or cowboy hats, and some sported fingerless gloves. What all had in common were the sidearms they carried on their hips. That, and the fact that all had turned toward the new arrival where he stood blinking as the door slammed shut behind him.

"Hey, neighbor. Come grab yourself a beer."

Logan advanced, studying the faces that studied his. He knew none of the men personally, but he recognized at least two of them. The speaker, a bearded bear of Logan's approximate age, ran the gun shop on Highway 491 while the man beside him, late thirties and rugged, was a Montezuma County deputy sheriff.

"No thanks," Logan said as the deputy pumped beer into a cup. "You boys expecting an invasion or something?"

The older man grinned. "Not tonight we ain't. But if it comes, you can bet your ass we'll be ready."

This engendered grunts of agreement from the troops, and a general hoisting of glasses.

"I know you received our summons," the deputy said, sipping the beer he'd pumped, "but let's go over the ground rules just the same. The first is, you were never here. The second is, this meeting never happened. Third and most important, whatever's said in this room stays in this room. Just like in Vegas. You got any problem with that, now's the time to say so."

Logan shook his head.

"All right then. I'll let the captain fill you in."

The older man had been lighting a cigar, twisting it under the flame of a vintage Zippo. His name was Carpenter, and Logan had heard a story about him from a neighbor who'd dated his sister. According to this neighbor, Carpenter had owned a dog, a big German shepherd that had bit him without provocation. Carpenter decided to punish the dog as a lesson to his other dogs by starving it. Not only that, he'd made a show of preparing food for the dog every day, and putting it in the dog's bowl, and then withholding it at the last minute. He'd done this daily for several weeks until the dog had finally died.

Or so the story went.

"The long and short of it," Carpenter said, watching the smoke as it curled to the rafters, "is that we're planning a little security operation out your way, at that gas field above your ranch."

"On my grazing allotment."

Carpenter nodded. "That's why we asked you here. To discuss logistics."

"What's this operation involve, exactly?"

"On a date of our choosing," the deputy said, "in the not-too-distant future, armed patriots from the Militia of Montezuma acting in coordination with other like-minded individuals and organizations will establish a perimeter around the drill site and set up various roadblocks. The details don't necessarily concern you. The point being that once the site's been secured, there won't be any traffic moving in or out without our permission."

"My access is from the south, off a dirt track that follows the west fork of Red Rock Creek."

"And you're welcome to come and go as you please, just as long as you keep the BLM off your property. You let them, or the FBI, or any other federal agents use your access during the operation and we'll have no choice but to close it off."

"If you knew anything about me you'd know I got no truck with the feds."

"We do know that," Carpenter said, cuffing Logan's shoulder. "We do. The thing is, we also know you got a man at your place who's the one started this whole situation."

"And what situation is that?"

"Christ almighty, Decker. That Sommers boy is fixin to shut down every drill rig on the West Slope. You ever heard of the Western Warriors?"

"Should I?"

"They're radical enviros. Monkey wrenchers and socialists. They're the ones brought them wolves back to the Gila. They're the ones agitatin to make the sage grouse an endangered species so's they can retire every grazing permit from here to California."

"So what's that got to do with Sommers? He's some kind of a college professor."

"He's one of 'em, that's what. He's on their damn payroll! And now he's got the Oil and Gas Commission comin down here in a couple weeks to try and put Archer-Mason out of business. You got any idea what that would do to this part of the state?"

Logan reddened. He'd had a vague understanding that the professor was up to something involving Archer-Mason but hadn't known what, exactly, it involved. Now it appeared he'd gotten Addie mixed up with some troublemakers who'd gotten themselves tangled up with this bunch of wingnuts.

The deputy asked, "Ever heard of Agenda Twenty-One?"

"Can't say as I have."

"It's a UN program that requires member countries to promote what they call sustainable development. Once Agenda Twenty-One is fully implemented the US will become part of a one-world government whose goal is to resettle rural residents into cities and turn the American Southwest into a network of national parks and monuments with no grazing or drilling or mining or timber cutting. Just read the UN website. It's all there in black and white."

"That sounds like crazy talk."

"Nothin crazy about it," Carpenter said. "Hell, it's already started. Just look where you are in McElmo. First they made it a monument, and now they're squeezin out the oil and gas. You can bet grazing will be next, and after that they'll come for your guns."

"I served two tours in Afghanistan," the deputy said. "I swore an oath to preserve, protect, and defend the Constitution against all enemies, foreign and domestic. A domestic enemy in my book is any American who conspires to put the interests of the United Nations over those of the United States. I'm willing to die before letting that happen, and so is every man in this room."

The troops murmured their assent, though with notably less enthusiasm.

"Then why would you want to shut down the drill site?"

"We ain't shuttin it down," Carpenter said. "We're protecting it. Protecting it and using it to shine a light on what's goin on around here. Just like at Grants Pass and Bunkerville and Malheur. This is *our* land, Decker—yours and mine and our families' before that. Our children's forever, God willing. Ain't no pencil pushers in Denver or no tree huggers from Los Angeles gonna dictate what happens in Montezuma County. And if they think otherwise, well, we aim to show 'em different."

"Let's say I got no quarrel with any of that. And let's say I don't give a rat's ass about Sommers except that he happens to be dating my daughter. But I'll tell you right now, and you damn well better hear me. If anyone so much as touches one hair on my little girl's head—"

"Relax," the deputy said. "Unless the feds try something stupid, ain't nobody gonna get hurt."

"That's another reason we asked you here." Carpenter pointed at Logan's chest with his cigar. "You got to keep Sommers and his people off that drill site and out of our way. He pokes his nose inside the perimeter and all bets are off. And that includes anybody that's with him."

Logan felt the hot rush of blood return to his face. "Who'd you say is in charge of this operation?"

Carpenter read his watch. "The commander should've been here by now. But don't you worry about that. We may look a little ragtag, but I guarantee we're a disciplined unit that's been meeting and planning and drilling for months."

"You're missing my point," Logan told him. "I don't give a shit about your unit or your discipline or your plans. What I want to know is if anything happens to my daughter, who it is gets the first bullet."

"Easy, Mr. Decker," the deputy said. "Nothing's gonna happen to your girl, and I'll guarantee that. We're all on the same side here. But as far as Sommers goes—"

The door banged open and the men all snapped to attention. Logan turned to where the two uniformed sentries now stood inside the doorway flanking a pint-sized figure backlit on the threshold.

"As far as Sommers goes," the figure said as it stepped into the light, "I get half a chance, I'll turn that boy every way but loose."

17

Being a big-picture guy by nature, Bradley dreaded the sort of micromanagement that operations like this one entailed. Normally it fell to Stacy, his departmental secretary, to make up the spreadsheets and track down the phone numbers and even to schedule and brief the less significant players. Stacy, with her freckled cleavage and the front-tooth gap Bradley found so oddly alluring, was to the minutia of office administration what du Pré had been to the cello. But for this particular operation it fell to Bradley, with a major assist from Addie, to perform these quotidian tasks, and to the Western Warriors to foot the bill.

Office space: $800/mo. furnished. Util. and Wi-Fi: $275.

A successful mission: Priceless.

Now that's a budget I can work with.

In your dreams Professor.

Smiling, he powered off his phone just as the glass door sucked open and Addie looked in from outside.

"How's the signal?"

"Three bars, or waves, or whatever you call them."

"Good. Now come out here and tell me what you think."

He rose from behind his scuffed metal desk and followed her onto the sidewalk. The storefront they'd rented was tiny—barely three hundred square feet in total—and it smelled of recent paint and a vaguely uric tang he preferred not to think about. But it was situated on Main Street within two blocks of the theater and stood therefore to capture a modicum of much-needed pedestrian traffic.

They stood together with their backs to the street and studied the message Addie had lettered onto the storefront glass in water-soluble paint.

PROTECT OUR RURAL LIFESTYLE
COME IN AND FIND OUT HOW!

"You're a woman of many talents."

"But you already knew that."

"Do you think 'lifestyle' is a little too . . ."

"Hoity-toity?"

"Somehow it makes me think of Gwyneth Paltrow."

"I considered 'our rural ways,' but to change it now, everything would be off-center."

"Then lifestyle it is."

Back inside, they returned to their respective desks. On a low table between them Addie had arranged a fan of folded handbills whose layout and production had occupied most of their morning. Printed on glossy paper stock, each handbill featured four-color images of various gas wells photographed from above. Three of the photos were drone shots of freshly scraped well pads while the last was a fixed-wing panorama taken near the Durango airport. It depicted a houndstooth pattern of interlocking wells and service roads stretching to the far horizon through formerly pristine forest like a scabrous pox on the skin of the earth.

The accompanying text explained the various objectives of the local public forum. Its precise language was a matter of no small importance, framing as it did the arguments to be made to the Colorado Oil and Gas Conservation Commission. For that reason, Bradley and Addie had spent the better part of Monday evening at the Triple-R batting ideas and catchphrases—Conservation or resource management? Global warming or climate change?—like so many shuttlecocks over a dining room table cluttered with take-out Chinese, their precious privacy the result of Logan Decker having been called to some meeting at the Elks Lodge in Cortez.

Perhaps it was the wine Addie had opened, or the warm afterglow of success with the county commission, or maybe it was just the absence of Addie's father who, like a noise you only notice once it finally stops, had been casting an intangible pall over Bradley's libido. But as the grandfather clock chimed ten, Bradley stood and circled the table and planted a lingering kiss on Addie's lips.

"Wow. Does that mean we're finished?"

"It means we've only just begun," he said, and to drive home the point he lifted her standing and swept a space on the table, sending cartons and chopsticks clattering to the floor.

"Wait. Are you sure . . ."

He was positive. Setting her on the table, he began unbuttoning her jeans.

"This isn't the greatest idea," she said, glancing over her shoulder.

"This is a fabulous idea."

"Okay, but just not here."

A low growl stayed Bradley's hand. Waylon had appeared in the open passage to the living room with his teeth bared and his hackles raised in a hedgerow. Addie twisted free and slid to her feet, gathering up the cartons and chopsticks and leading Bradley by the hand.

"Come on, let's go upstairs."

Inside her darkened bedroom, in the canted moonlight that shone through her window, he undressed Addie with the eager dexterity of a man unwrapping a prize. Even Colt Dixon, he was willing to bet, had never breached the castle keep; never braved the snarling Cerberus of Jess Olsen and Logan Decker to lay claim to the damsel within.

When both at last were naked he stretched beside her and saw in her eyes neither longing nor lust nor a gleam of playful insouciance, but a different look entirely.

"Are you all right?"

"I guess."

"You guess?"

He looked to where her gaze had strayed—to the mirror over her dresser where the dimly reflected image of the leaning cowgirl and the wobbling barrel transformed before his eyes from advertisement to allegory.

He rolled to his back beside her. "What's wrong?"

"It's nothing. Really."

But it wasn't nothing, and already he felt himself softening.

"I'm sorry," she offered.

"What's the matter?"

"It's just . . . I keep thinking about my father walking in."

"I locked the door."

"I know. It's just . . . this house. This *room.*"

"Your house," he reminded her. "Your room."

"Somehow it doesn't feel that way. Not yet anyway."

He sighed. The irony here was that some of his faculty colleagues and most of his friends outside academia assumed that Bradley slept with his students. How could you resist, they kidded, plucking an occasional grape from that coed cornucopia? But they weren't really joking so much as inviting Bradley to share with them some juicy tale of conquest, some ribald confession of Eros run amok in that sun-kissed Gomorrah beyond the far horizons of parental supervision.

Ducks in a shooting gallery, they said. Fish in a barrel. And while it was true that the opportunities had been many, even after the #MeToo movement had worked its saltpeter effect on virtually every other American workplace, the anodyne fact was that Adelaide Decker of Cortez, Colorado, had been the first and only student with whom Bradley Sommers had ever, in his nine-plus years of university teaching, deigned to transgress.

"Our plan," he reminded her, keeping his voice even, "was to spend one or two nights here and then find a hotel."

"I know. But it would almost be hostile to move right now. Plus I'd like to spend more time with my grandfather. Plus it'd be dumb to pay for a hotel when, like you said, this is practically my house."

"Where we can't be together."

"We can." She rolled to her side and rested a hand on his chest. "I don't care what my father thinks."

But that, he knew, was a lie. Enough so to leave Bradley flaccid and wanting and looking ahead to the day when their work here would be finished; when at last he could put the thin air and the nosebleeds, the bad coffee and the heavily armed boyfriend behind him.

He shifted to face her. "The last thing I want is to come between you and your family. You know that, right?"

"You're not, I promise. Daddy likes you. Really. It may not seem that way, but that's just how he is."

"Antagonistic?"

"Protective."

"Misanthropic?"

"Fiercely parental."

He lifted her hand and kissed it and rolled his weight from the bed.

The door sucked open again and a woman entered pulling an oxygen tank on wheels. She was over sixty and morbidly obese and wore hot pink sneakers adorned with some sort of silver glitter. She hovered over the fan of brochures with her lips pursed as though trying to decide which card to draw from a magician's hand.

Bradley and Addie shared a look.

"Help yourself," Addie said, rising from her chair. "There's a public meeting coming up next month. It concerns oil and gas drilling here in Montezuma County."

The woman made her selection. She unfolded the brochure and frowned as she examined the photos.

"Have you been impacted by oil and gas where you live?"

The woman looked up. "I thought this had to do with the 4-H."

"No, ma'am. It's about keeping gas wells away from our farms and ranches and protecting our water supply."

The woman studied the brochure. She turned it over to read the back. "My Norbert was in the 4-H," she said. "Only we raised chickens. We couldn't raise stock on account of our land was too small."

Addie looked to Bradley, who shrugged. To the woman she said, "Well, why don't you take that home and tell your family and friends about the public meeting. They can find the exact date and time on our Facebook page. It's right there on the back."

But the woman had already replaced the brochure and was wheeling her tank in a hasty three-point turn.

"Running to tell her friends," Bradley said when the door had closed behind her.

"Which explains the shoes."

"Nothing explains those shoes."

Addie straightened the brochures. "This all seems so analog. How many people can we expect to reach this way?"

"We need both local and national publicity. And as we know from bitter experience, many Four Corners residents are without internet access."

"But why national publicity? I thought the goal here was a big local turnout."

"Publicity is the goal. The more heat we can generate, the more likely Archer-Mason will feel it."

As the day progressed, filtered sunlight angled through the office window and the words Addie had painted there began a slow and backward crawl across the floor. Perhaps a dozen more visitors interrupted Bradley's telephone calls and Addie's internet work; Addie in each case the one to rise from her desk and engage with the visitor, employing her radiant smile and her down-home charms to coax a reluctant promise of attendance. Then at four thirty the door sucked open again and a ham-faced man leaned his bulk into the office.

"Have you all seen my mother by any chance?"

"What does she look like?"

"About yea high? Oxygen tank?"

"Pink sneakers? She was in around two hours ago. I think she headed east."

The man nodded and started to leave when Bradley pressed his phone to his chest.

"Hey! Are you Norbert?"

"That's right."

"How're those chickens doing?"

The man squinted. "Chickens?"

"Never mind," Addie said. "But please take a brochure."

At the stroke of five Addie closed her laptop and unplugged her power cord and wound it in a tight figure eight. "Sure you won't reconsider?"

"Positive."

"So you'd rather hang out with my father? Maybe help with the irrigation?"

Bradley read his watch. "I need to talk to that reporter. Then I thought I'd take a little drive."

"What drive?"

"Pleasant View. I want to see the Archer-Mason operation up close."

"You can do that from the ranch."

"If I felt like schlepping a mile uphill."

"That's why God created horses. We could ride up together. Maybe tomorrow evening?"

"God also created four-wheel drive."

Addie slung her laptop bag over her shoulder and tossed her hair. She circled the desks and patted Bradley atop the head.

"Your God, maybe, but not mine."

18

She stood on the corner and waited for her grandfather's pickup. When at last it rolled into view, a wisp of oily smoke trailing behind it, she waved her arms and watched in horror as it veered into the adjoining traffic lane, setting brakes screeching and car horns angrily blaring.

"Damn tourists," he said to Addie as she climbed into the passenger seat.

"You need to be more careful."

"Me? I been drivin this road since before it was paved."

"And before it was striped, apparently."

It was less than a mile to the Denny's on Highway 160 that had played host to her grandparents' weekly date nights since the old M & M Truck Stop closed back in 2001. As they swung into the parking lot Addie asked whether this particular Denny's, chrome-clad in the retro style of a 1950s diner, harkened back somehow to Jess and Vivian's courtship days.

"Nah," he said, setting the brake. "Your grandmother was just partial to the bacon chicken sandwich is all."

The hostess greeted Jess by name and led them through the half-empty dining room to a booth by the window where a passing waitress set a white china mug at Jess's elbow and filled it with steaming coffee.

"For you, hon?"

"Iced tea, please."

The waitress hesitated, as if searching for the right words, and then patted Jess on the arm before trundling back to the kitchen.

"That's Dotty," he said. "When your grandma and me didn't show up last week, she called the house to make sure everything was all right."

While Addie scanned the oversized menu, Jess gazed out the window to the EconoLodge across the highway where, in a tableau pixilated by the flash of passing cars, a couple stood arguing in the parking lot. A suitcase rested on the blacktop between them with its handle extended as the woman leaned forward, poking the man's chest with a finger.

"Some things never do change," Jess said, shaking his head.

Addie watched what he was watching. "Did you and Grandma ever used to fight?"

"Oh, my. Like cats and coons, till I learned a valuable lesson."

"What lesson was that?"

"That gettin your way ain't nearly half as important as gettin along."

Addie enjoyed this shared confidence. She tried to recall her grandparents as a couple, the way they'd behaved in each other's company. Vivian, of course, was a woman of strong opinions readily voiced, and yet there was an unspoken deference she seemed to pay only where Jess was concerned. Addie thought of Waylon and how as a young dog full of bark and bluster he would trot ahead of Feather on a trail ride, a study in self-confidence. Until, that is, he noticed horse and rider had turned, at which point he'd dash to resume his position, always following from the lead.

Was her grandma Vivian's canine fealty to her husband always reciprocated? Addie could not recall a single instance of Jess talking over her grandmother or chiding her in public or disparaging something she'd said. Then again, two trucks traveling in the same direction rarely collide, and if ever they do, the impact is generally minimal.

"I was terrified of her when I was little," Addie confessed. "It was like I knew I could wrap Daddy around my little finger but Grandma Vivian could see right through me. Then as I got older and started driving and staying out later on weekends, I noticed she was always up when I'd get home. I'd see that light in the cabin and I'd see her in silhouette in her rocker with a book in her lap and I thought, boy, she must be some reader. It wasn't until college that I realized she'd been up all those nights just waiting for me to come home. Looking for the light in my bedroom, making sure I'd made it back safely."

Jess chuckled. "I remember she told me once, 'If I had half that girl's looks I'd carry bear spray in my handbag. And if I did, you'd have never gotten to first base.'"

Addie laughed. She delighted in stories like these—x-ray glimpses into a life that while lived right under her nose had been all but opaque to her younger self. Not that her younger self would ever have thought of her grandparents in quite that way: intimate, flirtatious, sharing an inside joke. It was, she supposed, a conceit of youth that love was an elixir of which they alone partook.

"You look like a woman with things on her mind."

"I'm sorry."

"If it's that carbon dioxide, you're allowed to have second thoughts. I reckon you'd be crazy if you didn't."

"I don't," Addie said, and meant it. "I was actually thinking about you and Grandma. About what it takes to make a marriage last sixty years."

Jess tasted his coffee. "First of all, sixty years ain't but the blink of an eye. I know you hear that all the time, and maybe it's hard to believe at your age, but it's true. The second thing, and I think it's the important one, is that if you want a long and happy marriage, you need to find yourself a partner who suits your gait."

"Your gait?"

"Sure. Take that Feather horse of yours. Remember when your pa and me took you to the sale barn and there was that tobiano you thought was so flashy? Oh my, but you had to have that horse. Never mind that anybody with eyes in his head could see that horse fit you like a boot that's a half-size too small. And then you rode that mare and it was like watching Cinderella slide right into her slipper."

"And I pouted about it for a week."

"That's right. A flashy horse is like a beautiful woman. You think, wouldn't I look fine astride that little darlin. And so you turn yourself inside out tryin to overlook its flaws. Then after a while you come to realize you're only foolin yourself and that a solid cow horse is worth ten of that lot."

"And that was Grandma? A solid cow horse?"

He returned his gaze to the window. "We're not talkin about your grandma now, are we?"

"Excuse me?"

"I seen you and that Dixon boy at the funeral parlor."

"Really." Addie could feel her face warming. "And what did you see, exactly?"

"Looked to me like a rider who'd come to a fork in the road."

"From clear across the room you could see that?"

"I'm old, honey, but I ain't blind."

"The way you drive, you could've fooled me."

The lines at his eyes deepened. They were startling eyes, pale and milky, the color of glacial ice. The color of marbles she'd played with as a child.

"Then again," he said, "I suppose it could turn out like them curly fries."

"Curly fries?"

"For years this place served regular fries. Then a while back they switched to curly fries. No warning, mind you. One day you order your supper and *boom*: curly fries. As if regular fries wasn't fancy enough. Or maybe curly fries was all the rage in Durango or Telluride so they figured it was a public service they was doin to save Cortez from gettin left behind."

"Fry-wise."

"The thing of it was, the curly fries were greasy, and sometimes they got stuck to themselves like a spring that's wound too tight. Anyway, your grandma didn't like 'em, and being your grandma she of course let the management know exactly how she felt about it. So where was I goin with this story?"

"Your guess is as good as mine."

"Fork in the road. That's it. So we had a choice to make. We either had to change restaurants again, which would've been a nuisance, or else your grandma had to eat the curly fries and be done with it."

"Or order rice."

"Rice? Lordy, no. So anyway your grandma, she decided to tough it out. But believe me, she wasn't happy about it. And then maybe a month or so later, *boom*: regular fries again."

"Hallelujah."

"The point of the story—the *moral* you might call it—is that sometimes you don't have to decide. Or maybe it's that you can go right ahead and decide all you want but it don't matter anyhow because fate or God or what-have-you just goes ahead and makes the decision for you."

"The decision being?"

"Colt or the professor, honey. Regular fries or curly."

"Yikes. Now you're starting to sound like Daddy."

"Between you and me, I wouldn't take relationship advice from your father. Logan's had himself a dozen women over the years, good women, practically toss a lariat over his head." He turned in his seat and signaled the waitress. "A regular eliminator is what I'd call him."

The waitress appeared with Addie's iced tea in one hand and a pad in the other. Addie ordered the avocado salad. Jess, apparently, didn't need to order.

"So," he said when the waitress had left, "which one is which?"

"I'm sorry?"

"The Dixon boy. Is he the tobiano that got away, or is he that solid cow horse you left behind for some flashy new stud?"

"I didn't come here to talk about me. I want to know how you're doing." She reached a hand across the table and laid it over his. "This must've been the hardest week of your life."

He didn't answer. Instead he looked across the highway to the motel where, save for the rows of shimmering cars, the parking lot was empty.

"What? Is something the matter?"

"Well. Since you brought it up, there is one thing I been meanin to tell you about. Just promise you won't go and make a big fuss over it."

"It doesn't involve onion rings, does it?"

"You remember Doc Milburn? Office on Park Street? I think you went once or twice with your grandma. Anyway, he tells me this thing that started in my prostate gland has gone and spread all the way to my bones."

Addie withdrew her hand. Then she replaced it. "My God, Grandpa."

"I said don't get excited. I'm a decrepit old man, and the fact is I wasn't too keen on livin without your grandma to begin with. So you might say it's just as well. Or if you was of a philosophical nature, you might say the decision got made for me."

"Like the curly fries."

He smiled.

"Did the doctor say—"

"A few months, maybe. Probably less."

"Oh, Grandpa."

"Now don't you go—"

"What about treatment options? Things like chemotherapy or radiation?"

"Hell. I got a damn drugstore still in my bathroom from your grandmother's illness, and what good did it do her?"

"I don't know. Maybe it bought her some time. Maybe it made her life a little more comfortable."

"The morphine did, there at the end. That I'm hangin on to."

"Daddy never told me anything about this."

"Well. I never did tell your grandma, so it could be I neglected to mention it to your pa."

"Jesus, you *men!*" She pantomimed strangulation. "This is like that time you almost cut your foot off. You remember that? If Grandma hadn't found you passed out in the bathtub you'd have bled to death."

"I recollect I nicked myself once with a chainsaw."

Addie buried her face in her hands.

"Speakin of your pa, I hope you noticed he's quit drinkin."

She looked up. "Since when?"

"Some years back. Pretty much since the day you left for college."

She didn't know what to say about that, or how to feel. On the one hand it was exactly like Logan to quit drinking only after the years Addie had spent making excuses for him or worrying he'd gotten into some fight or some wreck. Reluctant to have her friends sleep over or for their parents or her teachers to see him in town or to hear about some scene he'd made somewhere. On the other hand she *had* noticed a change, a more open demeanor, and was happy for that—happy for him—and flattered her departure might have been the catalyst for something so life-altering. Something so positive, like that silver lining you always hear about but rarely get to see.

"That's good," she said. "I'm glad to hear it."

"Don't be angry with him. For years after your mother died, old Logan didn't know if he'd found a rope or lost a horse. And don't you be angry with me, neither. I wasn't tryin to hide anything. I wanted you to be first to know is all."

What Addie wanted right then was to scream. At the same time she was determined not to—to demonstrate to her grandfather she was a grown woman, a strong woman like Vivian, capable of handling not just his news but also her own affairs and those of the ranch. But at the thought of the Triple-R, and of owning it, and of dealing with her father and Bradley and the mineral rights, she wanted to scream all over again.

"We need to tell Daddy," she finally said. "*You* need to tell him. Tonight."

"I will," he said, twisting in his seat. "Now who's a man got to know to get himself a cheeseburger in this place?"

19

The auto shops and the liquor stores and the farm supply mega-centers along Highway 491 gave way to listing barns and weathered houses and then to the occasional grain silo as Cortez receded in Bradley's rearview mirror and a flat expanse of farmland opened up before him. Soon he was speeding through a patchwork of cow pastures and hayfields, bean fields and cornfields—pastoral acres of green or gold or freshly plowed umber and all of it stitched together with miles upon miles of barbed wire.

He lowered his window and extended a bladed hand. He remembered driving like this as a boy in his parents' Volvo, fast and unimpeded and with the same agrarian smells, through the Santa Ynez Valley—past the vineyards and the horse farms and the oak-studded hillsides toasted gold by summer sun. Traffic-choked now like the rest of Southern California, which had fused together like hot asphalt during his lifetime into one enormous city. Here in the rural Southwest, in one of the nation's last remaining outposts of empty roads and broad horizons, he understood how the looming threats of overpopulation and resource depletion might fail to evoke the sense of urgency they did in urban America.

Although he consulted his phone's map application it was the blue contours of the Abajos, low peaks on the western horizon, that guided him northbound toward Pleasant View, a farming community on the northern edge of the county soon to enjoy the dubious distinction of having more gas wells than residents.

Despite the scenery, despite the childhood reverie, it was the newspaper interview that played like a loop in Bradley's head. The *Cortez Journal* reporter, young and earnest, had read him a series of pointed questions about tax revenues and unemployment statistics from a spiral notepad held in her lap. Wasn't poverty a greater threat to local health and safety than any alleged environmental issues? Wouldn't the kinds of setbacks for which he was advocating effectively bar oil and gas exploration altogether in Montezuma County? What right did an academic from Los Angeles have to challenge a centuries-old Western tradition like natural resource extraction?

"Sounds to me like you've been talking with Bud Wallace," Bradley said, to which the reporter had replied, in a line she'd probably heard on television, "I'm afraid I'm not at liberty to reveal my sources."

Heading to inspect am
gas field in pview.

How did it go with the
paper?

Rough sledding. The knives
are already out.

Nothing we didn't anticipate.

The cutoff road when finally he found it was marked by a hand-painted sign reading ARCHER-MASON TRUCK TRAFFIC. After ten more minutes on teeth-chattering washboard that took him past farms and fields and orchards heavy with fruit, Bradley feared he'd gone astray.

Then he began seeing the signs. Century 21. RE/MAX Realty. 4 Corners Properties. Infrequent at first but soon, it seemed, alongside every third mailbox he passed.

Proving exactly the point he'd tried to make to that reporter. You want to talk economic impacts? There'd been hundreds of fires and explosions at drill sites and pipelines across Colorado in recent years—nearly one per month by some estimates. So what about the families whose homes, whose nest eggs, lose half their value overnight when industry comes to a neighborhood? Who foots the bill when a well blowout or a pipeline rupture requires emergency response and cleanup? What are the lost opportunity costs to a county like Montezuma when hikers and bikers, rafters and anglers depart for less spoiled environs?

Bradley quoted statistics. How outdoor recreation employs over six million Americans each year, driving over $650 billion in direct consumer spending. How Mesa Verde National Park, one of only two dozen UNESCO World Heritage Sites in the entire US, attracts roughly six hundred thousand visitors each year to the community. How the Canyons of the Ancients—the scenic red-rock corridor connecting the cliff dwellings of Mesa Verde with the ancient stone towers of Hovenweep National Monument—was uniquely positioned to capitalize on this economic bonanza if only the national, state, and local governments would quit trying to turn it into a giant industrial park.

If one thing had become clear to Bradley, it was that local experience had failed to enlighten. In 2015, for example, the EPA's attempts to remediate years of acid leaching from the shuttered Gold King Mine in nearby Silverton had caused an explosion of mine waste—zinc and cadmium, arsenic and iron—to flood the Animas River. For days after the event, the Animas and the San Juan had run fluorescent orange as millions of gallons of toxic sludge flowed through Durango and Farmington and onto the Navajo Nation. States of emergency were declared in Colorado and New Mexico, and although litigation was still ongoing, impacts ranging from recreational closures to crop losses were expected to tally in the tens of millions of dollars.

So what lesson was learned from the incident? Was it that hard rock mining in a sensitive watershed is a bad idea to begin with? Was it that mine operators who, thanks to an obsolete 1872 law, pay nothing in federal royalties on the billions they extract from public lands should finally be charged for the privilege? Alas, it was neither. Public anger, stoked by industry, was instead directed against the EPA itself, leading to calls not just for its elimination but for turning all federal lands over to the states and to cash-strapped counties for further mismanagement.

Or consider the wildlife question. Where Bradley had grown up, on the outskirts of a city of ten million people, he'd heard coyotes yip-yipping in the night and glimpsed the occasional bobcat or mountain lion. His parents to this day told stories of neighbors waking up to find a black bear in their hot tub. Yet after five days in Colorado, amid red-rock canyons and high-mountain vistas, Bradley had yet to see or hear a single predator.

And why was that? In part because Wildlife Services, a shadowy arm of the US Department of Agriculture, employed aerial gunning, sodium cyanide bombs, and iron leg-hold traps to maim and kill some two million carnivores annually—nearly six thousand animals per day—at the behest of ranching and industry.

So much, Bradley thought, for rugged self-reliance and disdain for the federal government.

Blame the Marlboro Man, or country-and-western music, or Wrangler blue jeans. It was hard to blame the ranchers— men like Jess Olsen or Logan Decker—or the miners, or even the drill rig owners for suckling on the twenty billion dollars in annual subsidies that flowed like mothers' milk from a feckless Washington bureaucracy either too calculating or too callow to buck the hoary Western mythos.

But all politics is local, he reminded himself. Here in Montezuma County, Bud Wallace had a financial incentive for opposing a public forum while Hawkins and Holcomb, in Bradley's corner for now, both would need to be managed. He made a mental note to touch base with each of them on a daily basis. Once the

Cortez Journal article appeared, the community pushback would be furious. He made a second mental note, to work up a set of talking points for their use in dealing with angry constituents.

This, after all, was what Bradley did best. He'd long ago learned that nothing in this world is all black or all white—that even the most rapacious industrialist might enjoy his weekend cabin while the most militant enviro might blanch at the high price of gasoline. If compromise was a mountain, then these were the cracks—the imperceptible toeholds—by which an experienced climber might summit. And Bradley Sommers was nothing by now if not an experienced climber.

The gravel road ended abruptly at a chain-link gate bracketed by rock outcrops and fronted by a flimsy guard shack. The gate appeared closed at this hour, the guard shack shuttered and dark.

Bradley pulled his Prius alongside an older Toyota sedan. He stepped from his car and approached the gate and rattled the chain and padlock. The fence in which the gate was set stood twelve feet in height. The flat horizon beyond it was, he realized, just an extension of the tabletop mesa—a huge plateau, really—that overlooked the Red Rocks Ranch some dozen miles to the south.

Buildings—new-looking trailers with blue porta-potties—flanked the dusty dirt road that continued on to the gas field. Vacant now, just as he'd hoped. The fence, however, was something he hadn't anticipated. Frustrated, he turned back to his car just as a *thunk* from the guard shack stayed his retreat. The upper half of its plywood door creaked open.

"Help you?" called a voice from within.

"Hello!" Bradley approached warily. "I thought I was almost to Hovenweep when I hit this gate."

The shaggy-haired kid in the shack was college-aged. Hispanic probably, or else Native American. He removed a white earbud as he leaned his forearms on the sill. His left eyebrow was pierced by what looked like a silver exclamation point.

"To get to Hovenweep you gotta go back to 10, then west again on CC. But the visitor center's probably closed this late in the day."

"Darn it." Bradley faced west with his hands on his hips. He read his watch. "I was supposed to meet my parents there, like, ten minutes ago. I don't suppose you could let me cut through?"

"Dude, I'd like to help, but I doubt you could even get there from here. Not in that, anyway."

They both looked to the Prius, small and out of its element.

"So what is this place, anyway?"

"Gas wells," the kid said, leaning forward. "Carbon dioxide."

"No kidding. I don't smell anything."

"That's because it doesn't smell. Except when they drill a new one, then you can smell it for miles."

"Like a giant fart?"

The kid laughed, and Bradley laughed with him, edging closer. There was a desk and a chair and a gooseneck lamp inside the booth, and in the cone of light from the lamp, a familiar sight.

"Studying?"

"Yeah." The kid turned to his open textbook. "Intro to Psychology. I'm a freshman at Fort Lewis."

"So this is, what, a night gig?"

The kid nodded. "Six p.m. to two a.m. Twenty-five bucks an hour to sit here and do my homework. It's great, because nobody ever bugs me. Well, except for tonight."

"I'm sorry."

"No, man, it's okay. You weren't the first."

"I wasn't?"

"Nah. Couple of dudes came by earlier. Hunters, with camo and rifles and shit. Said they were tracking an elk. Which is weird 'cause I never seen any elk around here."

Bradley turned to study the road behind him. The shadows were lengthening, the light beginning to fade.

"What did they look like, these hunters?"

"I don't know. White dudes, scruffy beards. Old beater truck."

"The reason I ask is I'm surprised you can hunt around here at all. This close to the farms I mean."

The kid shrugged. "They wanted me to open the gate. Got all in my face about it. I told 'em I couldn't, that I'd lose my job."

"Plus an elk would need wings to get over this fence."

"Exactly. Hello?"

"So what did they do when you refused?"

"Nothing. They just got in their truck and left. Oh, but the one dude, he said something weird. He said it was okay, because the hunting was gonna be way better tomorrow."

20

He was on the tractor when the old man's pickup rounded the driveway and stopped, still idling, in front of the house. He watched Addie alight and duck her head to wave before bounding up the steps as Jess continued around back to the cabin.

The professor must be off somewhere on his own, Logan figured, meaning now was the chance he'd been waiting for.

By the time he'd garaged the tractor and turned out the horses and hiked back up to the house Addie was barefoot on the front porch, rocking and sipping a drink. She'd left teabags floating in a Mason jar that morning, setting it in the sun by the kitchen window, and it was little touches like that—the changing flower arrangements and the fruit bowls and the neatly folded dishtowels—that for the past several days had been stopping Logan and making him smile and leaving a lump in his throat.

"Hello, Daddy," she said as he mounted the steps, blotting his neck with a kerchief. "Here, let me fix you some tea."

Logan sat and rocked and studied the field he'd left half-mown like the work of a drunken barber. Above the ridgeline, a skein of Canada geese flapped and honked in a ragged *V*. There were thundershowers in tomorrow's forecast, the first since August, but he figured the mowing could wait. He thought it would have to wait.

"Here," Addie said when she returned. "You look like you could use this."

The drink she'd handed him, lukewarm despite the ice, was garnished with an orange slice and a sprig of mint. "Thanks," he said, taking a sip and resting it on his thigh. "I believe that's just what the doctor ordered."

"Speaking of which, when was the last time you went to a doctor?"

"Why, do I look sickly to you?"

"Please. You look amazing. You do know my girlfriends all had a crush on you, right? I swear I could've sold tickets."

"The one I remember was that teacher—what was her name? Sort of cross-eyed?"

"Oh, God. Miss Nelson. Remember she used to bake cookies and brownies and send them home with me? 'Your poor father,' she used to say. 'All by himself in that great big house.'"

"She was determined."

"But I mean it. For one thing, you shouldn't be smoking."

"I don't smoke but a pack a month tops. Probably less."

"I don't believe that for a minute. Even so, that's a pack too many. A man your age needs to take care of himself."

"A man my age?"

"Aren't you about to turn sixty?"

"Don't remind me. And I do take care of myself. I'd better, 'cause this ranch don't exactly run itself."

"What about Grandpa, doesn't he still help?"

"Oh, yes. He helps himself to my coffee. He helps himself to my newspaper. Of a cold night he's been known to help himself to my dog."

"Have you ever considered what would happen if Grandpa were laid up?"

"Laid up? Your grandfather? I don't think that's even possible."

She didn't respond. He took another sip to order his thoughts on the topics whose sequence and phrasing he'd spent the better part of the day rehearsing.

"Speaking of the ranch. I hope you know I got no hard feelings about your grandparents' wishes. I couldn't be happier for you. You know that, right?"

"Of course I do."

"Good. Only here's the thing you need to understand. There's a reason there was no cash in that trust. The fact is this ranch's been running on fumes for the better part of a decade. There's only four or five meatpackers left in the whole country now, and they're the ones calling the shots. Vertical integration is what they call it, like what happened in the poultry industry. Was a time we'd get ten, maybe fifteen bids on our stock. Nowadays we're lucky to get one, and it's a take-it-or-leave-it proposition. Plus we need a new side-roll and a new baler and around two or three miles of new fencing. That waterer in the horse barn is shot to hell and there ain't a vehicle we got that's less than seven or eight years old. Truth be told, I don't know how much longer the Triple-R's got as a working cattle ranch."

He waited for her to say something. When she didn't he took another sip.

"I know you and Bradley have strong feelings about oil and gas. I understand that. But to my way of thinking that's like a patient telling the surgeon she's opposed to sharp objects. There has to come a point, in other words, when the principle gives way to the practical."

"Or else the patient dies?"

"Or wishes she had."

"And by practical, you mean turning the Triple-R into a gas field?"

Logan shook his head. "You're young, Addie. You got sixty, maybe seventy years ahead of you. There's not a thing in this world I'd like more than to have you spend them here, making a home and raising a family. You already know that. With the money Archer-Mason's offering, you could turn this ranch into a showplace and still have a million left over. You could hire help for the heavy work and spend your days doing whatever it is you want. It doesn't have to be cows. Matter of fact, I say to hell with cows. You could train cutters, for instance. Heck, you could train unicorns. And if that means having a few wells tucked away here and there, then what of it? I know a hundred men in this county who'd give their right arm for a proposition like that."

She rose and crossed to the railing and stood with her back to him. Slender, like her mother, with those same broad shoulders.

"I know how you feel about it," she said. "I get it, okay? But let's talk about something else."

"Why? What's the matter?"

She turned toward the pasture where Feather and Lightning, their tails swishing, grazed in the low sunlight. "When I came here with Bradley, I thought we'd just stay for Grandma's funeral and then move to a hotel until our project was finished. I thought it would be nice to see you and Grandpa and maybe a few friends and to show Bradley where I grew up. And honestly, I thought it would be nice if you and I could bury the hatchet."

"We can, honey. We are."

She nodded, examining her feet. "What I didn't count on was getting you or Grandpa or Colt mixed up in any of this. Especially Colt. Then come to find out the ranch is mine but that Grandpa wants me to keep it just like it is. And now you're telling me that without Archer-Mason's money, it's pretty much a goner. And Colt and Brenda both say that without Archer-Mason's jobs, the whole town's a goner. But if I drill the ranch then I'll be betraying Grandpa, not to mention Grandma Vivian. Not to mention Bradley and everything he stands for. Everything *we* stand for. And it just feels like whatever I do, whoever's side I take, it'll be my fault something bad will happen to someone I care about."

"Addie . . ."

"It's not *fair*, that's all. The only thing I ever wanted was to get out there and see the world and try to do right by it. To be a whole person and a good citizen. And maybe, if I was lucky, to make a difference. And I have to say that owning a gas field feels like the exact opposite of that."

Logan set his drink on the decking and rose and crossed to where she stood hugging herself. He hesitated, unsure of his boundaries.

"You've always been hard on yourself," he told her, "ever since you were little. That hasn't changed. But I think you'll find out that things have a way of working out for the best."

"Or maybe we just say that. Maybe we say it's the best when really it's not. We say it to fool ourselves because we can never know for sure what might've happened otherwise."

"Is that all you're worried about?"

"Isn't that enough? Last week the only decisions I had to make were which shoes to pack."

He moved beside her and rested his hands on the railing. The sun had slipped behind the mountain and shadows were fading across the canyon.

"Let me tell you something I've learned from my almost sixty years on this planet. When you're young, you think there's all these choices out there, and that once your parents or your teachers quit telling you what to do then they'll all be yours for the making. Only to find out it's just the opposite. That the older you get, the fewer choices you have, and then fewer still, until one day you wake up and you realize there's no more choices left."

"Thanks. That's the most depressing thing I've ever heard."

"But the choices you make now, when you're young, those are the important ones. And they need to be the right ones. And I'm not talking about the ranch now, or gas wells, or Archer-Mason Industries."

"Oh, Daddy."

"I'm serious now."

"But look at you." She turned to face him. "You thought you'd made the right choice when you married Mommy, but it turned out to be no choice at all."

"Tell you what. The choice I made to marry your mother? Even knowing what I do now, I'd make it again in a heartbeat.

And you want to know something else? Our choice to have a baby? I'd make that again too."

She hugged him then, fierce and sudden, with her face warm on his chest. He stood as though paralyzed, his hands loose at his sides.

"I don't know what I should do," she said.

"About which, honey?"

"About any of it."

"Including Colt?"

She didn't answer. He gripped her shoulders and held her at arms' length. "Hell, honey, that's the easy one. Just follow your heart."

"Oh, sure. People always say that, like it's so obvious."

"Isn't it obvious?"

"No! It's the least obvious thing in the world."

"All right then, how about this? Picture yourself married to Bradley and living in Los Angeles but thinking about Colt Dixon. Then picture yourself married to Colt and living here at the ranch but thinking about Bradley. Then ask yourself which of those two would hurt the least."

"As if those are my only choices?"

"That's not what I—"

"Good, because they're not. It's a big world out there, Daddy. I can go anywhere and I can be anything. It's high time you realized that a woman is more than just the man she chooses to marry."

She returned to her chair and took up her drink and resumed her silent rocking. Logan, stung by her accusation, remained rooted in place.

"What was I like as a baby?"

"What do you mean?"

"I mean did I fuss and cry a lot?"

"No more than the usual, I guess."

"But no less?"

"I don't know, honey. You were just a regular baby."

Silence. And then, "What about when Mommy died?"

That Logan remembered. How Addie would lay sprawled on her mother's bed playing with her little toy horses as Carole read her to sleep, Addie blissfully ignorant of the chasm that was opening under her feet. Oblivious to the fact that her mother was shrinking by the day, and turning a sickly shade of yellow, and growing less and less coherent as her meds failed to keep pace with her pain. Vivian offering to take the girl but Carole refusing, clinging to Addie like a life vest until the day the doctor came and it fell to Logan to pry her one final time from her mother's skeletal grasp.

She never did cry. In much the way that a horse or a dog looks Death in the face and knows him for what he is, Addie accepted her mother's passage with the blue-eyed wonder of the innocent. What was it like in heaven? she wanted to know. Would Mommy be happy there? Could we go there and see her? Those were Addie's questions, each a dagger to her father's heart.

"You were very brave," he told her now. "We were all so proud of you."

"What about you? What was it like for you when Mommy died?"

"That's what I'd call a man-sized portion. You sure you want me to go there?"

"Please? I think I need to know."

He crossed the porch and joined her where she sat. Both were rocking now, discordant at first but soon finding a common rhythm.

"I guess the first thing I felt was guilty," he told her. "The doctors, they said in so many words the cancer would never've got started if not for the pregnancy."

"That makes it my fault."

"No it doesn't. It was nobody's fault, although it took me a while to see that. And you know it's not hereditary, right? I told you that?"

She nodded. "That was the first thing. What else?"

"What else. I reckon the next thing I felt was scared. That was the big one. Scared of raising a little girl by myself. Even more scared of raising a young woman. Scared of someday having to sit you down and explain the birds and the bees."

"Which you never actually did."

"Which I wisely delegated to your grandmother."

"Guilty and scared. Okay, what else?"

"I guess the last thing was anger."

"Anger?"

"Hell, yes. Why her? Why me? What did we ever do to deserve this? I reckon I might've done some real damage, either to myself or to somebody else, except for the one thing."

"What thing was that?"

"You, honey. It was me holding you, and reading to you, and tucking you in at night that got me through those years. I guess you could say it's what got me through my life."

"Okay, now you're trying to make me cry."

"Go right ahead. And while you're at it you might want to think for a minute about the man you'd want beside you when times get as tough as that. And then as you grow older together and your choices narrow and your life gets smaller and smaller, ask yourself who's that one person you'd want there beside you at the end. Because really, it's no more complicated than that."

Addie composed herself and sipped her drink and sat sideways like she did with her legs folded beneath her.

The night was cooling quickly. Addie studied the canyon—the pasture and the horse barn and the hayfields beyond—and Logan hoped that as she looked into the darkness she might be measuring the dimensions of a reimagined future.

"There's more to him than you think," she finally said.

"How's that?"

"Bradley. You think he's some kind of a sissy, but you're wrong about that. You can't blame him for how he grew up or who his parents were any more than you can blame Colt Dixon. The important thing is that Bradley had every advantage. He could've done a million different things with his life, but he chose to work for others. He chose to work for the planet, and for all of us who live here."

She told him a story then, of how while still in high school Bradley Sommers had stopped some housing development from getting built by staging a publicity stunt with a fawn.

"That took courage. I think you'd really like him if you gave him half a chance. And yes, despite our age difference. He's a good person. He loves nature and he loves the planet and he cares about the future. I like to think that if I'd known him when he was in high school I'd have been right there beside him."

"If you knew him when he was in high school you'd have still been in diapers."

"That's not even funny."

"Well what do you expect me to say?"

"You could say you respect him at least."

"I suppose I've met worse."

"But you don't trust him."

"Trust? I trust the neighbors, honey, but I still brand my calves."

It was nearly dark now, with the moon yet to rise. He asked her, "Where is the professor, anyway?"

"Pleasant View. He said he wanted to drive up there and see firsthand what Archer-Mason was doing."

Logan grunted. That was perfect. If the professor was up at the gas field, he'd have no reason to go back again. Which meant if there was more to the Militia of Montezuma than keg beer and bullshit, then at least he'd be out of harm's way. And by extension, so would Addie.

"Promise me one thing. I want you to keep away from the grazing allotment while that drilling's in progress. You saw what happened to them calves. I don't want you or anyone else getting sick or worse from whatever the hell's up there."

Addie nodded, distracted, signaling to Logan their conversation was over. That she had things to think about, more important things, which suited Logan fine. He wanted her to think.

He finished his drink and stood and stretched. "I suppose you're waiting up?"

She nodded.

"Would you mind bringing them nags in before bed?"

"I will."

"Okay then. Well, I guess it's good night." He crossed to the door and opened it and paused on the threshold. "By the way, whatever happened to that girl?"

"What girl?"

"That girl in California who worked at that nature center. The one who let Bradley borrow the fawn?"

"How would I know?" She turned to where he stood with one foot still on the porch. "Why would you even think to ask me such a thing?"

21

Colt recognized the sensation, having known it for most of his life. It was the unmistakable feeling of being stared at, or whispered about, behind one's back. Of dipped heads and lowered voices. Of the lingering glimpse or the muffled guffaw.

From where he sat he could make out maybe half the tables in the mirror behind the bar and half of those were empty on a Tuesday night with no live music and nothing on the TV but hockey. Diners occupied three of the tables that he could see and another held what looked and sounded like an extended family of German tourists. A trio of girls was sitting somewhere behind him, as were some loudmouths in hunting camo determined to defend the national honor by out-drinking the Germans.

"Buy you a beer, cowboy?"

Without waiting for an answer, Carly the bartender snatched up his empty with the peeled-off label and replaced it with a fresh bottle.

"Careful, you might bankrupt the ownership."

"Not likely. And definitely not with that bunch in the house."

Her nod was over his shoulder, her mouth as tight as her T-shirt. Colt half-turned to see the four men directly behind him roaring and slopping beer and generally behaving like barnyard animals.

"Who are they?"

"Never seen 'em before. There was another bunch in earlier could've been their cousins."

"Texans?"

"I don't think so. Texans are pretty good tippers. These guys are cheaper than Chanel number six."

Though dressed as hunters, the men were strangers to Colt. All wore scraggly beards, and the one with a neck tattoo shot a scowl in his direction.

"Saw you dancing the other night with Addie Decker," Carly said as she polished the same section of bar she'd been polishing for the past twenty minutes.

"That was me."

"I like watching you dance. Always have liked it. Don't see it nearly enough."

On the TV behind her, the skaters who moments earlier had been rolling up and down the ice like marbles in a pan now tossed their sticks and gloves and began grappling and punching and stripping off each other's shirts. Colt was reminded of his father's line about the time he went to the fights and a hockey game broke out.

"So," Carly said, marking a circle on the bar with her fingertip. "Does that mean you two are an item again?"

"She came back for her grandma's funeral is all."

"And you believe that?"

"What do you mean?"

"I mean I loved my grammy and gramps, but I sure as hell didn't drive no thousand miles for their funerals."

"There's more to it than that. Plus she came with her boyfriend."

"You mean that older guy sitting with Brenda?"

He pried his eyes from the TV screen. "You don't miss a whole heck of a lot."

"It's what you call your perquisite of the job. I have a front-row seat to the human comedy, five nights a week."

"And a philosopher-poet to boot."

She placed a fist on her hip. "Colt Dixon, there's all nature of things you could learn about me if you put your mind to the task."

Order having been restored on the ice, the TV screen blinked to commercial.

"So. Does that mean there'll be no tearful reunions with Addie or Brenda?"

"Those boats have already sailed."

"And you don't figure on swimming after them, do you?"

"Hell no." He hoisted his beer. "I aim to keep high and dry."

Shattering glass made him turn in time to see Neck Tattoo standing and wiping his shirtfront. "Goddammit!" he bellowed, snatching a mug off the table and splashing the chest of his buddy. All were whooping and snorting when the oldest of the Germans, presumably the grandfather, said something over his shoulder.

The bearded men, hard-eyed and hostile, turned as one. A third man stood, and Colt could see he was strapped. The grandfather saw it too, his face registering the sort of abject terror you'd expect upon being confronted by drunken Americans with holstered handguns.

"Hey!" Carly had emerged from behind the bar. "Hey, shit-for-brains! Who do you think has to clean this up?"

"Fuck do I care? This asshole called me a name."

Colt, his back now to the bar, slid his boots to the floor.

"Okay, that's it, you're out of here." Carly pointed to the door. "All of you. Let's go, take a hike!"

"Bullshit." Neck Tattoo teetered like a man in a rowboat. "We paid for this beer."

"Not to throw it around you didn't."

"We bought it and we'll do whatever we want with it."

"I don't care if—"

"Here." Colt stepped between them, fishing a twenty from his pocket. He tossed it onto the table. "Now do like the lady says."

Neck Tattoo's eyes narrowed to slits. He stepped toward Colt with a hand on the grip of his pistol.

"Go ahead." Colt's hands had balled into fists. "See how far you get."

"Hey, hey!" The last of the drunken men was up and grabbing his buddy. "Forget it. This pissant ain't worth the trouble. C'mon, let's get out of here."

Neck Tattoo, still glaring, allowed himself to be dragged to the door. As he passed the last of the tables he kicked at a chair and sent it tumbling onto the dance floor.

In the silence that lingered after the door had closed behind them, the German grandfather stood. Pale, and visibly shaken. He walked to the dripping table and picked up the sodden twenty and handed it back to Colt.

"*Bitte*," he said.

"Yes, sir." Colt examined his hands. "I reckon I am a little."

22

Jess didn't appear for coffee that morning, and Addie imagined him holed up in the cabin with his quilt pulled up to his ears. Avoiding, or at least postponing, his promised discussion with Logan who himself seemed unusually chipper, offering to scramble their eggs and fry their bacon while holding forth on the virtues of real butter over margarine and apple juice over orange and cast iron over Teflon-coated aluminum.

Maybe it was the vulnerability he'd shown during their previous night's discussion, his willingness to expose the soft underbelly beneath his shell, that was making her father self-conscious and therefore chatty even as it had left Addie groping through a fog of remorse for the years she'd spent punishing this man, this basically good and decent man, for the crime of loving her too much. For the human sins of grief and fear and regret. Whatever the vibe that hummed beneath the surface, Addie could sense that a tectonic shift had occurred, altering the continental alignment and leaving her for the first time in years wanting to spend more time with her father.

The telephone rang as she was leaving. Bradley was already out at the car and Addie was chewing a last corner of toast while shrugging into her jacket when Logan lifted the phone from its base and read the caller ID.

"It's Brenda Holcomb."

She looked to the car before shaking her head. "See you tonight," she said, blowing a kiss and pausing long enough after the door had closed behind her to hear her father's voice raised in greeting.

The *Cortez Journal* appeared but twice weekly and had yet to arrive at the coin-operated vending rack down at the corner so their day at the office began pretty much as the previous one had ended, with each of them working at their respective desks on their respective assignments—Addie's mostly computer-related and Bradley's telephonic—until a trio of extraordinary events disrupted what semblance of routine they'd managed thus far to establish.

First, the Facebook page Addie had constructed to help publicize the local public forum—the page they'd decided to call Save Our Rural Water—had, by some alchemical reaction between the Western Warriors' listserv and Facebook's vaunted algorithm, appeared briefly in the latter's Trending news module. When Addie, alerted to the spike in viewership, accessed the page's Insights data she was astounded to find it had attracted over three thousand views overnight, generating dozens of lengthy comment strings.

"Oh my God!" she told Bradley, scrolling the comments. "We've been reposted by Mark Ruffalo!"

In the day's second development, Jimbo Hawkins telephoned Bradley to report that a woman from Colorado Public Radio had somehow gotten wind of the story and wanted to schedule an interview for tomorrow's news segment. Hawkins had stalled, stating that either he or a Mr. Sommers would get back to her shortly and, if Bradley didn't mind, would he please keep Hawkins' name out of it?

The third development, while no less exciting, was decidedly more alarming. It occurred at around three thirty, just as Addie was reminding Bradley they'd better get hopping if they hoped to finish their horseback ride in daylight. She had posted a link to the public radio website and was just logging off her laptop when with a resounding *crash* the street-side window imploded.

She instinctively ducked behind her desk just as the offending projectile—a rock the size of a grapefruit—caromed off Bradley's chair and skidded to rest midway between them.

"What the *hell*?" Bradley had dropped his phone as he'd jumped to his feet. "Are you all right?"

Outside, the revving of an engine faded into the background as first one pedestrian, then another ducked their heads into the jagged maw that read:

PROTECT	STYLE
COME IN	HOW!

"Are you all right?" an older man shouted. "Is everyone okay?"

There'd been no attribution for the assault—no note tied to the rock—and the officers who'd responded wrote it off as a teenage after-school prank. But for Addie and Bradley, the message had arrived with cold-water clarity: their mission was public now, and those who opposed it—those whose economic interests it threatened—knew exactly where to find them.

The clean-up and the police report and the boarding of the window delayed their return to the Triple-R by nearly two hours. But even with both still shaken by the incident—indeed, precisely because they'd been shaken—Bradley insisted they saddle the horses.

"You can't be deterred by bullying. That's what bullies want. Besides, you're the one who said the road turns to mud once it rains."

They could see Jess under a leaden sky driving the trailer rig in the alfalfa field while Logan, stooped and sweaty, bucked the forty-pound bales. The job looked nearly finished, assuaging Addie's guilt in sneaking off without offering to help. She left a note in the house for her father, ordered Waylon to stay, and led Bradley on a stealthy approach to the horse barn.

He would ride Feather, she told him, while she would borrow Lightning. With the haying in progress both horses were closed in their stalls where Addie brushed them and saddled them and led them one by one to the hitching post outside.

"Have you ever ridden before?"

"Ponies at birthday parties. And once on the beach in Costa Rica."

"It's not complicated. She'll be fine if you just stay out of her way. Sit quietly, stay centered, and hold a loose rein. Her natural instinct will be to follow behind Lightning."

"That's it?"

"Wait, there was one other thing. Oh yeah, try to keep the horse between you and the ground."

They'd each knotted slickers to their waists and Bradley had changed into jeans and his old running shoes. Without heeled boots, his foot could slide forward through the stirrup. She explained this, and the importance of keeping his weight off his toes.

"I'll try. Last time I rode I was barefoot."

"If you fall off here, you won't land in the ocean and you won't get any birthday cake. And if something goes wrong and your foot gets caught in the stirrup . . ."

"Okay, I get the picture."

She gave him a leg up before mounting her father's horse and turning it eastward onto the ranch road where Feather, good girl that she was, followed placidly in the big gelding's footsteps.

Storm clouds were banked to the north—dark thunderheads whose leading winds were swaying the cottonwoods. Flickers swooped and darted overhead while fallen leaves skittered in the roadway before them in golden swirls. Amped by the weather, her father's horse was coiled and prancing and had Addie been riding alone she'd have probably let him run. Instead she squeezed and softened her hands, pumping the reins like the brakes on a car until Lightning finally relaxed.

"How does she feel?" she called to Bradley behind her.

"Fine. Horse-like. Equine."

"We need to be back before this storm hits."

They'd reached the fork by six o'clock, and after ten strenuous minutes of uphill plodding they drew within sight of the four-wire boundary fence where it met the old cattle guard. There they dismounted and Addie walked her father's horse forward to open the gate beside it.

From atop the level mesa the clouds loomed high overhead, massive and dark, like a cold wave waiting to break. Grasses swayed and tumbleweeds danced to the low tympani of distant thunder. When Addie last had seen it with her father on Saturday morning, the mesa's wide horizon had been pierced by a crane-like contraption some eight stories tall rising from a freshly scraped well pad. Surrounding it that day were men and trucks, trailers and equipment—a hectic scene of ant-like industry.

Today, save for the wind, all was eerily quiet. The drill rig was gone and the compressor station and the newly graded roadway both were deserted. But two pickup trucks still fronted a single-wide office trailer.

"Does that mean people are still up here?"

"I don't know." Bradley surveyed the scene. "But it's your grazing allotment. We have as much right to be here as they do."

Still afoot, they led the horses forward. For as long as Addie could recall, the mesa-top had been a stark and desolate place—flat desert grassland dotted with sage and juniper, Mormon tea and mountain mahogany. A place where ravens might squawk or a silent vulture might kite overhead, its chevron shadow rippling over the redbrick landscape. She'd spent untold hours here on horseback, exploring or hazing cattle or just reveling in her seclusion. The sight of workers and trucks and equipment on Saturday had been as unexpected to Addie, and as unwelcome, as the wolf to Red Riding Hood.

The better to eat you with, my dear.

"Looks like they've already finished," Bradley said as they walked the horses past an evaporation pond bordered by flapping black plastic, the liquid within offering a rainbow reflection of the dark clouds gathered above. Despite the wind, a petrochemical stench still permeated the scene. "Here. Would you hold her for me?"

Addie took the reins, and Bradley scrambled up the low escarpment onto the pad. Where the drill rig had towered on Saturday morning stood a steampunk jungle gym of interconnected pipes and valves, casings and flanges. She watched as, turning a slow circle, Bradley photographed the layout. Addie took note of the dirt piles and the slash piles and the gravel piles, and she searched in vain for any sign of her father's cattle.

Thunder rumbled, closer this time, and she could sense the horses' disquiet, their instinctive fear not just of the impending weather but of the changes man had made to God's design.

"Think about this for a second." Bradley stood with hands on hips. "This isn't even fuel production. This is to *boost* fuel production a thousand miles from here. Can you imagine the madness of an energy policy that makes something like this cost-effective? Meanwhile, our sun provides a continuous fusion reaction with enough free energy to power all the earth's needs ten thousand times over."

"When you're finished here I'd like to go look for our cattle."

"And you know what's really ironic?" He descended the pad, and they remounted the horses. "Governments and think-tanks and universities the world over are spending millions to figure out ways to pump carbon dioxide underground. Carbon capture and storage—that's the whole concept behind so-called clean coal. And yet here we have industry pumping it right back out again."

She steered Lightning past the pickup trucks to the office trailer, dark and deserted, its sliding windows reflecting their jointed images as they moved slowly past.

"Do they just leave them here overnight?" Addie asked of the pickups.

"You wouldn't think so. Maybe they're still working on the road."

"One way to find out. You ready to trot a little?"

She gave Lightning a cluck and they jogged the horses forward. Archer-Mason had constructed what amounted to a perfect galloping track, one to which she might like to return someday and test. For now, however, she watched with amusement and misgiving as Bradley bobbed in her father's saddle, struggling to find Feather's rhythm.

"Sure you're okay with this?"

"I'm fine," he said. "Just trying to estimate how far it is to that gate I hit last night."

"And?"

He looked westward toward the Abajos, triangulating. "And I doubt we could make it before nightfall."

Less than a mile farther, a flash of lightning split the cloudbank. Seconds later, a thunderclap shook the ground and sent the horses prancing sideways. The wind suddenly freshened and rain began falling in cold leaden drops that pocked the sandy roadbed. They halted and untied their raincoats.

"What do you think?" she asked him.

"I think we've seen enough. Let's get out of here."

They were halfway back to the first well site with a hard rain on their necks when a new sound, low and steady, grew louder behind them. As she legged Lightning sideways, Addie turned to see Feather thunder past with her ears pinned and her eyes wild and rolling, horse and flopping rider followed by a jacked-up truck whose monster wheels spun twin fountains of sandy mud.

Addie shouted, shortening her reins and digging her heels into Lightning's ribs. The truck appeared to be weaving, intentionally driving the mare forward. At a gallop and closing, Addie watched in horror as the truck braked and skidded and Feather veered hard to the left with Bradley, his right foot caught in the stirrup, dragging and bouncing alongside.

"Jesus Christ!"

Addie took an angle on the runaway horse. Deep in the sage some hundred yards from the roadway she managed to pull alongside and grab a flapping rein and wrestle Feather to a halt.

Bradley lay muddied and motionless as Addie dismounted and circled the heaving animal and freed his foot from the stirrup. She stripped off her slicker and bunched it and eased it under his head.

Her hand came away bloody.

"Wake up," she said, shaking his shoulder. His upturned face was unmarred, his expression oddly placid. "Bradley! Wake up!"

Heavy footfalls crashed through the brush, and the horses spooked anew as four men in gleaming ponchos, rifles held at the ready, appeared from out of the rain.

23

Bradley woke to the sight of two rifle muzzles, wet and dripping, staring him in the face.

"He's all right," said a voice, low and gruff. "His eyes are open."

Addie was kneeling beside him, cupping his head in her hand. In the curtained face of her anguish he remembered exactly where he was and how, more or less, he'd gotten there.

He sat upright in the mud. Seeing the blood on Addie's hand, he touched the back of his head.

"He needs a doctor," Addie said over her shoulder. "He's suffered a concussion!"

"Put 'em in the truck," the gruff voice ordered. "You two bring the horses."

"Don't you touch those horses!" Addie shouted as Bradley was lifted to his feet and shoved roughly forward. Turning, still dizzy, he saw that two of the men had shouldered their rifles and were hazing the frightened animals with outstretched arms, trying to corral them.

"There's been a misunderstanding," he said to no one in particular. "That's Addie Decker. This is her father's grazing allotment."

"We know who she is," replied the gruff voice as a muzzle poked Bradley's spine. "And we know who you are."

Prodded at gunpoint, they were forced into the rear-seat compartment of a muddy truck that reeked of sweat and cigarettes, leather and gun oil. As the engine sputtered and caught, Bradley's captor extracted a walkie-talkie from the glove compartment and toggled it to life.

"Mobile three to base. Targets are in custody. Over."

Static. And then, *"Roger that, mobile three. Nice work out there."*

They bounced over rocks and sage stumps on their way back to the road, the truck's wipers carving fleeting glimpses of the muddy mesa that, shrouded by rain clouds, had dimmed to a russet brown. Soaked and chilly, his knees forced to his chin, Bradley's head cleared further with each jarring lurch. He turned to Addie beside him but her gaze was over her shoulder, at the quivering shapes of men and horses shrinking into the distance.

"Who are you?" she demanded, turning and addressing the front. "What do you want from us?"

The men ignored her.

"He needs a doctor. Can't you see that?"

"We got an EMT at base camp," the driver said without turning.

"We? Who are we?"

Again, neither man answered.

They continued in brittle silence, past other wells and other men in ponchos or slickers who nodded or waved or saluted in their wake. After another mile or two Bradley saw through the beating wipers a singlewide trailer and men at labor unloading boxes and crates and coolers from pickup trucks.

The scene was vaguely familiar to him, one that he recognized from . . . where exactly? News footage, that's where. From places like Oregon and Nevada.

"I'll see about that EMT," the driver said as he set the brake and climbed down into the rain. They'd stopped before the trailer where a phalanx of armed men in ball caps and cowboy hats crowded to meet the truck. The passenger door opened and the seat flipped forward and a gloved hand reached for Addie's hand to help her down.

"I don't know who you are or what you think you're doing . . ." Bradley heard her say over the drumming of the rain.

They next lowered Bradley and half-shoved, half-carried him up the steps and into the trailer, which was furnished as an office with desks and file cabinets, its once-beige carpeting soaked and muddied. A chair on wheels appeared, and they eased Bradley into it.

"You're some kind of sagebrush militia," he said to the man who'd captured them. The man was in his thirties, clean-cut and rugged, and he stood now over Bradley to examine the back of his skull.

"And you're a BLM stooge who's been causing a boatload of trouble."

"BLM stooge? The Western Warriors don't work with the BLM. Are you kidding me? We're the BLM's worst nightmare."

"Except when you're on the same page, like telling folks around here what they can and can't do with their land."

"Don't you mean the public's land?"

"That's right, it belongs to the public, not to the federal government. Read the Tenth Amendment."

"And not to a multinational oil and gas conglomerate?"

"Jobs, buddy. That's what the public wants. That means grass and timber, gas and oil. Not what your kind thinks is best."

Addie, sodden and breathless, burst through the door ahead of a man lugging an orange tackle box.

"Are you all right?" she asked as the man—the promised EMT—took a knee beside Bradley and opened his case and snapped on rubber gloves.

"I'll survive. But in case you haven't guessed, we appear to be prisoners of a paramilitary group that plans—" he looked to their captor "—what exactly?"

"To preserve the status quo. To prevent some judge or some bureaucrats in Denver from laying off two hundred men."

The EMT examined the wound on Bradley's head and grunted and dabbed it with a cotton ball. Then he returned to his case and opened a jar and applied a stinging salve. He stood before Bradley and shined a penlight in his eyes, first right and then left. Satisfied, he held the pen vertically and passed it back and forth, tracking his patient's gaze.

"Politicians back east, they live in a bubble," their captor said. "Democrat or Republican, it doesn't matter. They don't have a clue what's happening in places like this, and they wouldn't give a shit if they did. That needs to change. We aim to make 'em realize it's them who serve the people and not the other way around."

The paramedic pronounced that no stitches would be necessary, his ministrations ending with a gauze pad torn from its paper sleeve and pressed to Bradley's scalp. He could wrap it, he said, or else Bradley could just hold the pad in place until the bleeding finally stopped.

"Don't wrap it. Some nutjob out there might mistake it for a turban."

"That's it?" Addie demanded as the EMT repacked his things. "He needs an x-ray! His brain could be swelling!"

"I doubt that very much," the man said. "But if he develops a worsening headache or double vision or a nosebleed, be sure to let somebody know."

"I've had a nosebleed for four days now," Bradley said, holding the gauze in place.

Their captor left with the paramedic and returned moments later with an older man, bearded and ursine, and a pair of younger guards. The guards wore berets and tactical vests and carried assault rifles at the ready. They took up positions on either side of the door.

"Okay, Sommers." The big man removed his cowboy hat and flapped it against his thigh. "These men will escort you to your quarters."

"Quarters?" Addie again stepped forward. "Our quarters are on the Red Rocks Ranch, where people are looking for us. You can't hold us here. Who do you think you are?"

"Ask your father."

"What?"

"I said—"

"Try not to think of yourselves as prisoners," their captor interjected, "but more like our special guests."

"Right. Unless we try to leave."

He shrugged.

"This is insane." She turned to Bradley who was standing now with his hand on the back of his head. "Can't we do something?"

"Of course we can. We can lodge a criminal complaint, and we can file a civil lawsuit. But I suspect both will have to come later."

"This is ridiculous."

"Zip it!" the big man said. "Nobody asked your opinion."

Bradley examined the gauze pad and returned it to his head. "Maybe if you let her visit the horses and see they're being cared for?"

"I'm not your goddamn—"

"It's all right," their captor said. "I'll take them. I'd like to check on those horses myself."

Outside the trailer, the storm had mostly passed. Low tendrils of grayish mist hung over the encampment where the bustle of occupation continued. They tramped a muddy path through the laboring men with their captor in front and the two guards trailing behind, the heads of the men they passed turning to watch them.

They soon came to a clearing where a stock trailer was parked and where a rope as taut as a clothesline ran from the trailer's roof to a juniper snag. Five haltered horses were highlined to the rope like charms on a bracelet. Each of the horses stood ankle-deep in hay, and at the sound of their names Feather and Lightning raised their heads and nickered.

By the side of the trailer, a pudgy man in a canvas chair hopped to his feet at their approach. He wore camouflage pants and a Denver Broncos hoodie. After some perfunctory conversation he walked with Addie to inspect the lines he'd rigged, leaving Bradley alone with their captor.

"Kidnapping, you realize, is a federal offense."

"Only across state lines."

Bradley studied the man—his square jaw, his trim physique, and his quiet but commanding presence. "I take it you're in law enforcement. That is, when you're not breaking the laws you should be enforcing."

The man ignored the sarcasm, his attention focused on Addie. "Where's my saddle?" they heard her ask the pudgy man, who gestured toward the trailer. Addie circled the horses, assessing, examining their legs. Then with nothing further to inspect, she rejoined Bradley and their forced march resumed.

"You're lucky," she said to their captor. "If either of those horses was hurt, you'd be in a world of trouble."

"Then I'm glad they're not hurt."

"You think this is a big joke, don't you?"

"I think you need to calm down and take stock of your situation."

They approached a line of travel campers parked at the edge of an adjoining field. They appeared of various vintages and their arrangement suggested circus elephants standing trunk-to-tail, the effect heightened by the dozen or more tents that stood before them. Men from the tents were out building fires and stringing lanterns and lighting camping stoves. A trio of vultures circled high overhead, dark shapes kiting in and out of the mist. A shotgun boomed, and echoed, and one of the birds crumpled and dropped from the sky.

A cheer went up from the camp.

At the oldest and tallest of the campers their captor knocked and opened the door. It was tight inside, boat-like, with three sleeping bunks and a kitchenette with a small banquette table, all of it visible in the slanting light of a window above the sink.

"These are your quarters. There'll be a guard outside at all times, plus a dozen men behind him, so don't try anything stupid. Meanwhile, I'll try to find you some chow. We've got a big day tomorrow, so I'd advise you to turn in early."

"Why?" Addie asked him. "What happens tomorrow?"

"Tomorrow is when the shit gets real."

Addie perched on the bottom bunk as the door slammed shut and the screen door sighed and clanged. "How's your head?" she asked Bradley, who removed the gauze pad and examined it and tossed it onto the table.

He extracted his phone from a pocket and searched in vain for a signal.

"They let you keep that?"

"There's no service here anyway." He pocketed the phone and began to reconnoiter their surroundings, opening cupboards and drawers. "Not that that should surprise you."

Addie stripped off her slicker and tossed it on the bunk beside her.

Bradley asked, "What happens at the ranch when we don't show for dinner?"

"I don't know. Daddy's been haying all day, so I'm sure he'll be exhausted. What do you think the big one meant by 'ask your father?'"

"I have no idea."

"And what did this one mean about shit getting real? What do you think they're planning?"

Bradley found some playing cards and squeezed in behind the table and thumbed open the pack. "Near as I can tell they plan to act as some kind of security force for Archer-Mason. Similar to what they did at Grants Pass up in Oregon. If that's any precedent they'll set up a press center and brandish their weapons and spout some wild anti-government rhetoric. Then they'll sit back and wait for the news vans to arrive."

"And what about us?"

"Us?" Bradley halved the cards and shuffled. "I'm afraid we're the fat man and the bearded lady again."

"I have to say, you're being very cavalier about this."

"I prefer nonplussed. And that's because publicity is a two-way street."

"Jesus, Bradley. You sound like you *want* to be here."

"We were looking for attention, weren't we? And while this isn't exactly what I had in mind, you have to admit it fits the bill nicely."

A toilet flushed, and a narrow door banged open. The young man who stumbled forth wore a surprised expression punctuated by the silver exclamation point piercing his eyebrow.

"Excellent," Bradley said as he dealt out the cards. "Now we can play spades."

24

He found the note on the dining room table weighted under an ashtray.

Took B for ride to waterfall (I'll be on Lightning.)
Don't wait on us for dinner. Waylon not fed! xox

Logan read his watch. "Goddamn it," he said aloud.

"How's that?" The old man appeared from the kitchen. "I didn't hear you."

"It's Addie. She took the professor riding."

"There you go. Maybe he'll break his neck."

"Break his neck? I thought you liked him."

Jess disappeared back into the kitchen. "Never said I liked him. Never said I disliked him neither. Don't know as I have an opinion on the subject."

"That makes one."

He reappeared with two Cokes and handed one to Logan. "One what?"

"Subject on which you don't have an opinion."

Logan moved to the window. He took a long pull on the bottle. The rain, he figured, would be arriving any minute.

"She's a grown-up woman, you know."

Logan didn't answer.

"It's been my experience that a woman like that, with a good head on her shoulders, generally makes the right decisions."

"Is that a fact."

"Take my Carole, for instance. She ever tell you about that salesman who courted her out of high school? Jeffery something. Or Jeremy. Slicker than snot on a doorknob. Bull semen, that was his line. Drove a Lincoln as long as a Sunday sermon. Wanted her to move with him to Pagosa Springs. Didn't propose marriage, mind you. In my day we'd of called that a indecent proposal. Anyway, she turned him down, and when her mother asked her why, do you know what she said?"

"What's that?"

"She said any man who blow-dried his hair couldn't be trusted."

Logan turned from the window. "Blow-dried his hair?"

"Dried it with a goddamn blower!"

"I know what—"

"The point being that women have uncommon good sense. It's what keeps the species from going extinct. It was left up to men, our mothers would all of been strippers or cocktail waitresses. You think about that for a minute."

"You're making my brain hurt."

The rain arrived on schedule. Slow at first, the drops large and pelting on the flagstones, it swelled into a deluge that hammered the roof and gutters.

One quirk of the canyon, Logan knew, was that weather varied widely from place to place, such that a neighboring ranch could get rain or even hail while the Triple-R basked in sunshine. The waterfall being a thousand feet higher, it was entirely possible that all Addie and the professor were seeing right now was the top of a cloud ceiling. It was equally possible they'd been drenched for the past half hour. In that case they'd have taken shelter in the old hay shed or in any of the dozen caves and ledges whose locations Addie would still remember. Wherever they were, they'd be safe till it passed.

Unless, of course, they weren't.

"I don't suppose you're up for a little rummy? Or maybe break out the old chessboard?"

"Not tonight," Logan said, his breath clouding the window. "I'm gonna take a hot shower and go to bed."

"Don't tell me a little hay buckin's tuckered you out."

"I counted two hundred bales."

"There you go. You earned yourself a hot supper at least."

Logan turned around to face him. "You got something particular on your mind?"

"Me? Not that I recollect."

"'Cause if it's getting wet you're worried about, there's an umbrella back there in the mudroom."

The old man bristled. "Sonny, I've drove cattle from Dove Creek to the Weminuche in snow up to my stirrups, so don't be talkin to me about some pissy little drizzle."

"Suit yourself. It's just that the thought of you lying in bed with your hair all wet is enough to keep a man up of a night."

It was Addie, however, who kept Logan awake. He sat with his book and his heating pad, his ear straining for the telltale creak of the porch. He pinched his eyes and checked his watch. The rainstorm had ended around nine and he figured that even with the road a muddy mess they should've been down by ten. At ten thirty he stood and crossed to the window, the floorboards cold underfoot.

The barn lay dark and silent. The wind had risen, and the moon raced backward through a silvery scud. The barn, the trees, the fence posts stood in dark relief against a pale and shimmering nightscape.

Logan left the window to look for his cigarettes. He found the pack and shook one out and studied it and put it back again.

A thrown shoe, he told himself. Or maybe a stone bruise. Or else maybe the moonlight in the trees had signaled romance to a pair of young lovers who might or might not at that very moment be planning their future together.

Waylon appeared beside him and brushed against Logan's leg.

"I don't like it either," he told the old dog before returning to his book.

25

Addie woke with a start, nearly banging her head on the bunk above. To her right the first glow of sunrise lit the little window over the sink. Slow and measured breathing from the other bunks told her that Bradley and Oscar Montoya, the young college student who was their fellow captive, both were sound asleep.

She slipped to the floor and crept on stocking feet toward the bathroom, pausing to peer through the window. Outside, men were up and moving in the low sunlight, a shadow-play of elongated bodies. Inside the tiny bathroom, no more comfortable than its airline counterpart, the toilet seat was freezing.

Sitting there, inspecting her surroundings, Addie's eyes fell to the trapezoid of light on the wall beside her and, tracing it upward, to the skylight overhead. She stood and flushed the toilet and buttoned her jeans. Lowering the seat cover, she climbed and stretched on tiptoes but couldn't quite reach the latch. She removed her belt and looped it and hooked the latch on her second try, the plastic dome springing open with an audible *pop*.

Cold air and the murmur of outside voices filled the tiny space. That she could shimmy through the opening with a boost from Bradley or Oscar she had little doubt.

"Wake up," she whispered, shaking Bradley's shoulder.

He rose to an elbow, groggy, blinking the sleep from his eyes.

"There's a skylight in the bathroom."

"I know. I saw it last night."

"You saw it? Why didn't you tell me?"

Bradley threw aside his blanket and swung his legs over the edge. Behind Addie, Oscar stirred in his bunk.

"Because what's the point? There's a door right over there, and I don't even think it's locked. Addie, we're surrounded by armed men."

"That's it?" She stood with hands on hips. "We just stay here and do nothing?"

His silence, and the unspoken dismissal in it, irked her more than his words. It called to mind a news report she'd seen on television during her freshman year. Parents at a Compton public school had gathered to protest the abysmal condition of their children's classrooms. The accompanying video showed peeling paint and moldy ceilings interspersed with scenes from the auditorium in which a succession of angry adults shook fists and shouted into a microphone while dozens more sat fanning themselves during what, according to the voice-over, had been a contentious two-hour meeting.

And that, Addie thought at the time, perfectly illustrated the difference between urban and rural living. Had the same thing happened in Cortez, those parents would have come to the school that night with tools and brushes, buckets and ladders, and by the time two hours had passed there'd have been nothing left to be angry about.

"People will be looking for us," she told Bradley. "People who might get hurt trying to save us. We can't just sit around here and—"

A sharp rap, and then the door swung inward, flooding the camper with sunlight. A guard who was larger than a human but smaller than a bison set one lug-soled boot on the carpet.

"Up and at 'em!" he called with mocking cheer. "Rise and shine! You got exactly ten minutes to muster."

They took turns moving within the camper, from bunk to bathroom to banquette, and when at last they emerged single file into the sunrise the eyes of the camp were upon them.

"This way," Bison Man ordered as he led them past a charred fire ring where a half-dozen stamping men gathered around a coffeepot. Addie strained for a view of the field where Feather and Lightning had spent the night but the tents and the movement of men and vehicles blocked her line of sight.

Their march ended at an idling panel van, white and unmarked. Bison Man spoke to the driver, then into his walkie-talkie as the van's lone passenger stepped down and circled the vehicle and slid the rear door open, gesturing that they enter. After the door had slammed behind them the passenger resumed his place. Soon they were moving, bumping through the muddy field and onto the roadway.

"Where are we going?" Addie demanded, and the passenger turned to face her.

"Breakfast at the command center. Those are our orders."

They passed meandering cows and another well site and then, further north, several pickups headed in the direction from which they'd come. Unlike those of the militiamen, these trucks were new and white and emblazoned with the blue Archer-Mason logo, the men inside in hard hats and coveralls staring in wonder at the scene unfolding around them. Ahead lay another, larger cluster of office trailers and beyond that a chain-link gate manned by a dozen or more camouflaged men in cowboy hats and tactical gear with their omnipresent rifles and sidearms.

Oscar said, "This is where they got me." He was leaning forward between the front seats. "There's my car over there."

The van braked before a doublewide trailer and again the passenger climbed down. This time when the door slid open they were greeted by their original captor, the clean-cut man who may or may not have been a police officer but whom she and Bradley had taken to calling the Good Cop.

"Morning," he said, touching his hat brim. "Hope everyone slept well."

A cardboard sign on the trailer door read MEDIA in heavy black Sharpie. They stood for a moment to look on as each in the entering queue of Archer-Mason pickups and water trucks and equipment trucks of various types was inspected by the militiamen before being waved through the gate. The inspection process included handing each of the drivers a typewritten instruction sheet and, while he read it, passing what looked like a mirror taped to the end of a broomstick under the carriage of his vehicle.

As the panel van that had delivered them swung a U-turn, interrupting the flow of entering traffic, a pickup's window lowered and a familiar voice called, "Addie!"

Grant Hoover leaned his Clark Kent eyeglasses into the sunlight. "I heard you were back in town!"

"Hello, Grant."

He ducked back in and drove his company truck to where they stood.

"What the heck's going on around here?"

"Security operation," said the Good Cop. "It's all in your handout."

"I read the handout. Who do you think you're protecting us from?"

"Progress," Bradley said, ducking his head. "They're protecting you from the twenty-first century."

The Good Cop signaled to a gate attendant who trotted over and banged a gloved fist on Grant Hoover's hood while waving him forward again. As Grant drove onto the job site he craned his neck to watch as Addie and Bradley were escorted into the makeshift media center.

Inside the trailer, a trio of men was stringing cables and wiring a mismatched assortment of TV monitors and laptop computers on the five matching desks already burdened with landline telephones and, on one of the desks, an open box of donuts.

"Satellite dishes," the Good Cop explained, stepping over an extension cord. "It's the only way to get TV and internet this far out."

At the donut desk he opened a drawer and removed a key ring and tossed it to Oscar Montoya.

"Here you go, son. Sorry we had to detain you. I'd suggest you make a beeline back to Cortez. First go to the radio station on Main, then to the sheriff's office on Driscoll. Think you can find those?"

"Yes, sir."

"Go on then. Let the world know what's happening here."

Oscar hesitated, then disappeared through the door of the trailer.

"What *is* happening here?" Bradley stepped to the window and watched as Oscar trotted toward the gate.

"Right now breakfast is happening. That, and apprising the workers. After that it's mostly processing new recruits. We got men arriving from all over the West, and once the television folks get here we'll have dozens more. Oath Keepers, Three Percenters, various state and local militias. I expect by afternoon we'll have the sheriff and the BLM. After that it's the state police and the FBI. Maybe even the National Guard."

"You'll need more donuts."

The Good Cop smiled. "Then you'd better get those while you can. There's a coffeepot there in back."

Addie was starving. She and Bradley ate the donuts and watched the technicians work and the Good Cop deal with various issues brought to him for decision or approval. He appeared to be the man in charge, answerable only to Bluto, the name they'd given his bearded, bear-like boss.

Whenever an arriving or departing militiaman left the trailer door ajar, Addie considered making a dash for the gate. The problem, as Bradley had observed, wasn't the gate itself so much as the heavily armed men standing between her and freedom.

Not that she thought they'd actually shoot her. More likely they'd just chase her down and wrestle her to the ground and lock her up in the camper. So maybe Bradley was right. For now at least, maybe discretion was the better part of valor.

"Why are we even still here?" she whispered.

"I don't know."

"Maybe they plan to let us go."

"Maybe."

"But you don't think so."

When he didn't respond, an image of Colt Dixon with his newly broad shoulders and his same crooked smile flashed before Addie's eyes. Would he be arriving in one of those pickups? Was this even his worksite? Probably so, if Grant Hoover was here. Would Grant tell Colt that he'd seen her? Of course he would. And what would Colt do then? What *could* he do, realistically speaking, that they couldn't do for themselves?

More to the point, why would she expect Colt to do anything?

Then she pictured her father. Even if Logan had gone straight to bed, he'd be waking to an empty house and the realization that the horses were missing and therefore that Addie and Bradley had never returned. What would he do next?

That was a silly question. She knew exactly what he would do.

"My father will come looking for us," she whispered to Bradley. "There'll be trouble if they try to stop him."

"I suspect they realize that. Look around, Addie. Printed fliers, satellite dishes, at least a month's worth of provisions. This was no seat-of-the-pants operation."

"Do you think they'll take him hostage?"

"I suppose they might. Unless they've already reached some sort of arrangement."

"What are you talking about?"

"Has it occurred to you that these men were waiting for us yesterday? Or if not waiting, then at least keeping an eye out?

They knew exactly who we were and exactly where we'd come from."

"So?"

"So you heard what Bluto said. 'Ask your father.'"

One of the technicians waved the Good Cop over to a television monitor and Addie moved to stand behind them. The technician pointed a remote, and the TV blinked to life.

A network program of *The Today Show* or *Good Morning America* variety appeared on screen—a pair of over-caffeinated hosts bantered on a couch with a vaguely familiar guest.

"How many channels?" the Good Cop asked.

"Many as you want. Many as there are."

"What about the internet?"

"We'll start on that next."

The Good Cop checked his watch. "Okay," he said to his captives. "If you're finished with breakfast, they're waiting for us next door."

"Waiting for us for what?"

"For what you might call a little public service announcement."

Outside again, the rush-hour crush at the entrance gate had slowed to a half-dozen bored-looking men smoking and cradling their weapons and scanning for late arrivals. Two of the men straightened and saluted the Good Cop, who responded in kind.

Next door proved to be the trailer across the muddy road—a smaller version of the media center but with the same new-carpet smell. This too had once been an office of sorts only now a small conference table was shoved against one wall and its chairs against the other leaving a space in the room's center where a tripod-mounted video camera faced three empty folding chairs backed by an enormous yellow flag. Klieg lights on metal stands flanked the camera, each with a professional-looking umbrella device to diffuse its thousand-watt glare.

A kneeling man was duct-taping an orange extension cord to the carpet. Behind the man stood Bluto, and beside him a pint-sized figure in a Resistol cowboy hat. The two were engrossed in a conversation they interrupted long enough for the shorter man to turn around and acknowledge the new arrivals.

"Hello, Sommers," Bud Wallace said. The county commissioner touched the brim of his hat. "And hello to you, Miss Decker. So good of you to join our little group."

26

Sunlight splashed Logan Decker awake like ice water from a bucket.

He sat upright, groaning as he did, his book sliding to the floor. Waylon, alert to the sudden movement, lifted his head from his paws.

"Jesus Christ almighty."

Logan could barely move, so sore was his back. It felt as though his lower spine had been wrapped in barbed wire while he'd slept and then cauterized with a branding iron. He sucked a breath and gritted his teeth. He hooked a hand under his thigh and rocked his feet to the floor. Pausing there for a moment, he pushed himself upright and shuffled—an obtuse angle on legs—to the cold bathroom where he eased himself onto the toilet. "Like an old goddamn woman," he said to no one, bracing himself on the seat.

The heating pad had been a mistake, and now it was too late for ice. He considered a hot shower but knew that would have to wait. He pressed himself standing and shrugged into his bathrobe and made his way to the living room, grabbing furniture as he went.

At the foot of the staircase he stood listening, steeling himself for the climb.

"Addie? *Adelaide!*"

Once to the top of the stairs he knocked at her bedroom and waited and then nudged the door open to see exactly what he'd expected.

"Damn."

He heard a door close downstairs. Newly hopeful, he shuffled toward the sound. "Addie?" he called into the void.

"Just me!"

The old man was seated at the kitchen table with the newspaper folded beside his coffee mug. "You look like hell," he said as Logan entered. "What happened to your back?"

"What do you think happened to my back?"

"Sicker dogs have lived. Here." Jess pushed away from the table. "I'll fetch you some Advil."

"Never mind that. Addie and the professor never came home last night."

Jess turned from the open cupboard. "Say that again?"

"I stayed up past midnight and they never came back. Her note said they rode up to the waterfall. Do me a favor and check that horse barn while I get dressed."

It was easier said than done. The socks he managed by lying in bed, reaching with fingertips, but his boots were out of the question. He kept his rubber irrigation boots in the mudroom and was stepping into those when the front door opened and closed again and the old man called his name.

"Back here!"

Jess appeared in the doorway. He shook his head.

"Shit."

"You want I should run a quad up for a look-see?"

"We'll both go," Logan told him. "I'll drive up to the mesa."

"I thought they went to the waterfall."

"That's what her note said, but maybe they changed their minds."

Logan had to pause twice, hands on knees, on the long walk to the workshop. The old man, invigorated by being in charge, had trotted ahead and was waiting by the open bay door.

"Hell, son. You sure you're up to this?"

"I'll manage," Logan told him, holding on to the door track. "Sitting'll be better than standing."

"You think?"

"It sure as hell can't be worse."

It proved only marginally better, Logan bracing himself with gritted teeth and wincing at every twist and jounce of the ATV. They traveled side-by-side where the clearance allowed and in those places where boulders stood or where the cottonwoods narrowed he fell back to avoid getting splattered. The sun was up and the sky was clear and he was all the time checking for sign— for a print of hoof or boot—but yesterday's rains had washed the roadbed smooth.

Jess halted at the fork to the waterfall trail, waiting for Logan to pull alongside.

"We'll meet back at the house!" Logan called over the idling engines. "Be sure to check that hay shed. And be careful you don't slide off the damn road!"

Jess nodded and zoomed off and Logan felt an immediate pang of regret, picturing the old goat skidding and yawing and losing control of the heavy machine. Watching as it tumbled over the rocks into the canyon below with no one to know or rescue him.

But Logan had other, more pressing worries—worries that until now he'd dared not voice.

He figured Bud Wallace could be trusted. A decorated war veteran, and a leading businessman, and an elected public official. And hadn't that sheriff's deputy all but guaranteed Addie's safety? But that goddamned Carpenter . . .

If Addie and the professor had ridden to the drill site there was no telling what kind of trouble they were in. There was no telling if Wallace or the deputy were even up there. There was no telling any damn thing until he checked it out for himself.

Logan could read no sign of horse or human as the trail narrowed to twin tracks and began its steep ascent. The studded tires of the ATV slipped and spun in places, snatching his breath and sending shockwaves down his back. When he topped out on the final rise, he drifted to a halt.

A pickup blocked the cattle guard, with another blocking the gate. Four men, having long ago heard him coming, leaned behind their vehicles with rifles leveled.

Logan hocked and spat. He kicked the ATV back into gear.

"That's close enough!" one of the men shouted. Logan pulled abeam of the pickups, his engine idling, his hands gripping the controls.

"This is my grazing allotment!"

"You were warned," the man said, his eye glued to the gunsight. "Now it's off limits!"

"Like hell it is!"

"Don't test me, Decker! I got my orders, and I'll shoot your sorry ass!"

Logan revved his engine. Once, twice, as though to relieve the pressure building in his chest. Building in his head.

"Where's my daughter?"

"She's in no danger, and that's all I can tell you!"

Had this been a movie, now would be the part where Logan said something terse and threatening, like "I'll be back!" But really, why would he do such a thing? If these men had half a brain among them they had to know he'd be back, and back with a vengeance.

And if they didn't, well, then so much the better.

27

"This is a message to the American people, and to freedom-loving patriots everywhere."

Bluto read from a prepared text that he held in trembling hands. Bradley, seated to his left, glanced over at Bud Wallace who, perched on Bluto's right, was squinting into the void between the klieg lights where the camera's cyclopean eye, red and unblinking, was the only visible thing.

"All across this great country, we see our freedoms being eroded on a daily basis. We see miners getting run off their claims, and public trails being closed to motorized recreation, and national monuments springing up like so many weeds. We see Washington bureaucrats telling fourth- and fifth-generation ranchers they can't run their cattle anymore because of some fish or rodent or bird. We see, in short, a threat not just to our Western economy, but to our very way of living."

Bradley knew that beyond the lights, somewhere amid the featureless shapes of the half-dozen spectators, Addie was watching him, and she wasn't happy.

"Public lands make up more than a third of Colorado, almost all of it here on the West Slope," Bluto continued, licking his lips. "In Montezuma County that number is even higher, and yet the federal government pays no taxes on these lands, depriving local governments of badly needed revenue."

Bradley had to bite his tongue at that one, ignoring as it did the federal PILT funding—payments in lieu of taxes—the Department of the Interior doled out annually to rural counties like Montezuma for hosting federal lands. It was ironic how men like Bluto and Wallace—self-appointed watchdogs of the public treasury—never seemed bothered by the revenue lost to the dozens of tax-exempt churches in their communities.

"Meanwhile, in rural counties like ours, productive citizens are under assault. First the feds allow radical environmentalists to dictate how the state's land and resources are used, then they impose so many regulations on whatever's left that it becomes impossible for families who've worked the land for generations to make a decent living. And if by some miracle a business or industry does manage to gain a toehold, these same outside agitators swoop in to shut it down and put our local men and women out of work."

If that was a dig at Bradley—and it almost certainly was—then it was badly misguided. For one thing, the Oil and Gas Conservation Commission was a state agency, not a federal one. And as for groups like the Western Warriors exerting control over environmental policy, well, Bradley could only wish. The truth was that business and industry held virtually every lever of power in today's Washington. At best Bradley and others like him were mosquitos whose incessant buzzing and biting might merit an occasional scratch. More often than not they were simply shooed away without a second thought.

"So here's our message, both to Washington and to the outside agitators. Back the hell off! We don't share your values, we don't want your guidance, and we sure as hell don't like the America you represent. Our fathers and grandfathers settled this land and made it productive with nothing but the muscle in their arms and the sweat on their backs. Freed from outside interference, so will our children and our grandchildren for generations to come. So we say stand aside and let real Americans show the world what hard work and a little gumption can accomplish."

Bluto folded away the paper and looked directly into the camera.

"We are the Militia of Montezuma. We aim to keep this gas field open, even if that means a shooting war with the government. As you can see, we got two men with us today. One is a county commissioner, and the other's a tree hugger from California who came here looking for trouble. Both these men will be safe in our custody for as long as the feds stay out of our way. And if they don't, well, then any blood that's spilled will be on their hands, not ours."

Bluto sat blinking until a voice shouted, "Cut!" Wallace clapped his shoulder, then stood and snugged his hat into place.

"Okay people, listen up. Get that onto the internet as soon as we're up and running, and be sure to send a copy to the governor's office. Hell, send one to the White House. From this point forward we're at threat level Alpha. Tommy, I want things right and tight around here 'cause this is gonna get hot in a hurry. And I want some long guns on that high ground back of the trailer. And when the TV vans arrive, I want those horses up here!"

The men were already moving, already snapping to attention, when a handheld radio crackled. Wallace frowned as the Good Cop turned to the wall and spoke in low tones.

"What is it?" Wallace demanded, and the Good Cop raised a finger.

"Okay, roger that. We'll get back to you."

The Good Cop replaced the radio on his belt and motioned with his head. Wallace and Bluto followed him to the far corner of the room. Addie, meanwhile, joined Bradley where he stood watching the men converse.

"What are you *doing*?" she demanded.

"What should I be doing?"

"You just sat there and let them use you like . . . I don't know, like some *prop* in a hostage video. Why didn't you say something?"

"Say what, exactly? 'Help, I've been kidnapped?' I think they made that perfectly clear."

"You could've . . . I don't know. Asked to be rescued at least. Or you could've told them Wallace is in on it."

Bradley wrested his attention from the men in the corner. "Think for a minute. Anything I might've said they'd just have edited out or else done another take. At worst they'd have shot the piece without me. This way at least the world will know we're here. I'd say that's the first step toward getting rescued, wouldn't you?"

"So that's it? We behave like good little hostages and hope the cavalry comes to our rescue?"

"You've got a better plan?"

She turned a circle, like a frustrated child.

"Look, Addie. Like it or not, we're at ground zero of a national news story. Soon to be *the* national news story. You remember that Malheur occupation in Oregon? This could be even bigger. It seems to me we can play ball with these men and try to take some advantage of what they're doing or else we can sit in that trailer and stare at the walls all day."

"What does that mean, 'play ball'?"

"I don't know, but I know this much. The less cooperative we are, the better the odds we sit in the trailer."

The huddle in the corner broke and the Good Cop crossed to where they stood.

"I'm afraid I'll have to ask Miss Decker to return to quarters."

"Why?" Bradley asked. "What's going on?"

"Nothing that concerns you. And don't worry, I'll personally vouch for her safety."

"Hold on a minute. I played along with your little charade. I think I deserve some reciprocal candor."

"I'm afraid that's not my call. The commander will escort you to the media center. Miss Decker, you'll come with me."

He guided Addie by the elbow. Her parting glance, her look of stubborn dignity, seemed directed not at Bradley so much as at the situation in general.

Wallace, the county commissioner, appeared at Bradley's side.

"Commander?" Bradley said, still watching the door.

"That surprises you, does it?"

"Mostly it disappoints."

"Oh, yeah? And why is that?"

"Let's see. Because you hold an office of public trust? Because you lack the conviction to own up to your involvement here? Or is it because these people think you actually stand for something?"

"Save the lectures for college, Sommers. Come on, let's take a walk."

Outside the conference trailer, the armed gathering at the gate had swelled to over a dozen loitering men, all of whom turned and saluted Wallace when he stepped into the sunlight. Lacking only a swagger stick, the little man stood akimbo in the roadway, inspecting his troops like a half-pint General Patton.

"I want two pickups parked nose-to-nose blocking the gate," he said, pointing. "One-tons, with the keys left in the ignitions. I also want those lights from inside set up there and there. Remember, come nightfall those SWAT boys will have night-vision capability."

Satisfied with how his men sprang into action, Wallace's gaze drifted to the rocky ridgeline and to the lone figure on the roof of the media trailer adjusting a satellite dish. To Bradley he said, "This reminds me of Saigon in '75."

"You were there?"

"Did you know my wife is Vietnamese? She was all of sixteen when her family evacuated. Her mother worked at the US Embassy. Operation New Life they called it. Then after a couple of months in Guam her father got homesick and decided to go back. Phuong refused. There was a big to-do, a diplomatic stand-off, but she stuck to her guns. Her parents wound up in a reeducation camp. She ended up at Camp Pendleton."

They'd been strolling as he talked, and now they stopped at the front steps of the trailer.

"She told me a story once, about an apartment she'd rented in Orange County. She must've been eighteen or nineteen by then. There was a Hmong family living upstairs. Rural Laotians, mountain people. One day water started dripping through the ceiling of her unit, so Phuong called the landlady and they went upstairs to investigate. They knocked, but nobody was home so the landlady used her passkey. You know what they found when they opened the door?"

"No idea."

"Crops."

"Crops?"

"Corn, beans, lettuce. The entire apartment had been filled with around two feet of fresh topsoil."

The pickup trucks arrived and Wallace watched as the drivers maneuvered them into position.

"People who place their faith in governments do so at their peril, Sommers. That's one lesson Phuong learned before she ever got to America. The second was that if left to their own devices, people will generally do what comes naturally."

"I'm afraid you're losing me."

"These people—" his arm swept the compound "—they know three things. They know hard work. They know opportunity when they see it. And they know how to protect what's theirs. Google ain't coming to Montezuma County, Sommers, and neither is Amazon or General Motors. Hell, we're lucky to have us a Walmart. The thing that's here, the thing that keeps the potholes filled and the cash registers ringing, is oil and gas."

Wallace extracted a snuff can from his pocket and opened it and fitted a pinch in his cheek.

"People like you, from California or New York, you think you can come here and tell folks what's good for them. Well that's a fool's errand, my friend. These people know what's good for them, and it's high-paying jobs that don't require a college degree. In today's economy, those are rarer than hens' teeth. And you know what that makes you?"

"What's that?"

"The guest who shits on the birthday cake. The Grinch who steals the presents from under the tree."

Bradley shook his head, smiling.

"That's funny, is it?"

"I'll tell you something I've learned in the short time I've been here. You don't give your constituents enough credit. These are decent people, caring people, the kind that Faulkner might've written or Rockwell might've painted. They look out for themselves, sure, but they also look out for each other. And if adversity ever forced them to grow crops in their homes, I'm guessing they'd be mortified to learn that their neighbors were being impacted. So what happens when the good and decent people of Montezuma County figure out that the runoff from today's easy money is making the next generation's world uninhabitable?"

"Alarmist propaganda, Sommers. Pseudo-science bullshit."

"So let truth and falsehood grapple. If you think the science is on your side, then what're you so afraid of? All I'm doing is providing a forum."

"Smoke is what you're providing. Not even that if I have any say in the matter."

"Just listen to yourself. If it takes an armed militia to prevent the clash of ideas, then who's the one running the reeducation camp?"

Wallace leaned and spat. "You talk too much, do you know that?"

"At least I believe what I say. These men of yours do too, after a fashion. We may believe different things, but we *believe*. You, on the other hand, are just doing business. There's no poetry in that, Mr. Wallace. Capitalism has no soul."

"Come on, soul man. I got fish to fry."

Inside the media trailer, the three technicians were standing shoulder-to-shoulder, examining an open laptop.

"Status?"

"We should be online any minute now."

Bradley and Wallace joined them where they stood. After a moment the laptop chimed and the screen blinked from black to blue.

In Bradley's pocket, his cell phone vibrated.

28

Logan was on his knees with his head under the sink when Jess entered the cabin and stopped short in the doorway.

"There you are. You feelin all right?"

"I'd feel better if I could find some shells for that cannon of yours."

The old man's shotgun lay jackknifed on the kitchen table.

"Why? What happened?"

Teeth gritted, Logan leveraged himself to a standing position. "Did you know that bunch from the gun shop out on 491 are calling themselves a militia?"

"What of it?"

"They've got our fence line blocked at the cattle guard. I'm pretty sure they're holding Addie and the professor hostage."

"Say that again?"

"It's my own damn fault. I got a heads-up they were planning a stunt up at the drill site. I warned Addie to stay clear, but I didn't say why."

Jess slumped into a chair.

"So how about those shells?"

"Bedroom dresser. Third drawer on the left."

The old man's bedroom was neat as a pin with nothing much changed from before Vivian died. The same oval rug, the same quilted bedspread, even the same scent of rosewater. Only a thin scrim of dust on the dresser gave evidence to her absence. On the wall beside it a framed photo of Iron Jack Olsen, Jess's late father, cast a sepia frown on Logan's intentions.

The shells—two boxes of Wolf buckshot—were nested amid balled-up socks. Logan opened one of the boxes and stuffed his pockets full.

Back in the kitchen, Jess had set a thermos and wire cutters and binoculars alongside his shotgun. He stood at the sink filling a canteen from the tap.

"What's all this?"

"Provisions. We can't just tear-ass up there and start shootin. We'll need to park halfway and hike the rest. Maintain the element of surprise. Best if we wait till nightfall, you want my opinion. I don't suppose you considered callin the sheriff?"

"The sheriff might be part of it. One of his deputies is."

"In that case I wish't we had us a second gun."

"We don't need a second gun, because you're not coming."

Jess turned from the sink. "Say that again?"

"You heard me. I'm the one let Addie go up there. I ain't about to have you on my conscience too."

"Now listen here, bub—"

"This ain't a debate. I got the key to the one quad in my pocket. I'm taking the other, and I thank you for the loan of your weapon."

Logan grabbed for the shotgun as Jess, surprisingly agile, latched onto the barrel.

"Who do you think you're foolin?" the old man said. "You can't barely stand upright let alone fight."

"I don't aim to fight. I aim to shoot or get shot."

Logan yanked, but the old man held tight.

"Hell, son. Look at you. You're weak as a kitten."

"I'm strong enough to pull a damn trigger."

They stood that way, eyeball to eyeball, with neither man yielding an inch.

"Tell you what," Jess said. "I got some pills in the bedroom, some muscle relaxers. They work wonders for me when I'm sore.

You take two or three and wait maybe half an hour and I guarantee you'll feel good as new. You agree to do that and I'll give you my gun and my gear both. What do you say to that?"

Logan didn't answer, but he released his hold on the gun.

29

They drove in silence until Addie asked, "What does my father have to do with any of this?"

"What do you mean?"

"When I asked what was going on yesterday, your friend said I should ask my father."

"Oh."

"Well?"

"Nothing. He has nothing to do with this."

"Then why did your friend say he did?"

The Good Cop sighed. "First of all, he's not my friend. An ally, maybe, but just for the time being. What he meant was that we asked your father to keep the feds from using that road up from your place."

"Meaning he knew about this . . . whatever it is?"

"Only as of Monday night."

"At the Elks Lodge?"

"What?"

"Never mind. I'm getting the picture."

The picture—one of well-intended duplicity—was all too familiar. On the night Addie had opened her heart to her father and poured it into his lap, Logan had been lying to her face, concealing an armed invasion whose sole purpose was to thwart her every intention.

She allowed herself to marinate in self-righteous anger before certain artifacts—certain impurities in her logic—bubbled to the surface. Like, for instance, the fact that Logan *had* warned her against visiting the drill site, but that she'd ignored him. Also the fact that she'd sneaked the horses out from under his nose precisely for that purpose. And the fact that she'd lied about it in the note she'd left behind.

She'd done the wrong thing, in other words, for what she thought were the right reasons.

"What are you thinking?"

Addie said, "That he'll come looking for me."

"He already has."

"What?"

"We posted some men down at your property line. Your father drove up on an ATV this morning."

"And?"

"And they turned him back with a warning. That's why you're being confined to quarters."

When she didn't respond he added, "Believe me, I was against this from the beginning."

"You could've fooled me."

"Not the operation, but the idea of hostages. I told them, what's the upside? If we let the workers come and go and just use the site as a backdrop then no one'll be overly invested in shutting us down. But once you involve hostages, then the whole paradigm shifts. Now you have time and law enforcement and public opinion all working against you as a kind of force multiplier."

"But they didn't listen?"

He shrugged. "It happened too fast. Carpenter—that's the man you call my friend—he's a little gung-ho for my taste. He sells guns for a living. He talks tough and he hangs around with all these army vets and ex-cops, but he's never taken an oath in his life or put his own fat ass on the line for anything. He treats this like some kind of a game."

"And Mr. Wallace?"

"Wallace considers him a useful idiot, that's all."

"No, I meant how does he feel about having hostages?"

"Put it this way. If Wallace didn't want you here, you wouldn't be here."

She was digesting that morsel when the tents came into view. There were more than before, and like a spreading rash they now covered both sides of the road.

"Can we check on the horses at least? That won't take but a second."

He steered past the tents and the campers to the open field where a group of men had gathered. Feather and Lightning remained on the high line while the other three horses were being saddled.

"Looks like the show's about to get started," the Good Cop said, setting his brake.

Three riders were mounting up as they arrived. The men wore cowboy hats and camo, sidearms and fringed leather chinks. The pudgy man from the trailer was standing among them holding what proved to be a furled American flag that he handed up to the rider astride the largest of the horses. The men acknowledged the new arrivals with nods.

"Do us proud, boys," the Good Cop said, slapping a flank as the riders turned their mounts and departed three abreast. At the edge of the clearing they broke into a lope, and the flag unfurled, and a ragged cheer went up from the encampment through which they passed.

"Have they been watered today?" Addie asked the pudgy man in reference to her horses.

"'Course they have." He seemed offended. "What do you take me for?"

"I don't know. A horse thief? A kidnapper?"

"That's the thanks I get," he said to the Good Cop before trudging back to his trailer.

Addie thought to call after him, to apologize, but stifled the impulse. He *was* a kidnapper. They were all kidnappers, and thieves, and domestic terrorists, and what was most galling was that when all was said and done they'd probably be hailed as some kind of national heroes.

"If you want, we can walk them down to the creek," the Good Cop offered. "I'm not in any hurry."

"I'd appreciate that."

She loosened the lead rope from the high line and moved the clip-end to the tie ring of Feather's halter. The Good Cop watched her and did likewise. They set out together, leading the horses westward toward the row of red willows marking the creekbed some hundred yards distant.

"You're not a horseman," Addie said, and it wasn't a question.

"My sister had a pony when we were kids."

"Nice. Did you ever hold it hostage to get your parents' attention?"

"Ouch."

"Yeah, well."

The creek, normally dry this time of year, carried seasonal runoff from the draws and cuts that veined the mesa top. Today it held but a trickle, with yellow grasses streaming in fingers of muddy rainwater. The horses sniffed but they didn't drink. Instead they cropped at what weeds there were on the bank as the Good Cop looked north, monitoring the activity in the now-distant encampment.

"So they all follow your orders?" Addie asked, watching him. "That must come in mighty handy."

He half-smiled. The Good Cop was trim and handsome and hadn't shaved for days. Sexy, in a different context. His clothes were worn but clean, like those of a man who cared for himself.

"Even my dog," he said, "doesn't always follow my orders."

"Seriously. Aren't you afraid this could get out of hand? That you'll be blamed for whatever happens when it does?"

"Scared to death."

"And yet here you are."

He turned to face her. "It's not like there's anything in this for me. Personally, I mean. The fact is, it'll probably cost me my job."

"Then why are you even here?"

"For the same reason you are. Because I believe what I'm doing is right."

"Sorry, but that's false equivalency."

"What?"

"False equivalency. Professor Sommers and I are taking lawful action in response to what we regard as bad public policy. You're breaking the law to stop us. That's not even close to the same thing."

"Jefferson said that if a law's unjust then a man's not only right to disobey it, he's obligated."

"Unjust in whose opinion? Yours? Mine? Gun-shop guy's? That sounds like anarchy to me. We're not some banana republic where the gang with the biggest arsenal rules. In this country if you think a law's unjust then you show up on Election Day and vote for the candidate who'll change it."

"Except that all the candidates feed from the same trough. You think it really matters whether there's a Democrat or a Republican in the White House? A handful of billionaires still pull the strings, they just take turns doing it. They have the lawyers and the lobbyists and they buy off the politicians. The little guy's got as much chance in Washington as a frog on the interstate."

"I might agree except for the fact that Big Oil holds the strings in every administration. They're the ones whose lawyers write the laws. They're the ones who pay off scientists and buy ads on television to drown out climate science. It's grassroots organizations like the Western Warriors that're down in the trenches, fighting for the people. Fighting to make a difference."

"By putting the people out of work? By bankrupting their communities? Help like that we can do without, thank you."

The horses pricked their ears to an alien sound that arose from the north in a kind of stuttering whisper; a rhythmic pulsing that grew louder as it neared.

"What the hell?"

When the helicopter burst over the horizon, the horses spooked and planted. Addie watched as it approached, swinging low enough over the encampment to set the tent flaps dancing. After hovering there for half a minute it rose and banked and returned from where it had come.

"Time to go," said the Good Cop, already walking. "Not that this hasn't been interesting."

They hustled the horses back to the high line where Addie secured them as before. As they returned to the truck and wove their way through the encampment, men were standing beside their tents with weapons drawn, scanning the sky. At the camper that was her prison, the Good Cop left the engine running and escorted her to the door where Bison Man, her personal guard apparently, sat on a folding chair reading a *Playboy* magazine.

She said, "I guess the police are here then."

"That wasn't the police. I'm guessing TV news."

"From Denver?"

"Or Salt Lake or Albuquerque."

"Just like you wanted. Congratulations."

The Good Cop lingered for a moment, as if wanting to say more. That he wasn't like the others, perhaps; that his principles set him apart. Or maybe it was personal—that they'd made a connection, and that he cared what she thought, and that he hoped they might continue their discussion some other time, some other place.

"So what happens to me? I just sit here and wait?"

"I'm afraid so."

"I don't suppose you'd bake me a cake or something? Like with a hacksaw blade inside?"

He gestured to Bison Man. "You'd need a bazooka to get past him."

"Okay then, I'll take a bazooka."

He smiled. "I'm sorry Miss Decker, but those are my orders."

"Right." She turned and opened the screen. "And unlike the law, you always follow your orders."

30

The sound of the rotors was deafening from where he sat, the wash of the hovering chopper threatening to lift the porta-potty skyward, and Bradley along with it.

What's happening up there?
Please share an update.

That text was from 8:56 a.m., about the time Bluto had begun reading his videotaped message. About the time Naomi Lopez would have arrived to work at the Western Warriors' headquarters office in Santa Fe.

Helloooo? Anybody home?
I tried to call you.

He smiled. The time on that was 12:01. She would have been heading to lunch about then. The Shed, maybe, or Santa Café. And knowing Naomi, there'd have been a prospective donor waiting to join her.

Just saw the video. OMG!
I'm on my way.

That was more like it. Sent at 2:43 p.m., this last text roughly corresponded with the arrival of the first TV news van. If she were flying commercial her quickest options would be Albuquerque to Durango or else Santa Fe to Denver to Cortez. But Naomi

Lopez wouldn't be flying commercial. She'd have a donor or some other deep-pocket patron willing to pilot a straight shot in a private plane from Santa Fe to Cortez, less than two hours by air.

He checked his own watch, then took a chance and speed-dialed her number. It rolled to voicemail, and he tapped End without leaving a message.

Assume you're in the air.
Thanks for the rescue.
Hope you're camera-ready.

A pounding fist nearly shook the door from its hinges. "Let's go, Sommers! While we're young!"

When Bradley emerged into daylight, tucking his shirttail for verisimilitude, he found Bluto looking skyward. "That's a loud sonofabitch," the big man said. He wore fresh hunting camo and not one but two 9mm handguns, the first at his hip and another holstered to the tactical vest he'd donned for visual effect. Craning his neck, Bradley could glimpse the flashing scrum of police cars and firetrucks and news vans that seemed to have banked like windblown tumbleweeds just outside the gate.

Bluto followed him through the back door of the media trailer where, for the past half hour or so, selected reporters had been afforded a series of one-on-one interviews with Bud Wallace, ten minutes max, ostensibly under Bluto's watchful eye. Although still in hostage mode, Wallace was making no bones about his support for the message and tactics of his captors. It was ingenious, really—a sham Stockholm syndrome in which the oppressed, having seen the cold light of truth, becomes chief spokesman for his oppressors.

Bradley's assigned role in this Kabuki theater was to be present but not taking questions. He didn't doubt for a minute Wallace would have preferred him locked in the camper with Addie but, having included him in the hostage video—a strategic mistake, in hindsight—it would invite unwanted speculation were he to disappear from view altogether.

"I've got some people and equipment up here," Wallace was telling a *Denver Post* reporter, who scribbled furious notes, "and I sometimes drop by in the mornings to check on things. Little did I know I'd be walking into something like this. But I can't say I'm surprised. Resource development is under attack all over this country, from the coal mines of West Virginia to the rigs in the Florida gulf. It's got to the point where we've forgotten what it was like to be at the mercy of a bunch of sheiks in the Middle East. I can't for the life of me understand why anyone in this country would want to obstruct our path to energy independence. So yes, to answer your question, I do support what these good folks are doing, and so should every patriotic American."

The reporter spoke to Bradley as she wrote. "What about you, Mr. Sommers? Any comment on the situation?"

"Sure. Ask him what percentage of US coal is shipped abroad for private profit."

"That's enough for now," Bluto said, clapping his hands and shooing the reporter like a pigeon. "We've got a whole passel of you folks still waiting outside."

Which was certainly the case. From this better vantage Bradley could see through the blinded window to where the previous reporter now stood outside the gate surrounded by a circle of other reporters, their cell phones and recorders thrust in her face. Obscuring the tableau, a phalanx of armed men in cowboy hats milled inside the gate while, on the other side of the divide, a squad of SWAT officers, black-clad and helmeted, did the same. Every now and again a trio on horseback would circle past, one of them trailing a huge American flag, and the cameras would swing into action.

With its hyper-charged atmosphere and its massed lines of would-be combatants, the scene was reminiscent of a campus protest from the sixties, or one of those Black Lives Matter demonstrations whose rote choreography of charge and retreat had become second nature to the American public. But since his captors were white ranchers and farmers swaddled in Old Glory, Bradley doubted there'd be tear gas or rubber bullets flying anytime soon.

"Walter Cronkite is dead, Sommers." Wallace appeared beside him after the reporter had left. "So are Edward R. Murrow and Woodward and Bernstein."

"Better fact-check that last one."

"Facts? Nobody cares about facts. If the last few years have taught us anything, it's that. No my friend, nowadays it's whoever shouts first and loudest that gets the headline. Then the story becomes who said what about the shouter, never mind whether the shout was true in the first place."

"You're saying truth doesn't matter anymore?"

"Whose truth? Yours? Mine? Those people out there?"

"Objective truth."

"Truth is a relative concept. Haven't you ever read Nietzsche? We live in walled camps of our own construction where the voice on the loudspeaker is a continuous loop of soothing self-reinforcement. Democrats don't listen to Republicans and blacks don't listen to whites and Christians don't listen to Muslims. We only listen to ourselves, and if God forbid a different point of view finds its way over the wall, then woe unto he who gave it voice."

"Were you always this cynical, or did you have to work at it?"

"Not many optimists made it home from Nam, Sommers. Besides, a cynic is just an idealist with a little gray hair. You spend five years sitting through the public comment periods at county commission meetings and then come and talk to me."

"Call me crazy, but I still believe in the truth. I also believe in the power of the press to bring that truth to the people."

"Please. Most Americans wouldn't know truth if it sat in their laps."

"Maybe that's because it's gotten harder and harder to find. Like the way your industry spends millions on climate science disinformation and propaganda."

"That's your truth, Sommers. And as for climate science, nobody gives a shit about ice melting in the Arctic. Not compared to five-dollar gas down the street. Starving polar bears, now there's an image, but even that gets old after a while. What did whatshisname *say* about the polar bears, and what did whosawhatsis tweet about whatshisname? That's what kids today want to know. Clicks and shares are the coin of the realm, while truth is three for a dollar."

Bradley didn't respond.

"Your mistake was bringing a butter knife to a gunfight. A local public forum? Hell, son, I saw you coming a mile away. You or somebody like you. And I was two steps ahead before you even got here."

Out at the gate, some of the militiamen and a few of the SWAT officers had begun chatting through the chain-link. One of the cops accepted a cigarette. He took a drag and passed it back. At least it looked like a cigarette. This was Colorado, after all.

"Okay, so what happens now?"

"Now we sit back and watch the snake eat its tail."

From where they stood, observing the reporters interview one other, Bradley had to concede the analogy was apt. "I've been watching the TV coverage. You're on the chyron crawl of every news channel in the country."

"And it'll only get bigger. We'll dominate the cycle for three or four days. Longer, if it's a slow news week."

"And then what?"

Wallace shrugged. "It's like NASCAR racing on television. Nobody watches to see the cars go round and round. They're all just waiting for the crash, for the cartwheeling fireball. We'll fall off the front page for a while and then, when it all comes to a head, we'll be back."

"With a fireball?"

"Christ, I hope not."

"What then?"

"With a deal, Sommers." He turned to Bradley and showed his yellowed teeth. "With you letting me in on whatever scam it is you came out here to run."

PART THREE

31

Addie paced, and watched out the little window over the sink, and paced some more. At first she could hear the helicopter off in the distance, and then she couldn't. At around two o'clock Bison Man knocked to offer her lunch, which she refused in what she'd hoped was a principled show of defiance. She then lay on her bed to nap, but mostly she spent the afternoon staring at the bunk above her, lost in a jumble of thoughts.

About how children are exposed to different hazards in a rural setting than they are in an urban area.

About how adjacent mining uses can expand and cause negative impacts.

At five o'clock she was back at the sink watching Archer-Mason employees depart, their northbound column a mixture of company trucks and private vehicles. At the sight of Colt Dixon's old Bronco with its mismatched doors, her heart leapt. She wanted to shout, and to smash the window in hopes of raising a ruckus, but the moment passed in a heartbeat as the Bronco receded from view.

She returned to her bed in a funk. Afternoon bled into evening, and as inky dusk seeped into the camper her thoughts took a new and different turn.

"Come on, Addie," she said aloud. "This isn't Compton."

She inventoried the cupboards and drawers and the empty broom closet, finding cheap stainless flatware, a scarred cutting board, scorched potholders. Plastic plates. Two filthy mouse traps. A cast-iron skillet and a frilly apron. Coffee mugs and juice glasses. A dusty Monopoly set. The playing cards.

She checked at the window and saw Bison Man stand and yawn and amble toward the fire where others had gathered to cook. Dropping to her knees, she laid the apron strings across the camper's narrow aisle, stretching them taut and tying them off at ankle height. Then she returned to the banquette table to sit and wait in semi-darkness with her heart pounding, the skillet heavy in her lap.

It was darker still when Bison Man returned with a plate of spaghetti in one hand and a soda can in the other. He entered and paused inside the door, the pungent smell of tomato and garlic flooding the camper.

"Thank God, I'm starving," Addie said, making no effort to move.

"There's a light in here somewhere."

"I'll bet you'd like that. Then you perverts could watch me from outside."

He hesitated before moving forward. Then with his third step he tripped and the plate went flying and he landed face-first with the force of a fallen tree. Addie sprang to her feet with the skillet in both hands. She swung awkwardly for his head but Bison Man was already scrambling when the blow landed, grazing his shoulder.

"Ow! You little—"

His fist arrived backhand with the force of a mule-kick, sending Addie flying, smashing into the wall and onto the table. Sparks flooded her vision, bright and swirling, and just as they'd begun to clear she heard the metallic *klack-klack* of a pistol slide.

Bison Man stood heaving with his gun drawn, the muzzle pointed directly at Addie.

Time slowed to a crawl.

"Jesus!" he said, lowering the gun and rotating his shoulder. He turned and stomped the apron as he thundered back to the door.

Addie lay without moving, her head throbbing, her cheek already beginning to swell. Then with what seemed a great effort she slid onto the bunk and sprawled there in darkness cursing herself and cursing the Good Cop and cursing Bradley for good measure.

Bradley. What on earth was he doing? The horses had been standing, bored and tethered, for over eight hours. She was starving—a state of affairs only heightened by the smell of spaghetti. She desperately needed a shower, a change of clothes. Her father, meanwhile, would be worried sick, or worse, would be planning something reckless.

The door to the camper banged open and Bison Man reappeared. He sent a galvanized bucket clattering to the floor, followed by a mop.

"Here, bitch. Clean your own damn mess."

32

It was one thing to play with dynamite, Bradley thought, and another to keep it from detonating.

The ranks of the militiamen had swollen to God-knows-how-many and seemed to grow shaggier by the hour. Through a negotiated arrangement with the authorities they arrived by the truckload, or individually on motorcycles, and they brought with them enough guns and ammo to mount a full-scale invasion. Bradley looked on with alarm as an increasingly harried Bluto greeted the new men and, in consultation with the Good Cop, assigned them roles to play.

"Roles" being the operative term since, once it became clear that the SWAT teams and the federal agents and the national guardsmen massed beyond the gate weren't poised to invade anytime soon, the occupation took on a decidedly theatrical cast, a kind of improv atmosphere in which the audience—the assembled media—not only watched and applauded the performance but actively encouraged the players.

The influx of so many outsiders had forced Bud Wallace to remain in character so as to maintain what he called plausible deniability. He and Bradley, the supposed hostages, were holed up in the media trailer where Wallace, who'd procured a bottle of Jack Daniel's, sipped his drink and dipped his snuff and spit into a rubber wastebasket while receiving updates by messenger. Many of the cable news channels, which he and Bradley were monitoring in real time, showed a split-screen image of the so-called hostage trailer where Wallace's irregular appearances at the window—his jug-eared silhouette glimpsed behind parted blinds—were reported as anxious pleas for rescue or, in the assessment of one former hostage negotiator on CNN, as some kind of carefully coded message.

"Would you listen to this guy?" Wallace sneered, refreshing his drink. "I've got a notion to drop my trousers and hang a moon. What do you suppose he'd make of that?"

As darkness fell, the brightly lit area inside the gate became the stage from which all media interactions were conducted. Despite the authorities' best efforts to hold them at bay, the reporters managed to shout questions through the fence while their camera crews took positions atop their vans, giving them sightlines into the compound. Although Bluto remained the occupation's official spokesperson, other armed men—strangers to Wallace, men who'd been instructed simply to pose in the background and keep their mouths shut—stole cameos in the spotlight.

"Christ, this is just what I need," Wallace fumed, flipping the channels. "All it takes is one of these Idaho skinheads shouting 'white lives matter' into an open mic."

Bradley was not sympathetic. "You lay with dogs, you wake to doggerel."

At one point a scuffle broke out between two of the newer men, their rolling headlock captured by a TV crew's spotlight that, when trained on the combatants, froze them like bear cubs in the high beams. By the time Bluto arrived to restore order, both were dusting their clothes and smoothing their hair and mugging for their buddies back home.

It was nearly eight o'clock when a ripple of excitement passed through the crowd outside the gate. Cell phones flashed as the SWAT officers parted and a column of black SUVs rolled to a halt. Wallace upped the volume on a Fox News reporter's breathless on-scene commentary.

. . . significant development as what appears to be an official delegation is just arriving with at least one, make that two of the vehicles bearing federal government plates. From our position it's

difficult . . . wait . . . the gate is opening! The gate is opening! And Sheriff Janes from Montezuma County has just entered one of the vehicles . . .

Bluto, dirty and sweating, burst into the media trailer and addressed himself to Bradley.

"Okay, asshole. It looks like your people are here."

Wallace drained his glass and stood.

33

Addie was still at the window, still watching and listening to the muffled voices of the men outside arguing and laughing by the fire. Her back was sore, and her feet ached from standing, and the soda can she held to her cheek had grown warm an hour ago.

Finally Bison Man, who'd been making trips to the fire to chat and drink with his comrades, took his folding chair with him and sat with his back to the camper.

Addie donned her slicker and carried the galvanized bucket into the bathroom and upended it on the toilet seat. Using the mop handle she eased the skylight open to reveal a square of star-studded night. She climbed atop the bucket and jumped and grabbed the frame of the skylight, swinging gently at first, then dropped back to the floor, shaking her hands as she landed.

After she'd collected the potholders from the kitchen she stole another peek out the window. Bison Man was still at the fire. He was standing now, and laughing, and telling a story. He was probably telling her story, the one with the hilarious punchline.

"We'll see who laughs last, you bastard."

Back in the bathroom, cupping the potholders in her hands this time, she jumped and grabbed, hung and swung, then chinned her face into the cool night air. Keeping her grip with both hands, she shrugged an elbow through the skylight and jacked her shoulder upward. Then powerful hands grabbed her collar and covered her mouth as they hoisted her onto the roof.

"Shhh. Easy, cowgirl."

"*Colt*? What are you doing here?"

"Swimming after a boat."

"*What*?"

"Shhh. Never mind. Where's the professor?"

"I don't know. He never came back from this morning."

Colt Dixon took a knee, and Addie did likewise. They were side by side now, breathing in tandem, and although close enough to touch, Colt was barely visible to her in his dark coveralls.

"What happened to your face?"

"Nothing." She touched a hand to her cheek. "I bumped into something."

"Something or somebody?"

Over the lip of the camper's roofline Addie could see the singlewide trailer in which Bradley had received his medical treatment what seemed like ages ago. It stood now like a dark atoll in a sea of colorful tents—vibrant reds, blues, and greens—that glowed from within like Japanese lanterns.

"Come on," Colt said. "Watch how I do this." He laid out flat on his stomach, then used his palms to propel himself backward, feet first, toward the western edge of the roof until he hung there braced on his forearms. "Just drop and I'll catch you," he said, and disappeared from view.

Addie copied his maneuver, the metal roof of the camper cold where her raincoat rode up. Once her legs dangled free over the edge she paused for a moment, then took a deep breath and let herself fall and be hammocked in Colt Dixon's arms.

"Shhh. Wait here a sec," he said, standing her upright. He tiptoed to the rear of the camper, then tiptoed back.

"Now what?"

"I swapped Hoover for his truck. It's parked just over yonder." He pointed with his chin to a dark clump of junipers. "I figure to stash you on the floor of the cab and then drive us out through the gate. You can cover yourself with that slicker."

"What if they won't let us out?"

"Then we'll find someplace to park for the night. It'll be just like old times."

In his Cheshire cat's grin Addie felt a reassurance both forgotten and familiar. He took her hand and together they ran with their heads low. When they'd reached the white pickup with the Archer-Mason logo she stripped off her raincoat and wedged herself onto the floor on the passenger side.

She crouched there in darkness while Colt started the engine. She heard branches scraping as the truck eased forward over bumpy terrain.

"There's a wash up ahead," he told her, "then the road."

Once the rocking abated, the truck accelerated. Addie watched the occasional light drift past the driver's-side window. She estimated they were doing around thirty miles an hour.

"Whatever happens, thank you for doing this."

"Don't thank me yet."

"I mean it, Colt."

"I know you do. You don't have to say it."

Addie closed her eyes. She recalled that as a young girl crazy about horses, her grandparents had taken her out to Spring Creek to witness the annual mustang roundup. It had been a horrible experience. The BLM used helicopters to chase the horses, which in their panic and confusion trampled each other trying to escape. Mounted wranglers forced them through a gauntlet of whooping cowboys and into a pen where some of the mustangs were so terrified they just slammed through the panels, breaking bones and gashing flesh. Plus the confusion had jumbled the social order, separating studs from their mares and mares from their screaming yearlings. Then when the dust had finally settled they'd trucked the captured animals off to be slaughtered.

A vehicle passed them, its headlights filling the cab. Colt gave a little wave.

Addie said, "I was stuck in that camper for hours, and I did a whole lot of thinking. About the ranch, and about Bradley, but mostly about the future."

"This can wait."

"No it can't. No it can't. And the question I kept asking myself was, what would I regret? Like if something went wrong and people were killed. Or if I got killed. Or if the world changed somehow and there was no going back to the way it was. What would I regret?"

Colt's knuckles were white on the wheel. "And?"

Addie had been traumatized for weeks after that roundup. Years later she'd heard that the BLM had switched to a bait-trap method of collection in which the mustangs were lured with water and sweet feed into an open enclosure. Over the course of weeks, volunteers would add panels to the enclosure as the horses grew used to the arrangement. Eventually they just closed the circle, and those trapped within—intact bands and families— were quietly trucked to the penitentiary at Cañon City, there to be trained for adoption.

"And you were right the other night," she told him, "about Bradley using people. Only there's more to it than that. He's been a different person since we got here. A stranger almost. Or maybe I'm the one who's different, I don't know. Whatever it is, I've been making a big mistake."

She'd exhumed the memory of that roundup during her first weeks of college, donning it like armor when homesickness or regret followed her around campus like a shadow. Her father, she'd decided, had been running a helicopter roundup, using duress to try to control her. Colt, in contrast, had been a bait-trapper. Both men had wanted something from Addie she wasn't ready to give, so flight had been her natural response.

"I'm the one who made the mistake," Colt said, catching her eye. "Me. Five years ago. Biggest mistake of my life."

"We were just kids. Frightened kids, in way over our heads."

Now, years older and theoretically wiser, Addie sensed the contours of a different kind of trap—more sophisticated and less familiar—only with Bradley Sommers at the controls. But the circle hadn't yet closed, and her responsive instinct had changed.

"Not you," Colt said. "You were always an adult. And when you needed an adult to be there for you, all you got was me. That must've sucked. For what it's worth, a day hasn't gone by where I haven't kicked myself in the head. Where I haven't thought about you, and about us, and about what might've been. What should've been. I want you to know how sorry I am I messed that up. Sorrier still for what I put you through."

Addie closed her eyes again.

"I know," Colt said. "Too little, too late."

"No! I mean, that's not what—"

"Oh, shit."

"What?"

"Up ahead. It looks like a damn carnival."

"What do you mean?"

Colt shifted in his seat. "I mean there's cars and lights and a whole bunch of people. Plus they got two trucks blocking the gate."

"Turn around."

"Too late for that. Here, cover up."

The glow as they approached the entrance gate was punctuated by the flash of blue strobes on the window glass. Addie draped the raincoat over her head as the truck glided to a halt. Cold air flooded the cab when Colt lowered his window.

"Evening," he said, nice and casual. "Quite a deal you boys got going."

"How come you're still here?" a voice demanded.

"I was finishing up some paperwork on that number ten well and I reckon I must've dozed."

In the lull that followed, Addie could hear the muted commotion around her. As at the tent city they'd left, the crowd here seemed to have grown tenfold since morning.

"What's up?" said a new voice from outside the truck. "What the hell're you doin here? I thought you boys left hours ago."

"Yeah, well I got stuck doin safety reports, and like I was sayin to your man here, I guess I nodded off in the field office."

"Well, shit. You can see it ain't no simple thing to open that gate. I need to talk to somebody about this."

"Okay, but do me a favor? I got what you might call your hot date tonight, and I'm already runnin late."

"That ain't my problem, brother. Just wait for . . . hold on. What in the hell?"

Addie heard the urgent blaring of a car horn, the sound growing louder as it neared. Then a skidding vehicle, and doors slamming shut, and voices raised in warning.

"Brace yourself!" Colt shouted as their truck lurched into reverse. The engine roared, and a shattering impact slammed Addie into the passenger seat.

"Hang on!"

The truck jumped forward again, spinning into a turn. She threw off the raincoat and gripped the dashboard and pulled herself into the seat.

"What just happened?"

"That was your guard back there, the great big fucker. I hope we slowed him down some."

They were speeding back toward the tent camp, the rutted road rocking their high beams. Addie watched through the cab's rear window as the lights of the main gate faded into the distance.

"Plan B. We'll make a run for your dad's place. If that cattle guard's still blocked we can plow straight through the fence."

"They have radios, Colt. They'll just call ahead and stop us. We'll never get past those tents."

"Shit."

Colt checked the side-view mirrors. He drummed his fingers. He looked down, then down again, as if reading a book in his lap.

"What?"

"Cruise control," he said, fingering the wheel.

"What about it?"

"Here, take this." He reached under his seat and handed her a white plastic hard hat.

"What are you doing?"

"In a minute I'm gonna slow to around twenty-five and then steer us into that wash." He looked at her and smiled. "And then we're gonna jump."

"You can't be serious."

"Hell, we done crazier shit. Cow polo for starters. And remember that time we all dove off the waterfall in football helmets?"

"We could both break our necks."

"That wash is all sand, nice and soft from the rain. The trick is to get clear of the wheels. Just tuck and roll. No worse than fallin off a horse."

"You've done this before?"

"Not exactly. But I seen it on TV."

He glanced into the mirror. Addie turned to see headlights closing behind them. Up ahead, like a stand of flickering votives, the tent city rose into view.

"It's your call, cowgirl. Either we jump or give ourselves up."

Addie snugged the hard hat in place. She twisted the raincoat and wrapped her neck like a scarf.

Colt lifted his foot from the gas and the truck began to coast. He watched the drifting speedometer, then engaged the cruise control.

"We go on the count of three."

The truck bounced as he steered it into the wash. The tires bit, jerking them forward as though towed by an invisible cable.

"One."

He unlatched his seatbelt and drew his knees to his chin, working his feet up onto the seat. Addie got her boots beneath her and crouched on the passenger seat.

"Two."

Colt shouldered his door open, and Addie did likewise. A warning tone sounded, the shrill *beep, beep* lost in the cooling rush of wind. Through her whipping hair she watched him in the glare of the dome light. He turned to her and grinned.

"*Now!*"

Addie launched herself sideways, tucking and rolling and landing in a seated position. The truck rumbled onward, the cab doors flapping as it breasted the far bank of the wash, plowing like a juggernaut in the general direction of Hovenweep.

A hand gripped her elbow, lifting her to her feet. "They're coming!"

She snatched up the hard hat. Colt limped as he led her toward the same tangled copse from which they'd departed not twenty minutes earlier. Behind them the sound of heavy engines gave way to bouncing headlights, then to the dark bulk of a truck. A second truck, then a third, came roaring behind it, all of them chasing the fleeting ghost of Grant Hoover's pickup.

Running men, some with rifles, poured into the wash from the tent camp.

"Okay, now what?"

"I don't know," Colt said. "I guess we hide out for a while."

Lights from the receding trucks grew dimmer in the distance.

"Come on," Addie said. "I've got a better idea."

34

Bud Wallace sat at one end of the conference table, Naomi Lopez the other. From her red leather handbag the executive director of the Western Warriors had produced a slender black tablet on which her fingernails, scarlet and sculpted, clattered in rapid staccato.

"Number eight," Bluto continued, ignoring the sound as he read from a handwritten sheet. "No more national monuments, at least not west of the Rockies."

Naomi paused long enough to catch Bradley's eye where he sat opposite the bearded man. The corners of her mouth curled ever so slightly.

"Number nine. No more endangered species. Number ten. No more retiring grazing permits or issuing permits to folks who don't plan to actually graze."

Bluto refolded the sheet and studied the faces around him. Pleased, it seemed, with his performance. In the ensuing silence, all eyes had shifted to Naomi.

"Tell me something, Mr. Carpenter," she said, setting her tablet aside and composing her hands on the table. "What do I look like to you?"

What she looked like to Bradley was a university provost about to expel a shaggy undergraduate. Bluto shifted uneasily in his chair.

"I don't know. You look like . . . a woman." He swallowed and added, "A woman executive."

"But certainly not the President of the United States, who alone has the authority to designate national monuments under the Antiquities Act. Or to refrain from doing so?"

"No, ma'am."

"Nor am I a member of Congress, or the Secretary of the Interior, or a Supreme Court justice. Which means none of your so-called demands, even were I inclined to do so, are within my power to meet."

"Okay then, what about him?" Bluto pointed his beard to the nervous young man beside Bradley, the man whose business card, which he'd distributed to all in attendance, read Analyst/ Office of Surface Mining/Assistant Secretary for Land and Minerals Management.

"I've made note of your comments," the young man said, his eyes avoiding Bluto's. "And as I said at the outset, I'll certainly relay them to the assistant secretary."

"My *comments*? You'll *relay* them? Jesus H. Christ. Why am I wasting my time with you people?"

"Because you've got your tit in a ringer." Caldwell Janes, the silver-haired sheriff of Montezuma County and, not incidentally, the only law enforcement official whose authority Bluto said he and his men would recognize, pointed an accusing finger. "And because the Broncos are playing the Raiders on Sunday and you know as well as I do that half this crowd'll be home on their lounge chairs before kickoff. So quit horsing around and get to the point. What is it you boys really want? Bud? Maybe you could shed some light on the situation."

Wallace only shrugged, showing the sheriff his palms.

"Right. Okay then, I'll give it a shot. You're upset about some meeting these folks want to have with the Oil and Gas Commission. You'd like 'em to call it off, and maybe to go back to wherever they came from. They, on the other hand, would like Archer-Mason to scale back their drilling operations, at least in close to the monument."

"Not gonna happen," said the final man at the table, a bullet-headed Archer-Mason executive named Burwell.

"Not gonna happen," said Janes, returning to Bluto. "Okay then. Looks like no deals tonight. So how's about you pull your head out of your ass and let everybody go home to their families and I'll recommend that no charges be filed against you or your men. We'll just forget today ever happened."

Bluto glanced at Wallace, then shook his head firmly. "No can do."

"No can do. Okay. So maybe I leave here right now and go inspect that shop of yours and see that all your paperwork's in order. Make sure you ain't selling any guns without background checks. No automatic weapons stashed under that front counter of yours."

"Now hold on, Sheriff. Whose side are you on?"

"I'm on the side of nobody gets hurt. And in case you ain't noticed, there's around fifty state police and FBI out there who'd like nothing better than to shoot off a little tear gas and roll in here on their tanks."

"And I got a hundred armed men who'll see they die tryin."

"Bullshit. You got maybe five men dumb enough to get themselves killed. The rest are out here to get away from their wives for a few days and shoot guns and drink beer."

"Now hold on a sec—"

"You hold on. You hold on, because I got news for you and for anyone else was involved in planning this . . . whatever it is. If somebody gets killed, and I don't care if it's shot or hit by a truck or struck by a bolt of lightning, I'll see to it every last one of you gets tried for felony murder. You got that? Bud, are you listening over there?"

Wallace smiled thinly.

"Goddamn foolishness is what this is. From at least one man with sense enough to know better."

Outside the trailer, lights from the gate had turned nighttime into day. Strobes of blue and red splashed the windows as silence settled over the room.

Bradley looked to Naomi, who sat back with her arms folded. She stared down the table at Wallace, who imperceptibly nodded.

Bradley cleared his throat. "Passions are running high right now, but that can be a good thing in my experience because as in nature, heat is often the catalyst required for change."

"Oh, Christ," said Bluto.

"And while it's true the Western Warriors would like to see an end to oil and gas extraction in this area, rich as it is in fragile archeological resources, we also recognize that the McElmo Dome is a unique and valuable asset. So perhaps we might harness the heat of the moment and broaden our thinking to address issues of larger concern to all of us. Miss Lopez?"

Naomi pushed back from the table and stood. At six-foot-one in her tooled cowboy boots, hers was a formidable presence. *Striking* was a word Bradley had heard others use to describe her. Also *relentless* and *intimidating*. Tonight her raven hair was pulled into a long ponytail, her turquoise jewelry was understated but exquisite, and her manner, as always in situations like this, was coolly imperious.

"The mission of our organization," she began, "is to protect the health of our planet by any means necessary. So while it's true that carbon dioxide extraction in and around the Canyons of the Ancients is of grave concern to us, you may be surprised to learn that it's neither our only concern for the region's wellbeing, nor our greatest."

She circled the table and stood behind the blinking young analyst, who flinched as she touched his shoulder.

"I spoke personally with the Secretary of the Interior this afternoon," she continued, "and we agreed on the importance of defusing this situation as quickly and as peacefully as possible. Having met privately with the relevant stakeholders, I think it's fair to say that the broad parameters of a compromise are beginning to take shape—a compromise that will satisfy both Mr. Burwell's desire to protect the investment his company has made here and Sheriff Janes' goal of a swift and bloodless end to the standoff."

"Bullshit."

That was Bluto, newly red-faced.

"I beg your pardon?"

"I said bullshit. You know damn well you ain't met with me, private or otherwise. And as far as a swift and bloodless—"

"Shut up, Danny."

Wallace made his first, albeit brief, contribution to the discussion.

"What?"

"I said shut up and let the lady finish."

Bluto stood, knocking his chair to the floor. "Shut up? *I* should shut up? Why you pint-sized little turd. After all I done for you, settin this up while you sat on your—"

"Keep your big mouth—"

"—and pushed papers around on a desk—"

Outside the trailer, a truck horn blared. Doors slammed and an engine roared and the concussive *crash* of metal on metal rattled the trailer's windows, launching everyone to their feet.

The sheriff was first to the door. In the blinding glare of the spotlights, an Archer-Mason truck was carving a hasty U-turn, leaving a dented pickup in its wake.

"What the hell?" Bluto shouldered past the sheriff. "What just happened?"

"It's the girl!" One of the gate guards pointed. "She must be in the cab!"

"Well don't just stand there!" Bluto waved his troops into action. "Get them pickups started! And get that piece of junk out of the way!"

The collision and the ensuing commotion had awakened the TV news crews. Stiffly coiffed blondes toting handheld microphones rushed to the gate, shouting questions through the chainlink.

The dented pickup stuttered and caught and backed into a turn. Across the way, Bradley spied a familiar face on the steps of the media trailer. Their eyes held for half a second before the Good Cop ran through the scrum of flashing lights and frantic men to join Bluto in the cab of the second truck.

All three vehicles roared off in pursuit.

The sheriff turned. He grabbed two fistfuls of Bud Wallace's shirtfront and pinned him to the door jamb.

"*Girl?* What goddamn girl?"

35

More men from the tent camp raced toward the wash, some with flashlights, one with a flaming torch. Many were barefoot or in stocking feet, hopping as they ran. Most carried rifles or brandished handguns. All stopped to watch as the column of headlights disappeared at the far edge of the plain.

Addie led Colt into darkness. They dashed and waited, then dashed and waited again. When at last they'd reached the stock trailer, they crouched a final time to recover their breath.

"Feather and Lightning are high-lined in the clearing behind us," she told him. "Think you can tie a Macardy?"

"Long as I get the big boy."

"If we follow the creek it'll lead us straight to our gate."

"Then let's quit talkin about it."

Keeping low, they circled the trailer and ran to the horses that, spooked by the commotion around them, were snorting and stamping in place.

"Easy, girl." Addie held Feather's halter in one hand as she loosened the rope with the other. She moved the clip and tossed the rope over the trembling mare's withers. This would be her rein. Ducking under, she tied the rope off to the other side of the halter. She would ride without bit, saddle, or stirrups—just the unspoken trust that horse and rider had developed over their years and miles together.

"How're you doing?"

"Almost there," Colt said as the Appaloosa backed and jerked. "Hold still you big son of a bitch."

Addie threw her leg up and shimmied aboard, then watched as Colt did the same.

"Sure you don't wanna go that way?" Colt nodded westward, toward where the trucks had vanished. "They'd find us eventually, but it might take 'em hours to track us."

"I want to go home."

Behind them, a sudden light from the trailer threw shadows on the ground.

"Hey!" The pudgy man was striding toward them with a shotgun, speeding as he advanced. "Hey! What the hell're you doin?"

"Home it is," Colt said, digging his heels into the big gelding's ribs. Addie circled once and followed, leaning low on the mare's neck and bracing for the sound of the shotgun. When the blasts finally came she looked back to see the pudgy man firing into the air.

The clock in her head had started, and she calculated the odds. In the shape they were in, the horses could flat-out gallop for maybe two or three minutes, then trot for five, then gallop again. Absent a stumble or spill they should reach the Triple-R's fence line in twenty-five minutes. Meanwhile it would take at least five minutes for a posse to assemble, then fifteen more for a convoy to reach the cattle guard.

It would be close, and they were the longshots.

"How does he feel?" she shouted to Colt as she pulled abreast of the galloping Appaloosa.

"Like a runaway train!"

"When he starts to tire, bring him down to a trot!"

Again she glanced over her shoulder. The glow of the tent city receded, and there were no headlights in sight. Up ahead lay the first of the well pads, its maze of jointed piping now bathed in pallid starlight.

She called, "Do you think the gate is blocked?"

"It was at lunchtime! Two trucks! Four men with rifles!"

"Maybe they've already left!"

"I don't know! Maybe!" When she didn't respond Colt turned to her and grinned, his head nodding in rhythm with his mount. "Not that we'll make it that far anyway!"

Addie laughed. Incongruous though it was with armed men ahead of them and armed men behind, she felt an exhilaration that was more than just the sum of a close escape and impending danger and galloping horses. She felt a lightness of release—of a weight having suddenly been lifted.

"Okay, let's trot!"

Posting without stirrups as their horses blew and trotted, both riders were quickly exhausted. Out of shape though she was, Addie imagined herself an empath; that her exertions had a siphoning effect on Feather such that as Addie grew more and more winded her mare grew stronger beneath her.

"Listen! You hear that?"

Addie listened. At first she heard nothing over the clatter of hoofbeats and her own labored breathing. Then she made out a distant sound she was slow to identify.

"What is it?"

"I think it's that helicopter."

With a kick and a cluck she urged Feather back to a canter, twisting as she did to see the running lights of the chopper, red and blinking like alien stars on the horizon.

"It'll lead them straight to us!"

"They already know where we're headed!"

Again they hunched over the horses' necks, driving them with their heels as the sound above grew steadily louder. The helicopter followed a tracking course, zigging east and west along the roadway's southern axis. By the time it arrived overhead the *whop whop* of its rotors had sharpened to a piercing *soi soi soi*.

"Let's trot!"

With the aircraft directly above them, the horses wanted to bolt. Addie gripped the rope and leaned her weight backward as

Feather fought her at first, then finally yielded. Colt, for his part, was waving at the chopper as if to shoo it away.

The spotlight when it hit them was cold and white and it bathed the ground around them in a twenty-meter circle. Addie averted her eyes. She wanted to call to Colt but the rotor sound was deafening. It lasted less than a minute and then, as with the flick of a cosmic switch, the mesa went dark again and the helicopter lifted.

Colt was pinching his eyes. "I can't see shit."

"Let's walk for a second."

As the helicopter peeled away and her eyes readjusted to darkness, Addie again looked to the north, at the distant pinpricks of headlights.

"They're coming!"

She booted her horse to a canter, recalculating as she did. The posse had formed quickly and the trucks, twice as fast as the horses, would be on them in a matter of minutes. But horsemen, she knew, enjoyed at least one tactical advantage.

Still galloping, she drew abreast of Colt. "We need to be on the other side of that creek! Do you think you can jump it?"

"Do what?"

"The creek! Can you jump it?"

"Now why would I want to do a dumb thing like that?"

"He'll follow Feather! Come on!"

She veered toward the line of willows she knew to be somewhere off to their right. Chest-high and spiky, they bracketed the creek to a width of several yards, meaning the jump would span anywhere from ten to fifteen feet.

But that was only if the horses didn't balk, catapulting their riders headfirst into oblivion.

"You ever done this before?" Colt called ahead to her.

Addie smiled. "No, but I saw it on television!"

Still cantering, she steered Feather into a perpendicular approach with Colt and Lightning behind her. The willows when they appeared out of darkness were as a ribbon of greater dark. She lifted Feather's head to show her the question, then urged her forward again.

What happened next would be a matter of trust—Addie's trust in Feather to make the jump, and Feather's trust in Addie that a safe landing might lay on the other side.

"Come on, girl, we can do this."

She dug her heels and flapped the makeshift rein. Six strides, four strides, two. Addie threw her weight forward and the horse responded in kind, its bare back arching to catch her as they landed neatly in tandem.

She wheeled in time to see Lightning land heavily with Colt collapsed forward, draped on the big gelding's neck. They halted after a few strides with both horses lathered and blowing.

"Okay," Colt said. "Now what?"

"Now we keep going, using the willows as a screen."

The headlights swept past them. Addie counted four vehicles, plus the flashing red lights of the helicopter tracking above. If the pilot had noticed the horses moving in parallel, he did nothing to reveal their position. Minutes later, where the creek began its angle toward the cattle guard, they slowed to a halt.

The willows ended here, and the creekbed narrowed to a ditch. A hundred yards to their left, a dozen men mingled in the headlights of the still-idling pickups. The fence line dead ahead stretched in perpendicular to a sheer and sudden drop-off. They were effectively shelved, and any further progress would leave them exposed.

They slid from the heaving horses.

"I'm dark. I could crawl up there and cut the fence," Colt said.

"With what?"

"Shit." He patted the pockets of his coveralls. "I left my Leatherman in the Bronco."

"It doesn't matter. They'd spot you anyway."

"You think that thing can see us?"

High above and circling, the helicopter's rotors masked the sound of their voices.

"Probably."

"Then we need to do something. We're a couple of sitting ducks."

Addie turned a circle. They could abandon the horses here and scale the cliff down into the canyon, but the night was black and the thousand-foot drop nearly vertical. Or they could retreat on horseback and work their way west as Colt had suggested. That might delay their capture for several hours at least.

"This is my fault," she said. "We should've stayed where we were."

"You could take Feather and pony the big boy. Ride out and find someplace to hide."

"What about you?"

"I'll turn myself in. That should buy you some time."

"I can't let you do that."

"Why not? It's not like they're gonna shoot me or anything."

"We're in this together, that's why. Decker and Dixon. Come hell or high water."

Colt's smile lit the darkness. "Okay then, how about this? I'll walk out there with my hands in the air. When I get close enough I'll jump into one of them trucks and run it straight through the fence. You gallop through on Feather and just keep on going."

"That plan was just elected Least Likely to Succeed."

"You got a better idea?"

She turned back to the north. There were no good hiding places on the mesa and the horses, already exhausted, were easily tracked over ground still soft from the rain. But at least if they kept moving they could buy some time and hope for . . . something. Because to Addie's way of thinking, anything was better than being a prisoner again.

"Okay. I say we ride—"

But Colt had already left her, hopping the ditch with his hands raised in surrender. She started to follow but stopped. "Damn you," she said. She watched him for another moment then threw her leg over Feather's back and shimmied aboard.

From atop the horse she watched as the scene unfolded—a sequence that would stay burned in her memory as if by a white-hot iron: Colt walking toward the lights with his hands held high, the men oblivious to his approach until one of them points, then all turn as one. Rifle barrels lift. Colt still walking, speaking as he does, and the helicopter drifting lower, turning like a toy on a string.

When he was twenty yards out, the spotlight hit. Even from her remove, Addie shielded her eyes with an arm. Within the cone of glowing light the men appeared as holograms, and the hologram that was Colt dropped his hands and bolted for one of the pickups.

Colt slammed the driver's door just as the pickup was swarmed. Backing it sharply, he carved a muddy arc and then jammed it into drive. Dirt flew and men scattered, with two or three toppling like traffic cones.

Addie dug her heels into Feather's ribs. The mare leapt forward and took the ditch in a stride. Then gunfire erupted, pocking the commandeered pickup as it clipped the back of another truck. Muzzles flamed and glass shattered as dozens of rounds peppered the pickup's tires, its grill, its engine.

Feather stopped and reared, launching Addie backward. She landed hard and tumbled, then was nearly trampled by both galloping horses. But she rose again, staggering, running headlong toward the light.

"Stop! Stop it!"

The smoking pickup had drifted to a halt. Addie had nearly reached it when the thunderous *boom* of a shotgun blast shattered the windows of the neighboring truck, sending the armed men diving for cover.

"Drop your guns!" called a voice from the other side of the fence. Then a second *boom* rocked another truck, triggering its horn.

Addie reached Colt's pickup just as the scene blinked dark again and the helicopter lifted, the beating of its rotors replaced by another, shriller sound. To the north, a charging line of vehicles were spread across the mesa, their sirens screaming and their light bars wildly flashing.

She yanked the driver's door open. Colt lay splayed across the console, his lifeless body aglitter with broken glass like gems on a jeweler's velvet.

Addie recoiled. Then an impact drove her sideways, knocking the wind from her lungs and leaving her gasping, smothered beneath her tackler.

"Stay down," the Good Cop ordered. "You'll get yourself shot."

"He needs a doctor!"

"We'll get him a doctor. But first—"

A third *boom* rocked another pickup, and was answered this time by a fusillade of bullets.

"Hold your fire!" the Good Cop shouted. From where Addie lay beneath him she could see a hunched figure moving through darkness on the other side of the fence.

"Daddy?"

"You son of a bitch!" Bluto rose and fired again, the *pop pop pop* of his lone handgun barely audible over the blaring horn and the whopping rotors and the keening of the sirens.

Across the fence line, the darkened figure slumped. Addie screamed. The Good Cop sprang to his feet, charging Bluto and tackling him and wresting the gun from his grip.

Addie sat upright. Car doors slammed as the helicopter's spotlight again flooded the scene in a blinding supernova.

"Ten thirty-three!" the Good Cop shouted. "Gunshot victim in the blue pickup!"

Amid the commotion of bellowed commands and swarming officers, Addie stood and walked, trancelike, through the eerie daylight. On the other side of the four-wire fence her grandpa Jess lay sprawled like a broken doll, a shotgun by his side.

His eyes were wide open.

36

No one was supposed to get hurt.

That was the fly in the ointment, the loose bolt in the otherwise towering achievement Naomi Lopez was about to announce to the assembled media in the wee hours of the morning in the crowded atrium lobby of the office of the Montezuma County Sheriff.

A podium had already been rigged, the microphones that adorned it a kind of congratulatory bouquet from CNN, NBC, CBS, ABC, and half a dozen other national and international news outlets whose exhausted stringers and technicians crowded into a groggy semicircle chatting or texting or sipping stale coffee from Styrofoam cups. Sheriff Janes, bloodshot and haggard, stood to the side in a gaggle of senior deputies whom Bradley had come to know personally after the hours he'd spent fielding their questions in various offices and interview rooms as the details of the Sagebrush Siege, as the media now were calling it, were sifted, parsed, and probed.

For the most part the interrogations had been straightforward—who did what, who said what, and what happened next? The only delicacy required of Bradley was in relation to Bud Wallace, whose exact role in the affair seemed a point of contention among the competing law enforcement agencies. Fortunately for Bradley, the concussion he'd suffered from his equestrian mishap had allowed him to plead ignorance, or at least confusion, in that critical regard.

As for Wallace himself, the last time Bradley had seen him—outside the media trailer, just after he'd thrown the gate open to the screaming charge of police and news vehicles—the county commissioner had been sanguine, reasoning that his men were loyal and that if necessary he'd pit his veracity against that of Daniel Carpenter—aka Bluto—any day of the week.

It wasn't until hours after that conversation that the particulars of the evening's tragedy had filtered down to Bradley. The Good Cop, for instance, turned out to be an off-duty Montezuma County sheriff's deputy whose central role in the siege had so undermined Janes' authority that the FBI and the state police had quietly sidelined the old sheriff, reducing him to a bystander in his own jurisdiction.

As for the rank-and-file militiamen, none had fired on the police vehicles as they'd roared through the tent camp and all had surrendered peacefully—mitigating circumstances that had facilitated their swift passage through the distended bowel of the local criminal justice system.

The dozen possible shooters—ballistics would confirm the actual number—who'd ambushed Colt Dixon were another story entirely. They, and particularly Carpenter, had emerged as the villains of the drama: the trigger-happy nutjobs whose disheveled mugshots even now were flashing across television screens throughout the English-speaking universe. Already Bradley had seen snippets of neighbor interviews, and coworker interviews, and ex-wife-in-curlers interviews attesting to the men's extremist leanings and to their fondness for heavy ordinance.

Finally there was Addie Decker, bruised and dirty and last glimpsed in bright florescence as she entered the sliding glass doors of Southwest Memorial Hospital. The grieving captive's story was the one that everyone wanted—the human interest angle, the "Shocking Twenty-Four-Hour Ordeal" of America's damsel in distress.

Or was she America's action hero? Some reports had Addie galloping bareback through a hail of gunfire, while others had her wrestling a shooter to the ground. All had her escaping,

Houdini-like, from a locked camper-trailer surrounded by heavily armed guards. Held but briefly for FBI questioning, she'd been granted special dispensation under the circumstances and, despite her status as the affair's most material of witnesses, released from police custody shortly before midnight.

Which suited Bradley fine.

"Ready?"

Naomi's hand lingered on Bradley's arm. He checked his watch before noting Burwell's bullet head reentering the lobby from the parking lot. The Archer-Mason executive was now accompanied by a spokesperson from the US Department of the Interior. Both men nodded in Naomi's direction.

"Ladies and gentlemen," she began, stepping to the microphones. "If I could have your attention, please. My name is Naomi Lopez, and I'm the executive director of the Western Warriors, a nonprofit organization dedicated to environmental advocacy and protection. I'm joined today by my colleague Bradley Sommers, whom you've all come to know by now. Professor Sommers chairs the Institute of the Environment and Sustainability at the University of California at Los Angeles. Also with us this morning are Malcom Burwell, an executive vice-president of Archer-Mason Industries, and Art Lowenstein, a deputy press secretary for the US Department of the Interior."

Cameras flashed as the last two men took up positions behind Naomi.

"The events of the past twenty-four hours have been profoundly unfortunate. It goes without saying that nobody should use or condone the use of violence or threats of violence in our public discourse. To be clear, we at the Western Warriors are appalled by what happened last night, and condemn those responsible in the strongest possible terms. That said, I'm pleased to report that the dark cloud cast by the so-called Sagebrush Siege has yielded at least one ray of sunshine, and for that I'll turn the podium over to Mr. Lowenstein for what amounts to a preview of a major environmental policy announcement."

Lowenstein fished reading glasses from a pocket and balanced them on his nose. He swiped to a screen on his cell phone and set it on the podium.

"Thank you, Ms. Lopez. Later today in Washington, the Secretary of the Interior will formally announce that the Navajo Generating Station, a coal-fired power plant located near Page, Arizona, will cease operations next year, a quarter-century ahead of schedule. This is pursuant to an agreement reached last night between the Environmental Protection Agency, the Bureau of Land Management, the Bureau of Reclamation, the Bureau of Indian Affairs, the plant ownership, and various interested stakeholders. Also slated for closure is the Kayenta coal mine on Black Mesa, which currently provides fuel to the Navajo plant. These closures—"

"Wait a minute. You call that sunshine?" The *Cortez Journal* reporter who'd interviewed Bradley on Tuesday had her hand in the air. "That plant provides nearly a thousand jobs on a reservation where unemployment is already at fifty percent."

Lowenstein removed his reading glasses. He returned the phone to his pocket.

"You make an excellent point. The fiscal impact of these closures on the Navajo and Hopi tribes is unfortunate, but it's important to understand that these events are driven almost entirely by market forces. The simple fact is that it's cheaper for the plant's customers to buy electrical power elsewhere thanks to the falling price of natural gas. That's why any further rollback of environmental regulations won't improve the situation, since the resulting increase in natural gas production will only widen the price gap between coal power and power produced by other means. The marketplace has spoken, in other words, and for that reason alone we can expect these closures to be permanent."

Naomi stepped forward. "We certainly don't wish to minimize the problem of Native American unemployment. We must, however, keep our eyes on the larger picture here. These closures will have the beneficial effect of eliminating some twenty million metric tons of carbon dioxide equivalent that the Navajo plant and mine produce each year, as well as obviating the approximately ten billion gallons of water consumed each year by plant operations. These represent huge benefits both for tribal health and for the environmental health of the entire Four Corners region, making this a truly landmark agreement. Are there any other questions? Yes."

"What does this announcement have to do with the siege?"

"If you mean directly," Naomi continued, nudging Lowenstein aside, "the answer is nothing. Indirectly, however, the siege brought certain parties face-to-face under circumstances that proved conducive to finalizing what had previously been a stalled negotiation. Speaking personally, the siege also helped open my eyes to the plight of rural communities like this as America continues the difficult task of navigating its way to a cleaner energy future. Yes?"

"Does this mean your organization is now open to expanded drilling for natural gas?"

"It means that under limited circumstances the Western Warriors recognize the need for natural gas as a bridge fuel during our nation's transition from coal and oil to clean and renewable energy sources. Yes?"

"What about the local public forum? Isn't that what started this whole thing in the first place?"

"That's an excellent question, and for that I'll turn it over to Professor Sommers, who, as you perhaps know, was the driving force behind that effort. For those unfamiliar with his background, Professor Sommers is one of the nation's foremost authorities on the environmental and health impacts of the fossil fuel industry." She turned to Bradley and smiled. "He looks a fright just now, but I think we can all forgive him under the circumstances. Come, don't be shy."

Bradley, still in his rumpled clothes from the siege, joined Naomi behind the microphones.

"Our goal in calling for a local public forum," he began, "was to raise awareness of the environmental consequences of oil and gas exploration not just on fragile archeological resources but also on farming and ranching operations here in Montezuma County. Those issues, by the way, are addressed at length on our Facebook page, Save Our Rural Water, and on the Western Warriors' website, both of which I'd encourage everyone to visit. The purpose of the forum was merely to highlight those issues and to invite a dialogue on the relative costs and benefits of fossil fuel extraction."

Here Bradley glanced at Burwell, who wasn't smiling.

"Fate, however, intervened, as it sometimes will. Since we have no desire to cause any further pain or disruption to the good people of Montezuma County, we've concluded it would be best if we withdrew our request for a local public forum. Suffice it to say that this matter has already garnered more than enough publicity."

Naomi returned her hand to Bradley's arm. "All right, then. That concludes our—"

"One final point," Bradley said. "Our sympathies go out this morning to all who've been affected by the events of the past twenty-four hours. In particular, I want to offer my condolences to Miss Decker. I hope she knows that she and those closest to her are in our thoughts and prayers."

There ensued a four-way handshaking ritual as the cameras rolled and the cell phones flashed. Over Lowenstein's shoulder Bradley caught a glimpse of Sheriff Janes, whose expression was that of a man watching sausage being made.

Which in a manner of speaking, he was.

37

As Logan was wheeled into the brightly lit lobby he found Addie sitting with her legs folded beneath her watching a wall-mounted TV with its sound barely audible. On the screen, the professor and two other men were shaking hands with a woman, all of them grinning like they were sharing an inside joke. Then the program cut away to the now-famous footage of the fatal shootout filmed from above in the white spotlight of the helicopter.

"Isn't this far enough?" Logan asked the orderly, who stopped pushing and circled the wheelchair and bent to lock it in place. He helped Logan to his feet.

"You take care, Mr. Decker."

Addie had turned at the sound of her father's voice. She stood and crossed to him, and they embraced.

"Okay, so where's he at?"

"Second floor." She hooked his arm and led him toward the elevators. "I'll take you."

"Wait a minute." Logan strode to reception and offered his arm to the woman behind the desk. She found scissors in a drawer and snipped the white plastic bracelet from his wrist.

"There you are," she said. "That makes you a free man."

As the elevator climbed, Logan studied his daughter in profile. *Haunted* was the word that had struck him when first she'd appeared at his bedside with the shiner under her eye. Only now he detected a different attitude, a more determined set to her jaw, as if grief and fatigue had combined somehow to imbue her with a newfound sense of purpose.

"Mr. D.!"

Colt Dixon grinned from where he lay in his hospital bed. Despite the poles and wires, despite the tubes and monitors, he reached to shake Logan's hand and seemed bemused to find a pulse oximeter clipped to his finger and an IV line running from his arm. His blue eyes followed the tubing to a bag hanging over his head.

"He's still pretty groggy," Addie said as she moved to his bedside. Colt's hospital gown was draped in a way that exposed his left shoulder, purple and swollen beneath the heavy padding that held his arm to his chest.

"I reckon I know the feeling," Logan said, studying the boy.

"Did you get shot?"

"You got shot." Addie pressed a hand to Colt's forehead. "Daddy got drugged. Probably the same drug they're giving you now."

Logan eased into a chair. "What do the doctors say?"

"That the bullet missed his lung but fractured his shoulder blade. That he lost a lot of blood, and that he's lucky to be alive."

Colt winked at Logan. "You can say that again."

Logan watched as his daughter ministered to the boy, fluffing his pillows and holding the clear plastic cup while Colt sipped from a straw like a baby bird.

"You know they can't keep him here. He'll need a place to recover, and he'll need someone to nurse him."

"I've been thinking about that."

"And?"

"And I was hoping you wouldn't mind having a housemate. At least for a while."

"Just one?"

The look she gave him was questioning.

"I could move upstairs. Or better yet, out to the cabin."

"You would do that?"

"I would like that. Does he even know . . ."

She shook her head.

"Know what?"

"Nothing," she said, touching his cheek with her hand. "Nothing you need to worry about."

38

They skipped the funeral home altogether—her father's decision—and instead used the simple barn-wood coffin they'd found on sawhorses in back of the cabin. Its discovery had vexed Logan in the way that Jess's behavior had vexed him on the night of the shooting. That was until Addie sat him down to explain the truth behind both.

His was a smaller service than Grandma Vivian's, with neither priest nor pallbearers nor reception to follow. Just Logan standing over the grave they'd dug together and into which he and Addie had already lowered the coffin before a handful of mourners—the last of the old-time ranchers from Jess's generation—had arrived in their jeans and canvas jackets, their hats doffed for the man one of them said was tougher than long division.

"Jess wasn't a big one for church," Logan began, scanning the downcast faces, "but if you took a notion to pray for him on Sunday, I'm sure he wouldn't object. For now though I just want to say that I'm a grateful man. Grateful because Jess and Vivian didn't have to treat me like a son, but that's exactly what they done. And I believe Jess forgot more about ranching than I'll ever know. But there's something else he knew a thing or two about, and that was being a grandfather to my little girl. Being a friend and an example, and for that I'm especially grateful. And now that both he and Vivian are gone, I know I've got some catching up to do in that department."

He looked to Addie at the foot of the grave and showed her a sheepish smile.

"We all know Jess was a frugal man. You'll recall that junker he drove, and you'll notice the coffin he made for himself. So I suspect he'd have been pleased to find out Vivian's headstone hadn't got started yet, which means he got himself a two-for-one discount right there. And that, come to find out, had more than a little to do with him getting himself shot."

Addie felt Colt's hand on the small of her back.

"But there's one thing Jess loved more than a bargain even, and we're all of us standing on it. His great-grandfather was one of the first white men to settle this country. This ranch belonged to his grandfather, who's buried right over there. So is his father and so is his mother. So is his wife and his daughter. I guess you could say this place was Jess's church, and that ranching was his religion, and that these were his saints. He devoted himself to this land and he worshipped his family, and damned if he didn't die defending both. He did everything in his power to preserve this place and to leave it in able hands. And now, ashes to ashes and dust to dust, he'll be part of it forever. And that's why today, despite our loss and our sorrow, all is right with the world."

Logan wiped at his nose and took up the shovel and began refilling the grave. The other men joined him, one with the mattock and one with the pry bar. None of them speaking, the others just kicking rocks and clods with their boots.

Hot tears streaked Addie's face. She left the men and led Colt past the still-fresh scar of Vivian's grave to her own mother's headstone, where they stood together in silence.

Look Mama, she wanted to say to the woman whose voice she could barely remember. Everything's right with the world. For while it had taken a while to get there, Addie had finally come to realize that her mother had never left her. Never did and never would. Instead it was Addie who'd almost left. Left her mother, her father, her family, all in pursuit of the fallacy that life is something that needs to happen somewhere else. Only to find that when she finally did cross that threshold, it had delivered her home again.

Below them, a horse whinnied. Addie turned to watch as first Feather and then Lightning kicked up their heels and tossed their heads and galloped around in a circle. Her gaze continued toward the house, to where a black Range Rover had pulled alongside Bradley's Prius. To where the doors of the Range Rover opened and two angular figures stepped into the sunlight.

"I'll just be a second."

They were transferring files from one vehicle to the other. Bradley, standing beside the Prius, looked up at Addie's approach. The tall woman with him had one knee on the backseat as she searched for something inside.

"I'm sorry," Bradley said. "We didn't mean to intrude."

"You're not intruding. Hello?"

The woman backed and straightened to her full height. She wore fashionable sunglasses and scarlet lipstick. "Hello," she said. "You must be Addie. I'm Naomi Lopez."

"I know. I saw you on television."

"And I you."

They regarded each other for a long moment before Addie returned her attention to Bradley.

"Your bag is upstairs. I think I packed everything."

Bradley looked to the woman before trotting up the flagstone path in his same running shoes, his same boyish manner. Both women watched him as he pushed through the door of the house.

"Just so I'm clear," Addie said. "The local public forum was just a ruse to get Archer-Mason's attention?"

"Not a ruse. Think of it more as a lever."

"Because they have the clout in Washington."

The woman nodded. "It's a little like judo. Whenever possible, you use your opponent's strength to your advantage."

"All because negotiations over closing the Navajo plant had stalled, and Washington needed a nudge?"

"A nudge we currently lack the weight to provide."

"And in exchange for its nudge you agreed to leave Archer-Mason in peace?"

"For now at least." She tilted her face toward the mesa. "Here, anyway."

When Addie didn't respond the woman added, "Do you have any idea how difficult it is to wrest an environmental concession, even a modest one, from this administration? Bradley is nothing short of a genius."

"That's one word to describe him. I'll bet the Navajo and Hopi tribes will have another."

"I suppose they might. Suffice it to say that the situation was not without nuance."

"And I suppose Mr. Wallace will have an expanded role with Archer-Mason going forward?"

The woman lowered her sunglasses. "Bradley was right about you. You're a very clever girl."

"And this whole idea, this *plan*, it all started when?"

"By any means necessary. That's our mission statement." The door to the house opened and Bradley emerged with his suitcase. The woman moved to the back of the Prius and opened the hatch. "Besides, I understand you'll be quite wealthy soon. Hardly grounds for complaint, I should think."

Bradley swung his suitcase into the Prius and lowered the hatch. The woman inspected Addie one final time before returning to the Range Rover and folding herself behind the wheel.

"I know I owe you an explanation," Bradley said, his voice lowered. "It's the least—"

"Don't. Please."

Waylon appeared from the shade of the house and waddled in their direction.

"All right, then let me say this. I hope you'll come back to campus. I really do. Or at least that you'll think about it. We'll be pushing for a national ban on single-use plastics this winter.

It's a perfect opportunity to get some congressional experience under your belt."

Addie looked to the gravesite where Colt, his arm in a sling and his back to the laboring men, gave a little wave.

"Thanks, but I have a fight to finish right here."

Bradley followed her gaze. "You have too much going for you to waste your talents in this place. And for what? So that someday with your cowboy boots and your callused hands you can be buried up there with the rest of them? Is that really what you want out of life?"

"That's exactly what I want." She turned to face him. "Of all the things you taught me, that was the most important."

The woman started her engine. "Come on, Bradley! We're already late!"

Waylon arrived at Addie's side. He growled and raised his hackles as Bradley slid behind the wheel of the Prius.

"Just tell me one thing." She closed his door and bent her face to the window. "That girl in the story, when you were in high school? The one with the little fawn?"

"What about her?"

"I was wondering what became of her."

His brow furrowed. "I don't know." He started the engine and put his car in reverse. "She got fired, but after that . . ."

She stepped away, and with Waylon beside her she watched as both vehicles backed and turned and drove off in a swirling cone of dust.

It was red clay dust, the kind that gets into your clothes and into your hair and sometimes, when you least expect it, into your heart.

Books on a shelf stretching back generations with each new chapter, each new entry, indelibly written. That was how Logan saw it. Some endings happy, some less so. Some with a moral, but many without. Some nice and long, and a few cut short before their time. But all of them influencing that which is yet to be written, yet to be lived.

It made a man think. About choices, mostly. Wise choices and poor choices. Those made and those avoided. Which in itself was a kind of choice, a kind of decision, the consequences of which could be just as far-reaching.

Men of Logan's generation feared Communism and the bomb and God knows what else. Sputnik. AIDS. Islamic terrorism. Threats that were all but unknown, or even unimaginable, to his parents or his grandparents but were no less urgent to him. More urgent, in fact, for their very novelty.

Now it was Addie's chapter. Her challenges, her choices. Her grandpa Jess had been right about one thing, though. Addie's generation, and its women in particular, seemed uncommonly sensible, uncommonly aware. And maybe it was that awareness that enabled them to see and to face the threats that old farts like Logan had ignored and avoided for too damn long.

Or maybe it was just the way of the world for each new generation to look ahead while those who came before, those whose chapters were already written, got stuck looking backward.

It was something to think about. And he would think about it, only later, when he had more time.

Right now the children were coming.

1. The book begins with Addie's reflections on Attachment Theory, which posits a connection between early parental interactions and later life relationships. How do you think the loss of her mother, and the experience of being raised by Logan, impacted Addie's relationship with Colt? With Bradley? With her hometown?

2. Did your feelings toward Colt, Bradley, and/or Logan evolve as the story progressed? How so? What specific incidents or passages caused you to reevaluate your initial impressions?

5. The term "character arc" is used to describe the ways in which a character evolves over the course of a novel. In what ways is Addie a different person by the end of the story than she was at the beginning? If you had to choose a word or phrase to describe her evolution, what would it be?

6. In a pre-publication interview, author C. Joseph Greaves described *Church of the Graveyard Saints* as "a book about place." Do you agree? To what extent does place—the tug of the land—influence Addie's decision to remain in her hometown? Conversely, to what extent do you feel her decision was influenced by Bradley? By Colt? By Logan? By Jess?

7. Early on, Logan fears that his fondness for Colt might have caused Addie to reject Colt "in the way the smell of a human hand can cause a mother bird to abandon her chick." By the end of the story, we find Addie at Colt's bedside holding a plastic cup

"while Colt sipped from a straw like a baby bird." What does the juxtaposition of these two images tell us about Addie's relationship with Logan? What does it say about their future together?

8. At the story's dramatic climax, Addie's grandpa Jess, having drugged Logan with his late wife Vivian's morphine, sacrifices himself in an effort to protect and rescue Addie. How did you feel about Jess's death? Was his conduct consistent with his character? Does the fact of his cancer diagnosis diminish the selflessness of his actions?

9. Both Logan and Addie do the wrong things for what each believes are the right reasons. Logan, for instance, hides Addie's college acceptance letter in an effort to keep her at home. Addie, for instance, lies to her father about riding with Bradley up to the well site. Are Addie and Logan more alike than either might want to admit? In what ways are they alike, and in what ways are they different?

10. References to environmental issues such as overpopulation, oil and gas exploration, and public lands cattle grazing recur throughout the story. Are their benefits and detriments presented in an evenhanded manner? Do you view any of these issues differently after reading the story? Did you learn anything about these issues that you didn't already know?

11. The Four Corners region of the American Southwest is described both as a place of astounding natural beauty and as a "national energy sacrifice zone" in which that natural beauty is under assault by industrial interests. Are you more or less likely to want to visit the Four Corners after reading *Church of the Graveyard Saints*? Might you want to learn more about, or become more involved with, these environmental issues?

12. Bradley and the Western Warriors strike a Faustian bargain with Archer-Mason Industries to abandon their opposition to Archer-Mason's gas drilling in exchange for its help in shuttering a coal-fired power plant. Setting aside the manner in which Bradley uses Addie to achieve that outcome, does this seem like a good deal for the environment? If so, can you justify the lengths to which Bradley goes to achieve this result? Was he doing "the wrong thing for the right reasons," or is his conduct unforgivable?

13. What do you think the future holds for Addie? Did she make the right decision by staying in her hometown to "finish the fight" against Archer-Mason?

14. For those who've read *Hard Twisted*, the author's 2012 novel also set in the American Southwest, how would you compare and contrast the two books?

15. If you were producing the movie version of *Church of the Graveyard Saints*, whom would you cast in the role of Addie? Colt? Bradley? Logan? Jess?

ACKNOWLEDGMENTS

For their encouragement, their assistance, or their inspiration in connection with this little story I owe a debt of gratitude to many people including Lynda Larsen, Mark Montgomery, Katie Greaves, Craig Johnson, Dan Greaves, and (belatedly) Richard J. Hawkey, with special thanks reserved for the gang at Torrey House Press—Anne Terashima, Rachel Davis, Kathleen Metcalf, Mark Bailey—and especially for my editor and publisher, Kirsten Johanna Allen.

Torrey House Press is a nonprofit publisher with the stated mission of supporting environmental conservation through literature. If you enjoyed this book, and if you might like to support that mission, you can begin by visiting them at their website: www.torreyhouse.org.

ABOUT THE AUTHOR

C. Joseph Greaves is an honors graduate of both the University of Southern California and Boston College Law School who spent twenty-five years as an LA trial lawyer before becoming a novelist. Sometimes writing as Chuck Greaves, he has been a finalist for many of the top awards in crime fiction including the Shamus, Macavity, Lefty, and Audie, as well as the New Mexico-Arizona, Oklahoma, and Colorado Book Awards. He is the author of five previous novels, most recently *Tom & Lucky (and George & Cokey Flo)*, which was a *Wall Street Journal* "Best Books of 2015" selection and a finalist for the 2016 Harper Lee Prize. He is also a member of the National Book Critics Circle and the book critic for the *Four Corners Free Press* newspaper in southwestern Colorado, where he lives and writes.

For more information you can visit him at his website: www.chuckgreaves.com.

ABOUT THE COVER

A native Southwesterner, artist Julia Buckwalter is drawn to the sweeping desert landscapes and majestic skies that made up her life from birth in Egypt to childhood in Utah and New Mexico. Moab, Utah, is the place she calls home, with a landscape providing endless inspiration via the intense variation of color and deep meditative stillness particular to the desert.

The drama of endless vistas, mountains, bodies of water, and sky are to her the embodiment of agelessness and the expression of the infinite. Mesmerized by rock and cloud formation, Buckwalter is deeply inspired and affected by the work of painters Georgia O'Keeffe, Maynard Dixon, Edgar Payne, the richness of the post-impressionist palette and brushstroke of Cezanne and Gaugain, and the cinematography of classic western films.

"Mt. Sinai" (30" × 24" oil on canvas, 2014) is used by permission of the artist.

TORREY HOUSE PRESS

Voices for the Land

The economy is a wholly owned subsidiary of the environment, not the other way around.
—Senator Gaylord Nelson, founder of Earth Day

Torrey House Press is an independent nonprofit publisher promoting environmental conservation through literature. We believe that culture is changed through conversation and that lively, contemporary literature is the cutting edge of social change. We strive to identify exceptional writers, nurture their work, and engage the widest possible audience; to publish diverse voices with transformative stories that illuminate important facets of our ever-changing planet; to develop literary resources for the conservation movement, educating and entertaining readers, inspiring action.

Visit www.torreyhouse.org for reading group discussion guides, author interviews, and more.

As a 501(c)(3) nonprofit publisher, our work is made possible by generous donations from readers like you.

This book was made possible by the generosity of the Ballantine Family Fund. Torrey House Press is supported by Back of Beyond Books, The King's English Bookshop, Jeff and Heather Adams, Jeffrey S. and Helen H. Cardon Foundation, Suzanne Bounous, Grant B. Culley Jr. Foundation, Diana Allison, Jerome Cooney and Laura Storjohann, Robert Aagard and Camille Bailey Aagard, Heidi Dexter and David Gens, Kirtly Parker Jones, Utah Division of Arts & Museums, and Salt Lake County Zoo, Arts & Parks. Our thanks to individual donors, subscribers, and the Torrey House Press board of directors for their valued support.

Join the Torrey House Press family and give today at
www.torreyhouse.org/give.